Edmond and Jules de Goncourt
Germinie Lacerteux

GERMINIE LACERTEUX

BY
EDMOND AND JULES DE GONCOURT

Translated from the French.

With an Introduction by
ERNEST BOYD

MONDIAL

Mondial
New York · Berlin

Edmond and Jules de Goncourt:
Germinie Lacerteux

Translated and with an introduction (1922) by Ernest Boyd.

Copyright © 2007 Mondial
(for this edition of
"Germinie Lacerteux")

Editor: Andrew Moore

Cover image: Uday K. Dhar

ISBN 978-1-59569-067-8

Library of Congress Control Number: 2007937019

www.mondialbooks.com

INTRODUCTION

MODERN FRENCH LITERATURE *is, I think, unique in the number of instances where brothers have made their names by work written in collaboration. The first of such partnership was that of Edmond and Jules de Goncourt, who have been followed by Paul and Victor Margueritte, "J. H. Rosny," and Jean and Jérôme Tharaud, all of whom have been associated in one way or another with their great predecessors. The two brothers "Rosny" and Paul Margueritte are members of the Goncourt Academy, while the Tharauds' first considerable work,* Dingley, l'illustre écrivain, *received one of the earliest of the Goncourt prizes. Since the honour of winning that Prize is almost equalled by the distinction of nearly getting it, it ought perhaps to be recorded that the brothers whose signature is Marius Ary Leblond achieved that degree of fame on the second occasion when the Goncourt Prize was awarded in 1904! However, I do not wish to stress unduly the natural interest which the Goncourt Academy must have in the work of brother collaborators, for the partnership of "J. H. Rosny" has resolved itself into the separate use of their joint pseudonym, with the addition of "Junior" and "Senior," while Paul and Victor Margueritte parted company after some years. Thus Jean and Jérôme Tharaud remain the most important examples of the method of collaboration which made Edmond and Jules de Goncourt famous. How closely the latter worked together, and how identical their minds were, has been attested by innumerable passages in that famous* Journal des Goncourts *which so largely occupied the closing years of the surviving brother's life. In the last volume Edmond has left an interesting account of their collaboration. "Our temperaments," he says, "were absolutely different: my brother's nature was gay, spirited and expansive; mine was melancholy, dreamy and concentrated," but if they looked at the exterior world with different eyes they received the same impressions. "My brother, I confess, was a greater stylist, he had more power over words, than I, whose only advantage over him was my greater capacity for visualising the world about us ... When we began my brother was under the influence of Jules Janin and I under that of Théophile Gautier, and in* En 18... *these two ill-assorted models are recognisable, giving to our first book the char-*

I

acter of a work from two distinct pens." As their work progressed there came *"the fusion, the amalgamation of our two styles, which united in the creation of a single style, very personal, peculiarly Goncourt." Finally it came about that Jules de Goncourt "attended particularly to the writing and I to the construction of the work. He was seized with a rather contemptuous disinclination to seek, to find and to invent, although he could always imagine a more striking detail than I when he took the trouble."* The younger brother always protested against the multiplication of books and Edmond declares that it was largely out of affection for him that Jules was induced to go on. *"I was born,"* the latter used to say, *"to write in a lifetime just one little duodecimo volume like la Bruyère, just one little volume."*

Their actual method of working together was described by Edmond de Goncourt in a letter to Georg Brandes. *"As soon as we had agreed as to the plan, we would smoke for an hour or two and talk over the section, or rather the paragraph, which had to be written. Then we wrote it, each in a separate room, and read to each other what each of us had written, either choosing without discussion whichever was the better, or making a combination of whatever was least imperfect in the two compositions. But even when one of the two was completely sacrificed, there was always something of both in the paragraph when definitely arranged and polished, though it might be only the addition of an adjective, the repetition of a phrase, or the like."* Out of that collaboration came Sœur Philomène, Renée Mauperin, Germinie Lacerteux, Manette Salmon *and* Madame Gervaisais, *not to mention their 'prentice efforts,* En 18..., La Lorette *and* Charles Demailly. *After his brother's death Edmond de Concourt wrote jour novels,* La Fille Elisa, Les Frères Zemganno, La Faustin *and* Chérie, *and it is on these twelve works of fiction that the fame of the brothers Goncourt rests, although as the social historians of eighteenth century France, and as connoisseurs of French and Japanese art, their achievements have been recognised by specialists.*

It would be difficult to find a body of first-rate fiction whose history has been more full of accidents and controversies than the novels of Edmond and Jules de Goncourt. They began their career with En 18... which appeared on December 2, 1851, the day selected for the coup d'état which gave France her Third Napoléon and her Second Empire. *The panic-stricken publisher, fearful of the political heresies which might be concealed in this youthful work, at once got rid of it, and in the turmoil of the times little attention was paid to the few copies which managed to circulate. Jules Janin, doubtless recognising the style of a disciple, gave the book a long review in the* Journal des Débats, *but Paris was busy with more pressing matters than the début of the brothers Goncourt. A year later the discretion of their publisher was proven by the fact that the authors were accused of publishing an article which was an outrage on public morals. They had quoted some lines by Tabureau from Sainte-Beuve's* Tableau historique et critique de la poésie française, *which the moral régime of the newly-fledged Empire regarded as obscene, although this work (now familiar in the college class-room) had been crowned by the French Academy! The case was going against them, but a postponement was secured, and in the interval a change in the judiciary gave the Goncourts a powerful friend in court, with the result that they were acquitted. The verdict was very like that delivered in the case of* Madame Bovary, *and is worth quoting, "Whereas the incriminating passages of the article suggest to the mind of the reader pictures which are obviously licentious and, therefore, reprehensible, nevertheless, it is evident from the article as a whole that the authors of the work in question had no intention of committing an offense against decency and public morals."*

In 1853 La Lorette, *a novel which has been allowed to lapse into the limbo of rare editions, caused the authors some apprehension, as the authorities had marked them as dangerous characters. An entry in the* Journal *states that this book, whose title indicates its nature, was "sold out within a week," and was "a revelation to us that it was possible to sell a book." This now unprocurable work is, by a characteristic irony of literary fate, the only publication of the Goncourts which gave rise to no difficulties, and about whose reception they have recorded no complaint.* Charles Demailly *(1860), which was originally entitled* Les hommes de lettres, *had little success and was denounced as an unfriendly attack upon the sacred order of men of letters by the ... journalists. It was not until 1861 that the first of their major novels,* Sœur Philomène, *appeared after many difficulties, having been refused by Michel Lévy on the ground that the subject was depressing. It eventually had what the*

Goncourts describe as the "triste succès" *of being issued by an unimportant firm, and of being more or less ignored. In this work, and its successor,* Renée Mauperin *(1864), Edmond and Jules de Goncourt definitely developed the method both in the selection of the theme and its development which was to be their special contribution to the modern French novel. But it was in* Germinie Lacerteux, *that they launched their most striking challenge to all hitherto accepted conventions.*

This work was published in 1864, with a preface which began: "We must apologise to the public for giving them this book, and warn them of its contents. The public like novels that are untrue. This is a true novel. They like books which seem to take them into society: this work comes from the streets. They like nasty little works, the reminiscences of prostitutes, bedroom confessions, erotic filth, the scandals indecently exposed in booksellers' windows. What they are about to read is severe and pure. They need not expect photographs of Pleasure in evening-dress. This is a clinical study of Love. Furthermore the public like harmless and comforting stories, adventures that end happily, ideas which disturb neither their digestion nor their peace of mind. This book, with its harsh and sad fable is designed to interfere with their habits and to upset their health. Why, then, did we write it? Was it simply to shock the public and to insult their tastes? No. Living in the nineteenth century, in a time of universal suffrage, of democracy, of liberalism, we wondered whether what are called 'the lower orders' were not entitled to a place in fiction, whether that world beneath a world, the common people, was to remain under a literary taboo, disdained by authors who have hitherto maintained a silence concerning whatever heart and soul they may possess."

Such, in part, was the manifesto with which the Goncourts invited a public previously preoccupied with the tragedies of kings and queens and the romance and sorrows of high society to contemplate the life below and about them. It was only seven years since Flaubert had shaken the literary conventions to their foundations with Madame Bovary, *but in* Germinie Lacerteux *a great step further was taken. The consequences are apparent in the reception which the book obtained. The mandarins of the time ignored it, while the orthodox reviewers surpassed themselves in the manner peculiar to their tribe. One of the chief articles, anticipating the English critics*

of Ibsen, described the book as "putrid literature," and the writer,
Professor Gustave Merlet, declared be had "hesitated before dis-
cussing the actions and reactions of Germinie Lacerteux, who does
not deserve to occupy the leisure time of decent people." Charles
Monselet, an author somewhat less obscure, if only because of his
contributions to erotica, *could find no better epithet than "sculp-*
tured slime" to apply to this work. But it had one admirer whose
fame was to grow out of the Naturalistic movement, which dates
from the publication of Germinie Lacerteux. *Emile Zola was a*
young and unknown author when he published in a provincial
newspaper an enthusiastic defense of the Goncourts, which was
subsequently included in the volume of essays Mes Haines, *and led*
to an exchange of letters, and three years later to a meeting and
a lifelong friendship. Zola's courageous article, in which he did
not hesitate to set the authors of Germinie Lacerteux *beside Bal-*
zac and Flaubert, had a supporter in that of another young writer,
Jules Claretie, whose article appeared in the Nouvelle Revue de
Paris. *Claretie showed himself equally appreciative but somewhat*
less rhapsodical than Zola, whose critical faculties never seem to
have been particularly subtle. He pleased the Goncourts specially
by his ingenious comparison of Germinie Lacerteux *with* Sœur
Philomène, *and his feeling for the peculiar quality of their minds.*
"This talent," he wrote, "supple and bold, charming and violent at
the same time, deliberately avoiding what attracts the mob, aris-
tocratic to the point of reproaching the Revolution, amongst other
misdeeds, of having scattered all the brilliant frills and furbelows
of the Old Régime, in love with what is bright, pretty, powdered,
silken, and also with what is harsh, ardent and virile, — this talent
which is sometimes bizarre, always superior; this talent so wide in
its scope and so complete, is one which I cannot resist and prefer
to all others." In this one sentence the whole essence of the Gon-
courts' contradictory appeal is aptly given.

Sainte-Beuve was as discreet as when Baudelaire's Fleurs du
Mal *was in trouble. He preferred to express his sympathy in a pri-*
vate letter rather than on the printed page. His critical acumen,
however, is evident in his recognition of the fact that a new era in
French fiction had begun, and that a new aesthetic was needed to
criticise the new literature. Flaubert and Victor Hugo were also
enthusiastic. The former wrote: "What I most admire in your work

is the gradation of the effects, the psychological progression. It is heartrending from beginning to end, and in places simply sublime ... The great question of realism was never so frankly propounded. Your book gives rise to some pretty arguments as to the purpose of art." Ten years or so later, when the book had slowly reached its third edition, the press was much more favourable, Madame Alphonse Daudet wrote a remarkable appreciation in the august columns of the Journal Officiel, *and Henry Céard, now of the Goncourt Academy, one of the oldest survivors of the original circle, risked his post at the Ministry of War by an article in praise of the work of the Goncourts. It was only a question of time for the authors of* Germinie Lacerteux *to find themselves saluted as the leaders of the Naturalistic School.*

The genesis of this work can be found in the second volume of the Journal des Goncourts, *where the brothers tell of the illness and death of their old servant Rose who had been with them for twenty-five years. They learn after the funeral that this trusted and devoted servant had led an amazing double life, that she was drunken and debauched, that she had stolen from them. While they were absorbed in their art this silent creature had lived through unspeakable fears and sufferings, through terrible joys and the lowest depths of despair. Out of that pitiful tale they built up this wonderful novel of a woman ruined through her craving for love and affection, which is simultaneously a masterpiece of imaginative reconstruction and a scientific work of documentation, as the entries in the author's diary of the period show. They turned from Marie-Antoinette to* Germinie Lacerteux, *and, as Henry Céard said, "in their eyes as artists the country girl arriving from Langres covered with lice was no less interesting than the French queen in her blue dress shot through with white. They brought to the novel the severity of their historical exactness."*

This is the book which made the Goncourts famous, though both brothers did not live long enough to witness their success. The younger brother, Jules, who was born in Paris in 1830, died in 1870, but Edmond, born at Nancy in 1822, lived until 1896, thus surviving by an entire literary generation. Zola began the Rougon-Macquart series in 1871 and the campaign of the Naturalists was in full swing when Germinie Lacerteux *had its success, which was confirmed after Jules de Goncourt's death by* La Fille Elisa, *the first novel which appeared without their joint signature, although Edmond declared that this powerful work was but the realisation of a plan thoroughly discussed by the two brothers.* When Zola's L'Assommoir *was published the indebtedness of the new school to* Germinie Lacerteux *was apparent and Zola, Huysmans, Céard and the others were only too proud to claim the Goncourts as their masters. Zola, however, represented the Left, or radical, wing of realism, while Edmond and Jules de Goncourt stood for the Right, or aristocratic, section. As Naturalism developed it became increasingly an appeal to mass suggestion, and relied more and more upon mass effects, the endless piling up of detail, the ceaseless extension of the field of observation and documentation. With this phase of the movement the Goncourts had nothing in common.*

They were essentially and primarily artists, and if they claimed for the novelist the right to transcribe reality, it was reality as seen through artistic vision, not through the eyes of a mere reporter. Life as the Goncourts saw it was far from the immense and crude reality of Zola. While they sought to reach the heart of things through a meticulous realisation of externals, Zola professed to be a scientist, a social anatomist, whose novels would have the precision and practical value of scientific studies. It did not take long to demonstrate that this conception of realism led through monotony and repetition to the inevitable assumption of a democratic mission. Zola ended as reformer and a Messiah with a panacea and a message for humanity. Oblivion was imminent. Edmond de Goncourt resolutely held aloof in those last novels, La Faustin, Les Frères Zemganno *and* Chérie, *from the current practice of his disciples. And so his work and that of his brother — for to the end they remained indistinguishable — still survive with that of Flaubert, because they created works of art in which reality endures through the spirit of life breathed into them by imagination that embraces and transcends the exterior world.*

ERNEST BOYD
New York, June 1922.

I

"Saved! so now you are saved, mademoiselle!" joyfully cried the maid who had just shut the door after the doctor, and, rushing to the bed in which her mistress was lying, she began in a frenzy of happiness and with passionate caresses to embrace, bed-clothes and all, the old woman's poor wasted body, which seemed as small for the size of the bed as the body of a child.

The old woman took her head silently between her hands, pressed it to her heart, heaved a sigh, and ejaculated: "Well! so I am to live some time longer!"

This scene took place in a small room the window of which showed a narrow strip of sky intersected by three black iron pipes, by lines of roofs, and, in the distance between two houses which nearly touched each other, by the leafless branches of a tree which could not itself be seen.

In the room there stood on the mantelpiece a clock with a square, mahogany case, a large dial-plate, big numbers, and heavy hours. At the sides, and under glass, were two candlesticks, each formed of three silvered swans stretching their necks round a golden quiver. Near the fire-place, a Voltaire easy-chair, covered with one of those chequered antimacassars which are worked by little girls and old women, extended its empty arms. Two small Italian landscapes in the manner of Bertin, a water-color drawing of flowers with a date in red ink at the bottom, and a few miniatures hung on the wall. On the mahogany chest of drawers, in the style of the Empire, stood the figure of Time in black bronze, running with his scythe advanced, and serving as a watch-stand for a little watch with diamond figures on blue, pearl-bordered enamel. On the floor stretched a flaring carpet with stripes of black and green. The window-curtains and bed-curtains were of old-fashioned chintz with red patterns on a chocolate ground.

At the head of the bed, a portrait bent over the sick woman and seemed to bear down upon her with its gaze. It represented a harsh-featured man, whose countenance showed above the high collar of a green satin coat and one of those loose, flowing cravats, one of those muslin scarfs which it was fashionable to tie slackly round the neck in the early years of the Revolution. The old woman lying in the bed resembled this face. She had the same thick, black, imperious eyebrows, the same aquiline nose, the same distinct lines of will, resolution and energy. The portrait seemed to be reflected in her as a father's face is in that of his daughter. But in her the harshness of the features was softened by a ray of rugged kindness, a flame, as it were, of manly devotion and masculine charity.

The daylight which illumined the room was such as is common in early spring towards five o'clock in the evening, which has crystal clearness and silver whiteness, which is cold, virginal and gentle, and which expires in the rosy hue of the sun with the paleness of limbo. The sky was filled with this light which is like that of a new life, as charmingly sad as the still naked earth, and so tender that it impels happiness to weep.

"Why! is my foolish Germinie crying?" said the old woman a moment afterwards drawing back her hands which were wet from her maid's kisses.

"Ah! dear lady, I'd like to cry like this always! it's so nice! It brings back my poor mother to me, and everything, if you only knew!"

"Well, well," said her mistress to her, closing her eyes to listen, "tell me about it."

"Ah! my poor mother!" The maid paused. Then with the flood of words which springs from happy tears she went on, as though in the emotion and the outpouring of her joy her whole childhood were flowing back to her heart: — "Poor woman! I can see her the last time she went out to take me to mass, — it was a 21st of January, I remember. They were reading the king's will then. Ah! she went through a great deal for me, did mother! she was forty-two years old when she had me, and father made her cry so! There were three of us already and not too much bread in the house. And then he was as proud as anything. If we'd had nothing but a pod of peas, he'd never have looked for help from the priest. Ah! we didn't have bacon every day. No matter; mother loved me a little more for it all, and she always found a bit of dripping or cheese somewhere or other to put on my bread. I wasn't five years old when she died. It was a misfortune for all of us.

"I had a big brother who was as white as a sheet, with a yellow beard, and so good, you can't think! Everyone liked him. They had given him names — some called him Boda, I don't know why; and the others Jesus Christ. Ah, he *was* a workman! It made no odds that his health was as bad as could be; at daybreak he was always at his loom — for you must know we were weavers — and he kept to his shuttle till the evening. And so honest, too, if you only knew! They came to him from all parts with their thread, and always without weighing. He was a great friend of the schoolmaster's — it was he made the speeches at Carnival time. My father was very different: he would work a minute or an hour or so, then he would go off to the fields, then when he came in again he would beat us — and hard too. He was like a madman — they said it came of being consumptive. It was a good thing my brother was there: he used to prevent my second sister from pulling my hair and hurting me, because she was jealous. He used always to take me by the hand to go and see the skittles played: indeed, he was the sole support of the house.

"How he slaved for my first communion! Ah, he turned out his work so fast that I might be like the rest, with a white figured frock and a little bag in my hand, for that was the custom then. I had no cap: I had made for me, I remember, a pretty wreath, with favors of the white pith you get by peeling reeds — there's plenty of it about our home in the place where the hemp is put to rot. That was one of my great days, that was, that and the drawing for pigs at Christmas, and the times when I used to go and help them to prop the vines, — it's in the month of June, you know. We had a little vineyard on the top of Saint-Hilaire. One of those years was a very hard one — you remember it, mademoiselle? — the hail of 1828, which destroyed everything. It came down as far as Dijon, and further still — they were obliged to put bran into the bread. Then my brother just buried himself in his work. My father, who at that time was always out roaming in the fields, would sometimes bring us home mushrooms. It was misery all the same — we were hungry more often than not. When I was in the fields I'd look to see whether anyone was watching me, then I'd slip along very gently on my knees, and when I was under a cow I'd take off one of my wooden shoes, and begin to milk her. You see it wouldn't have done to be caught.

"My biggest sister was in service with the mayor of Lenclos, and she used to send home her twenty-four francs of wages — it was so much to the good. The second used to work at sewing in the houses of the towns-people, but prices were not then what they are now — you'd go from six in the morning till night for eight sous. Out of that she tried to save something for dressing herself in holiday style on Saint Remi's day. Ah, that's how it is with us. There's many a one eats two potatoes a day for six months, in order to have a new dress on that day. Misfortunes came upon us from all sides. My father died. It had been necessary to sell a little field and a vineyard that gave us a cask of wine every year. The notaries cost something. When my brother was ill there was nothing to give him to drink except some stum, which had had water thrown into it for a year past; and then there was no linen left for a change for him: all our sheets in the cupboard, where there used to be a gold cross above them in mother's time, were gone, and the cross too.

"To make matters worse, my brother, before he fell sick, went to the Clermont Fair. He heard them say that my sister had been seduced by the mayor: he fell upon those that said so. He wasn't very strong and there was a number of them, and they threw him on the ground, and when he was on the ground they kicked him with their wooden shoes in the pit of the stomach. He was brought back to us like a dead man. However, the doctor set him on his feet again, and told us he was cured. But he only lingered — I could see myself that he was going when he used to kiss me. When the poor, pale darling was dead, Cadet Ballard had to use all his strength to drag me away from the body. The whole village went to his funeral, mayor and all. My sister, who had not been able to keep her place in the mayor's house on account of the way he used to talk to her, had left for a situation in Paris, and my other sister followed her. I was quite alone. A cousin of my mother's then took me with her to Damblin; but I was like a fish out of water there. I used to spend the night in crying; and when I could escape, I always returned to our own house. Just to see the old vine at our gate as I entered the street had such an effect on me! It gave me new legs.

"The good people who had bought the house used to keep me until someone came to look for me; they were always sure to find me there again. At last they wrote to my sister in Paris that if she did not have me with her I should not be long for this world. In fact I was like wax. I was placed under the charge of the driver of a small conveyance which went every month from Langres to Paris; and that was the way I came to Paris. I was then fourteen years old. I remember that during the whole journey I lay down fully dressed because they made me sleep in the common room. When I arrived I was covered with lice."

II

THE old woman remained silent. She was comparing her maid's life with her own.

Mademoiselle de Varandeuil was born in 1782. Her birth took place in a house in the Rue Royale, and Mesdames of France held her over the baptismal font. Her father was intimate with the Count d'Artois, and held a post in his household. He was a member of his hunting parties, and one of those familiar friends in whose presence, at the mass which preceded the hunt, the man who was to be Charles X. would hurry the officiating priest, saying to him in an undertone:

"Hist! hist! parson, be quick and swallow up your Bon Dieu!"

Monsieur de Varandeuil had made one of those marriages to which his time was accustomed; he had wedded a sort of actress, a singer who, without any great talent, had succeeded at the Concert Spirituel by the side of Madame Todi, Madame Ponteuil, and Madame Saint-Huberti. The little girl born of this marriage in 1782 was of a weakly constitution, and ugly, with a large and already ridiculous nose like her father's on a face as big as a fist. She was nothing that the vanity of her parents would have wished her to be. After a pianoforte fiasco made when she was five years of age at a concert given in her mother's drawing-room, she was relegated to domesticity. Only for a minute in the morning used she to go to her mother, who made her kiss her under the chin, that she might not disturb her rouge. When the Revolution came, Monsieur de Varandeuil, thanks to the protection of the Count d'Artois, was a collector of taxes. Madame de Varandeuil was travelling in Italy, whither she had had herself sent under the pretense that her health required it, abandoning the charge of her daughter and of a very young son to her husband.

The heavy cares of the time, the threats muttered against money and the families that had the control of money — Monsieur de Varandeuil had a brother who was a Farmer-General — left this very egotistical and unfeeling father little of the necessary leisure or heart for looking after his children. Then, embarrassment began to show itself in his home. He left the Rue Royale and came to live at the Hôtel du Petit-Charolais, which belonged to his mother who was still alive, and who allowed him to take up his abode there. Events progressed; the beginning of the years of the guillotine had been reached, when one evening he was walking behind a pedlar crying the newspaper called "Stop Thief!" The pedlar, according to the custom of the time, was announcing the contents of the edition, and Monsieur de Varandeuil heard his own name mingled with the coarsest expressions. He bought the paper and read in it a revolutionary denunciation.

Some time afterwards his brother was arrested and shut up with the other Farmers-General at the Hôtel Talaru, His mother, in a fit of terror, had foolishly sold the Hôtel du Petit-Charolais in which he lodged for the worth of the mirrors, and being paid in assignats she had died of despair on seeing the increasing decline in the value of the paper currency. Fortunately, Monsieur de Varandeuil obtained from the purchasers, who were unable to let, permission to live in the rooms which had formerly served for the stablemen. He took refuge here in the rear of the house, discarded his name, posted on the door, as he had been ordered, his patronymic "Roulot," beneath which he buried the "de Varandeuil" and the former courtier of the Count d'Artois. There he lived solitary, effaced, entombed, hiding his head, never going out, crouching in his den, with no servant, waited upon by his daughter and allowing her to do everything.

They lived through the Terror in a state of expectancy, trepidation and continual anticipation of death. Every evening the little girl went to a little grated dormer window to listen to the condemnations of the day, the "List of winners in the Lottery of Saint Guillotine." At every knock, she would go to open the door with the thought that they were about to seize her father in order to lead him to the Place de la Révolution whither her uncle had been led already. The time came when money, — money which was so scarce, — could no longer procure bread, when it had to be carried off almost by force from the baker's door, when it was necessary to win it by spending hours in the cold, keen nights amid the press and crush of crowds, by making one of a file from three o'clock in the morning. Her father did not care to risk himself in the throng of people. He was afraid of being recognized, of compromising himself by some of those outbursts such as the impetuosity of his temper would have caused him to utter in any place, no matter where.

Moreover, he shrank from the weariness and hardness of the labor. The little boy was as yet too small; he would have been trampled upon; and accordingly the task of obtaining bread every day, for the three months, fell to the girl.

She did obtain it. With her little, thin body lost in a large, knitted waistcoat belonging to her father, a cotton cap pulled down over her eyes, and her limbs hugged together in order to retain a remnant of warmth, she would wait shivering, with eyes blue with cold, amid hustlings and pushings until the baker of the Rue des Francs-Bourgeois placed in her hands a loaf which her benumbed fingers could scarcely grasp. At last this poor little girl, who came back every day with her face suffering and her trembling emaciation, moved the baker to pity. With the kindness of heart which is to be found among the people, she sent her man to the little girl as soon as she appeared in the long file, with the bread which she came to obtain. But one day, as the little girl was about to take it, a woman, jealous at the favor and preference shown to the child, gave her a kick with her wooden shoe which kept her in bed for nearly a month. Mademoiselle de Varandeuil bore the mark of it all her life. During this month the family would have died of hunger, but for a store of rice which it had happily occurred to one of their acquaintances, the Countess d'Auteuil, to lay in, and which she was willing to share with the father and the two children. Monsieur de Varandeuil thus escaped the Revolutionary Tribunal through the obscurity of a buried life. His escape was assisted by the accounts of his post, which he was to render, and which he was fortunate enough to have postponed and put off from month to month. Moreover, he averted suspicion by his personal animosities against certain great personages of the court, hatreds which many servants of princes had imbibed from the King's brothers against the Queen. Every time that he had had occasion to speak of this unhappy woman, he had used violent, bitter, and abusive language in so impassioned and sincere a tone that it had almost made him appear an enemy to royalty; so that those to whom he was only the citizen Roulot looked upon him as a patriot, and those who knew him under his former name almost excused him for having been what he had been — a noble, the friend of a prince of the blood, and a placeman.

The Republic had reached the patriotic suppers, those meals of an entire street in the street, whereof Mademoiselle de Varandeuil, in the mingled terrors of her confused recollections, could see the tables of the Rue Pavée standing in the stream of September blood issuing from La Force! It was at one of these suppers that Monsieur de Varandeuil devised a scheme which finally assured him of the safety of his life. He told two of his table companions, warm patriots, one of whom was intimate with Chaumette, that he found himself in great perplexity, that his daughter had been only privately baptized, that she lacked civil status, and that he would be very glad if Chaumette would have her entered upon the registers of the municipality and honor her with a name chosen by himself from the republican calendar of Greece or Rome. Chaumette soon made an appointment for this father who was so "well up to his part," as people said then. Forthwith Mademoiselle de Varandeuil was shown into a room where she found two matrons who were instructed to satisfy themselves as to her sex, and to whom she showed her bosom. She was then brought back into the great Hall of Declarations, and there, after a metaphorical address, Chaumette baptized her "Sempronia;" a name which custom was to make her own and which she never laid aside.

Screened and reassured to some extent by this, the family passed through the terrible days which preceded the fall of Robespierre. At last came the 9th of Thermidor and deliverance. But poverty remained great and pressing in the home. They had lived through the hard times of the Revolution, and they were about to live through the unhappy time of the Directory with nothing but a very unexpected resource, a godsend in money which came to them from Folly. The two children and the father could scarcely have subsisted but for the income from four shares in the Vaudeville, an investment which Monsieur de Varandeuil had been inspired to make in 1791, and which turned out the best of transactions for those years of death, when people needed to forget death every evening, for those final days when every one was fain to laugh his last laugh at the last song. Soon these shares, coupled with the recovery of a few debts, gave the family something more than bread. They then left the Hôtel du Petit-Charolais, and took a small lodging in the Rue du Chaume, in the Marais.

For the rest, there was no change in the habits of the home. The daughter continued to wait upon her father and her brother. Monsieur de Varandeuil had gradually become accustomed to see nothing more in her than was denoted by her costume and by the work which she performed. The father's eyes were no longer ready to recognize a daughter through the dress and the low occupations of this servant. She was no longer one of his own blood, one who had the honor to belong to him: she was a servant whom he had there, under his thumb; and his egotism became so strengthened in this harshness and this mode of thought, he found so much convenience in this filial affection and respectful service which cost nothing, that he had all the trouble in the world to surrender it later on, when a little more money reverted to the household; battles were necessary to bring him to hire a maid, who should replace his daughter and spare the young girl the more humiliating labors of domesticity.

There was no news of Madame de Varandeuil, who had refused to rejoin her husband at Paris during the first years of the Revolution; but soon it was reported that she had married again in Germany, producing the death-certificate of her brother-in-law, who had been guillotined, and whose first name had been changed, as that of her husband. Thus, the young girl grew up forsaken, uncaressed, with no mother but a woman who was dead to all her relations, and whom her father taught her to despise. Her childhood had been spent in never-ceasing anxiety, in the privations which wear away life, in the fatigue of toil which exhausted her feeble, childish strength, in a looking for death which at last became an impatience to die. There had been moments when the temptation had come to this girl of thirteen to act like some woman of that time, to open the door of the house and cry: "God save the King!" into the street, in order to put an end to it all.

Her youth followed upon her childhood with less tragic cares. She had to endure her father's violence of temper, his exactingness, his harshness, his storms which hitherto had been somewhat subdued and restrained by the great tempest of the time. She was still subjected to the fatigues and humiliations of a servant. She continued to be under restraint and kept down, isolated in the society of her father, driven from his arms, and from his kisses, her heart big and sorrowful with the desire to love and with having nothing to love. She began to suffer from that chilling void which is formed around a woman by youth that cannot attract or seduce, youth that is stripped of beauty, and of sympathetic grace. She could see that she inspired a sort of commiseration with her large nose, her yellow complexion, her withered leanness. She felt that she was ugly, and with a pitiful ugliness in her wretched attire, — her sad-colored woollen dresses, the material of which her father never paid for without tokens of ill-humor; for it was not until she was thirty-five years old, that she could obtain from him a small dress allowance.

What sadness, what bitterness, what loneliness did she experience in her life, with this sour, morose old man who was ever grumbling and growling in their lodging, who had no amiability except in society, and who left her every evening to visit at the houses that had been re-opened under the Directory and at the beginning of the Empire! Rarely, and at wide intervals, did he take her out, and when he did so it was always to take her to the everlasting Vaudeville where he had seats. His daughter, however, used to be in terror of these outings. She trembled, the whole time that she was with him; she was fearful of the violence of his temper, of the old-fashioned style which still belonged to his passions, of the readiness with which he would lift his stick upon the insolence of the vulgar. On almost every occasion there were scenes with the ticket collector, wordy wars with the people in the pit, threatenings with the fist which she would terminate by letting down the grating of the box. The same demeanor would be continued in the street, even in the cab with the cabman, who, unwilling to drive for the fare offered by Monsieur de Varandeuil, would let him wait an hour or two hours without proceeding, and sometimes would impatiently take out his horse and leave him in the vehicle with his daughter, the latter vainly beseeching him to yield and pay.

Considering that these pleasures ought to be sufficient for Sempronia, and being moreover jealous of having her all to himself, and constantly under his thumb, Monsieur de Varandeuil did not allow her to become intimate with any one. He did not take her into society, he did not bring her except on days of official receptions and family gatherings to see their relations who had returned from exile. He kept her closely at home; it was not until she was nearly forty years of age that he considered her sufficiently grown up to have permission to go out alone. Thus the young woman had no friendship, no relationship to sustain her; she had no longer even her young brother, who had left for the United States, and had entered the American navy.

Marriage was forbidden her by her father, who refused to allow that she could so much as entertain the idea of getting married and forsaking him; every match that might have presented itself was combated and repulsed by him in advance, so that he did not even leave his daughter the courage to speak to him did an opportunity ever offer itself to her.

Meanwhile our victories were accomplishing a clearance in Italy. The masterpieces of Rome, Florence, Venice were thronging to Paris. Italian art was throwing everything into the shade. Collectors had ceased to pride themselves on anything but pictures of the Italian School. It appeared to Monsieur de Varandeuil that an opportunity of making a fortune was afforded by this movement in matters of taste. He too had been taken with that artistic dilettantism which was one of the refined crazes of the nobility before the Revolution. He had lived in the society of artists, and virtuosos; he was fond of pictures. He thought of collecting a gallery of Italian works and then selling it. Paris was still filled with the sales and dispersals of objects of art caused by the Reign of Terror. Monsieur de Varandeuil began to haunt the pavement — which was then the market for great pictures — and every step brought a discovery; every day he purchased something. Soon there was not room enough for the furniture in the little apartment, which was encumbered with old black pictures, so large, for the most part, that they could not be attached to the walls with their frames. Each was baptized a Raphael, or a Vinci, or an Andrea del Sarto; they were all masterpieces, and the father would frequently keep his daughter in front of them for hours, taxing her with his admiration, and wearying her with his ecstasy. He would rise from epithet to epithet, would grow intoxicated and rave, would finally believe that he was dealing with an imaginary purchaser, would dispute about the price of a masterpiece, and cry:

"A hundred thousand livres, my Rosso! yes, sir, a hundred thousand livres!"

His daughter, alarmed by the amount of money taken from the housekeeping by these big, ugly things, covered with great, frightful, perfectly naked men, tried to remonstrate and sought to stay such waste, but Monsieur de Varandeuil would fall into a passion, display the indignation of a man ashamed to find so little taste in one of his own blood, and tell her that this would make his fortune later on, and that she would see whether or not he was a fool. At last she induced him to sell. The sale took place; it was a disaster, and one of the greatest disillusions ever witnessed by the glazed hall of the Hôtel Bullion.

Wounded to the quick, furious at this check which not only involved a loss of money, and a rent in his little fortune, but also a defeat as a connoisseur, a slap dealt at his knowledge on the cheeks of his Raphaels, Monsieur de Varandeuil declared to his daughter that henceforth they would be too poor to remain in Paris, and that they must go and live in the country. Reared and cradled in an age which disposed women but little to love of the country, Mademoiselle de Varandeuil tried in vain to combat her father's resolution; she was obliged to follow him whither he wished to go, and, by leaving Paris, to lose the society and friendship of two young relatives to whom, in interviews that were too infrequent, she had half unbosomed herself, and whose hearts she had felt come out to herself as to an elder sister.

At L'Isle-Adam Monsieur Varandeuil rented a small house. Here he found himself close to old memories in the atmosphere of a former petty court, in the neighborhood of two or three mansions which were beginning to be peopled again, and the owners of which he knew. And then, here on the ground of the Contis, there had come to be settled, since the Revolution, a little society of substantial citizens and rich-grown tradesmen. The name of Monsieur de Varandeuil sounded big in the ears of all these worthy individuals. They bowed low to him, they disputed for the honor of entertaining him, they listened respectfully, and almost religiously, to the stories that he told of the old society. And flattered, loved and honored as a remnant of Versailles, he had the position and consideration of a lord among these people. When he dined at the house of Madame Mutel, a retired baker, who had an income of forty thousand livres a year, the mistress of the house would rise from table in her silk dress to go and fry the salsify herself. Monsieur de Varandeuil did not like it unless it was done in his own way.

But it was not these advantages which had especially fixed Monsieur de Varandeuil's retreat at L'Isle-Adam; it was a plan. He came there in quest of leisure for a great work. What he had been unable to do for the honor and glory of Italian art by means of his collections, he wished to accomplish by means of history. He had learned a little Italian from his wife; he took it into his head to give Vasari's "Lives of the Painters" to the French public, to translate it with the assistance of his daughter who, when quite a child, had been able to speak Italian with her mother's maid and who still remembered a few words. He buried the young woman in Vasari, shut up her time and thought in grammars, dictionaries, commentators, and the scholiasts of Italian art, kept her stooping over the thankless task, over the weariness and fatigue of groping out the translation of words.

The whole book devolved upon her; when he had cut out her work for her, he would leave her alone with the white vellumbound volumes and set out for a walk, or pay visits in the neighborhood, or go and gamble in a mansion, or dine with the citizens of his acquaintance, to whom he would complain pathetically of the effort and labor which the enormous enterprise of his translation cost him. He would come in again, listen while the portion translated was read to him, offer his observations and his criticism, and spoil a sentence to insert a mistranslation which his daughter would remove when he was gone; then he would resume his walk, or his gadding about, like a man who had done a good day's work, swaggering as he walked with his hat under his arm, wearing thin pumps, enjoying himself, the sky, the trees, and Rousseau's God, who is gentle to nature and tender to the plants. From time to time impatience like that of a child or of an old man would possess him; he would require so many pages for the next day, and would compel his daughter to sit up during part of the night.

Two or three years were spent in this work, upon which finally Sempronia's eyes were fixed without intermission. She lived buried in her father's Vasari, more solitary than ever, alienated by lofty, innate repugnance from the burgesses of L'Isle-Adam with their Madame Angot manners, and too poorly dressed to visit at the mansions. There was no pleasure, no amusement for her that was not thwarted and tormented by the irritating singularities of her father. He pulled up the flowers which she planted secretly in the little garden. He would have nothing in it but vegetables, and he cultivated them himself, setting forth grand utilitarian theories the while, arguments which might have served the Convention for the conversion of the Tuileries into a potato-field. The only comfort she had was a week which came at wide intervals, and during which her father granted her permission to receive a visit from one of her two friends, a week which would have been seven days of Paradise for Sempronia had not her father poisoned its joys, its diversions and its entertainments with his ever menacing rages, his ever aggressive humors, and his difficulties about trifles, — a flask of Eau-de-Cologne requested by Sempronia for her friend's room, a dish for her dinner, or a place to which she wished to take her.

At L'Isle-Adam Monsieur de Varandeuil had taken a servant who had almost immediately become his mistress. Of this connection was born a child whom the father, in his cynical carelessness, had the shamelessness to have brought up under his daughter's eyes. As years went on the maid had gained a firm footing in the house. She ended by ruling the household, father and daughter. A day came when Monsieur de Varandeuil wished to have her sit at his table and be waited upon by Sempronia. It was too much. Mademoiselle de Varandeuil revolted at the outrage, and drew herself up in all the loftiness of her indignation. Secretly, silently, in misfortune, and isolation, and the hardness of the things and people around her, the young woman had developed a soul that was straight and strong; tears had tempered instead of softened her. Beneath her filial docility and humility, beneath her passive obedience, beneath an apparent gentleness, she concealed a character of iron, a man's will, one of those hearts which nothing can bend and which never yield. At this insult she proved herself to be her father's daughter, set forth her entire life, flung the shame and reproach of it in his face with a flood of words, and ended by telling him that if the woman did not leave the house that very evening she would leave it herself, and that, thank God! she would be at no loss to live anywhere with the simple tastes which he had given her.

The father, stupefied and astounded at this revolt, yielded and sent the servant away, but he kept up a cowardly spite against his daughter for the sacrifice which she had wrung from him. This resentment betrayed itself in harsh speeches, in aggressive words, in ironical thanks, in smiles of bitterness. Sempronia tended him better, more gently, more patiently, for all his vengeance. A final trial awaited her devotion; the old man was stricken with an attack of apoplexy which left him with the whole of one side of his body stiff and dead, with a lame leg, and with a dormant understanding accompanied by the living consciousness of his misfortune and of his dependence upon his daughter. Then, all that was bad at bottom within him was exasperated and unchained. He displayed ferocities of egotism. Under the torment of his suffering and his weakness, he became a sort of wicked madman.

Mademoiselle de Varandeuil devoted her days and nights to the sick man who seemed to bear her ill-will for her attentions, to be humiliated by her care as by her generosity and forgiveness, to suffer inwardly at seeing this indefatigable and watchful figure of Duty always at his side. Yet what a life was hers! She had to combat the incurable weariness of the patient, to constantly keep him company, to take him out, to sustain him during the entire day. She had to play cards with him when he was at home, and to see that he neither lost nor won too much. She also had to contest his inclinations and his greedy longings, to take the dishes from him, and for every thing that he wanted, to undergo complainings, reproaches, abuse, tears, furious despairs, rages, like those of a passionate child, and such as are displayed by the old and powerless. And this lasted ten years! — ten years during which Mademoiselle de Varandeuil had no other recreation or relief than to lavish the tenderness and warmth of a maternal affection upon one of her two young friends who had lately been married, her "chick" as she called her. Mademoiselle's happiness consisted in going every fortnight to pass a short time in this happy household. She would kiss the pretty infant in its cradle, and already in the arms of sleep; she would dine at racing speed; at dessert she would send for a carriage, and hurry away with the haste of a schoolboy who is behind his time. However, during the last years of her father's life she ceased to have permission to dine: the old man would no longer permit so long an absence, and kept her almost continually beside him, telling her repeatedly that he was well aware that it was not amusing to look after an infirm old creature such as he was, but that she would soon be rid of him. He died in 1818, and the only words that he could find before dying in which to bid farewell to her who had been his daughter for almost forty years were these:

"Ah, I well know that you have never loved me!"

Two years before her father's death, Sempronia's brother had returned from America. He brought back a colored woman who had nursed him and saved him from the yellow fever, and two daughters who were already grown up, whom he had had by this woman before marrying her. Notwithstanding that she had the old-fashioned ideas about black people, and although she looked upon this uninstructed colored woman, with her negro speech, her harsh laugh, and her linen-greasing skin, as absolutely a female ape, Mademoiselle de Varandeuil had striven against her father's obstinate horror of receiving his daughter-in-law; and it was she who had induced him, in the last days of his life, to allow her brother to present his wife to him. Her father being dead, it seemed to her that this household was all that remained to her of the family.

Monsieur de Varandeuil, to whom on the return of the Bourbons the Count d'Artois had caused to be paid the arrears of his office, had left an income of nearly ten thousand francs to his children. Before inheriting this, the brother had nothing but a pension of fifteen hundred francs from the United States. Mademoiselle de Varandeuil calculated that five or six thousand francs a year would not be sufficient for the comfort of this household which comprised two children, and it immediately occurred to her to add her own share in the inheritance. She proposed this contribution in the most natural and simple way in the world. Her brother accepted it, and she came to live with him in a pretty little dwelling at the top of the Rue de Clichy, on the fourth floor of one of the first houses built on that soil, which was still almost a waste, where the country air passed gaily through the framework of the houses under construction. Here she continued her modest life, her humble toilets, her frugal habits, content with the worst room, and not spending on herself more than from eighteen hundred to two thousand francs a year.

But soon a secret and slowly hatched jealousy began to show itself in the mulatto woman. She took umbrage at the friendship between the brother and sister, which seemed to withdraw her husband from her arms. She was hurt by the communion effected between them by speech, mind and recollection; she was hurt by the talks in which she could take no part, and by what she heard in their voices without understanding it. The consciousness of her own inferiority roused in her heart the wrathfulness and fiery hatred which burn in the tropics. She employed her children for her revenge, and impelled and urged and incited them against her sister-in-law. She encouraged them to laugh at her, to make fun of her. She applauded that evil littleness of understanding which is characteristic of children, in whom observation begins with naughtiness. Once let loose, she allowed them to laugh at all their aunt's absurdities, her physique, her nose, her clothes, whose poverty, however, was caused by their own elegance.

Thus directed and supported, the children soon arrived at insolence. Mademoiselle de Varandeuil was as quick as she was kind. With her, hand as well as heart belonged to the first impulse. Moreover, she thought with her time respecting the mode of bringing up children. She tolerated two or three impertinences without saying anything, but at the fourth she seized the laugher, turned up her petticoats, and in spite of her twelve years gave her the soundest whipping that she had ever had. The mulatto uttered loud shrieks, and told her sister-in-law that she had always detested her children, and that she wanted to kill them. The brother interposed between the two women and succeeded in patching up a reconciliation. But fresh scenes occurred in which the two little girls, enraged against the woman who had made their mother weep, tortured their aunt with the devices of naughty children combined with the cruelties of little savages.

After several superficial reconciliations, it had become necessary to separate. Mademoiselle de Varandeuil resolved to leave her brother, who, as she could see, was most unhappy in the daily trial to his dearest affections. She left him to his wife and children. This separation was one of the great heart-breakings of her life. She who had been so strong against emotion, who had been so self-contained, who had apparently taken a pride in suffering, was nearly giving way when obliged to leave the dwelling where, in her own little corner, she had had a short dream of happiness beside the happiness of the rest; and her last tears rose to her eyes.

She did not go far away, so as to be still within reach of her brother, to nurse him if he were sick, to see him and to meet him. But a void remained in her heart and life. She had begun to see the members of her family after her father's death: she drew closer to them, allowing those relatives whom the Restoration had again placed in high and powerful positions to return to her, and going herself to those whom the new authority left insignificant and poor. But above all she returned to her dear "chick," and to another little cousin who was also married and had become the "chick's" sister-in-law. Then her existence and her external relations were ordered in a singular fashion. Mademoiselle de Varandeuil never went into society, to an evening party or to the play. It required the brilliant success of Mademoiselle Rachel to induce her to set foot in a theatre, and she ventured into one only twice. She never accepted an invitation to a large dinner party. But there were two or three houses to which, as to that of her "chick," she would invite herself unexpectedly when no one else was there.

"Bichette," she used to say without ceremony, "you and your husband are doing nothing this evening? I will stay and taste your stew."

Regularly at eight o'clock she rose, and when the husband took his hat in order to see her home she would make him drop it with a:

"Nonsense! my dear; an old stager like me! why, it is I who frighten the men in the street."

And then they would be ten days or a fortnight without seeing her. But did any misfortune come, the news of a death, or sadness in the house, or did a child fall ill, Mademoiselle de Varandeuil always heard of it in a minute, no one knew how. She would arrive in spite of the weather, or the hour or anything else, give her own loud ring — it had finally become known as "cousin's ring" — and, instantly laying aside her umbrella, which never left her, taking off her clogs and throwing her hat upon a chair, be quite at the service of those who had need of her. She listened, she spoke, she inspired courage with a sort of martial tone, in language energetic after the manner of military consolations, and as warm as a cordial. If it was a little one who was not well she would come straight to its bed, laugh at the no longer frightened child, hustle the father and mother, hurry to and fro, give orders, assume the management of everything, handle the leeches, arrange the plasters, and bring back hope, mirth, and health at a gallop. Among all her relatives, the old maid would appear in this providential and sudden manner in days of pain, weariness and grief. She was never seen except when there was need of her hands to cure, or of her devotion to comfort. She was an impersonal woman, so to speak, from sheer goodness of heart, a woman who did not belong to herself at all. God seemed to have made her in order to give her to others. The everlasting black dress which she persisted in wearing, the worn and twice-dyed shawl, the ridiculous hat and the poorness of her whole attire, were for her the means which enabled her, with her slender fortune, to be rich in doing good, to be a dispenser of charities, to have her pocket always open to give the poor, not money, for she was afraid of the public-house, but a quartern loaf which she would purchase for them at the baker's. And then with this poverty she indulged further in what was her greatest luxury: the joy of her friends' children when she loaded them with Christmas boxes, presents, surprises and pleasures. Was there one, for instance, whose mother, being away from Paris, had left him at the boarding school on a fine Sunday in summer, and who, young urchin that he was, had for spite got himself kept in? He would be quite astonished to see cousin marching into the court-yard at the stroke of nine, and in such a hurry as to be still fastening the last hook in her dress. And what affliction on seeing her!

"Cousin," he would say piteously, in such a passion as makes one feel inclined to simultaneously weep and to kill one's pedagogue, "I am kept in."

"Kept in? Ah! very likely, kept in! And you think that I am going to put myself out like this — does this schoolmaster of yours fancy he'll make a fool of me? Where is the old bear that I may speak to him? Meanwhile do you go and dress yourself, and be quick."

And while the child was still afraid to hope that a lady so badly dressed could have the power to cancel a detention, he would feel himself seized by the arms; it was his cousin carrying him off, tossing him perfectly stunned and amazed with joy into a cab, and taking him away to the Bois de Boulogne. She would have him ride on a donkey the whole day, herself urging on the animal with a broken bough, and crying: "Gee!" Then, after a good dinner at Borne's she would bring him back again, and, kissing him at the entrance to the school, put a large crown-piece into his hand.

Queer old maid! The trials of her whole existence, the pain of living, the never-ending sufferings of her body, one long physical and moral torture had detached her, as it were, and set her above life. Her education, what she had seen, the sight of the extremity of things, the Revolution, had moulded her to contempt of human misery. And this old woman, to whom only breath was left, had risen to a serene philosophy, to a manly, lofty, and almost ironical stoicism. Sometimes, she would begin to be incensed with a pain that was somewhat too keen; then, in the midst of her complaining, she would abruptly throw out a word of anger or raillery at herself, where upon even her face would grow calm. She was cheerful with a natural, effusive and thorough cheerfulness, the cheerfulness of experienced devotion, like that of an old soldier or of an old hospital-sister. Exceedingly good, there was nevertheless something which her goodness lacked — forgiveness. Never had she been able to sway or bend her temper so far as this. A hurt, a bad action, a trifle which touched her heart, wounded her for ever. She did not forget. Time, death even, failed to drown her memory.

Of religion she had none. Born at a period when women dispensed with it, she had grown up at a time when there was no longer a church. The mass had no existence when she was a young girl; nothing had habituated her to a belief in God, or made her feel that she needed Him; while to priests she had always felt a hostile repugnance that must have been connected with some secret family history of which she never spoke. All her faith, strength, and piety consisted in the pride of her conscience; she considered that it was sufficient to be anxious about self-esteem in order to act well and never err. She was completely moulded in this singular fashion by the two centuries in which she had lived, compounded of them both, steeped in the two currents of the old régime and the Revolution. After Louis XVI, who had not mounted his horse on the tenth of August, she had lost esteem for kings; but she detested the mob. She desired equality and she had a horror of upstarts. She was a Republican and an aristocrat. She blended skepticism with prejudice, the horror of '93, which she had seen, with the vague and generous ideas of humanity in which she had been cradled.

Her externals were all masculine. Her voice was rough, her speech frank, her language that of the old dames of the eighteenth century set off by the accent of the people — a rompish and highly-colored elocution of her own which overlooked the modesty of words and was bold enough to call things plainly by their names.

Meanwhile the years passed, carrying away the Restoration and the monarchy of Louis Philippe. One by one she saw all those whom she had loved depart, and all her relations take the road to the cemetery. Solitude was falling around her, and she remained astonished and sad that she should be forgotten by death, she who would have offered it so little resistance, she who was already quite disposed for the grave, and was obliged to stoop her heart to the little children brought to her by the sons and daughters of the friends whom she had lost. Her brother was dead. Her dear "chick" was no more. The "chick's" sister-in-law alone was left her. But hers was a tremulous existence and one ready to take to flight. Crushed by the death of a child that had come after years of waiting, the poor woman was dying of consumption. Mademoiselle de Varandeuil shut herself up with her from twelve o'clock until six every day for four years. She lived by her side all this time, in the close atmosphere and in the odor of fumigations. Not allowing herself to be stayed for an hour by gout or rheumatism, she devoted her time and her life to the gentle dying creature, who kept looking to heaven where all dead children are. And when at the cemetery Mademoiselle de Varandeuil had kissed the dead woman's coffin in a last embrace, it seemed to her that no one was left about her, and that she was alone on the earth.

From that day, yielding to the infirmities which she had no longer any reason for shaking off, she had begun to live the narrow and confined life of those old people who wear out the carpet of their room in the same spot, no longer going out, no longer reading on account of the fatigue to her eyes, and most frequently sunk in her arm-chair, engaged in reviewing and reviving the past. She would maintain the same position for days with open and dreamy eyes, far from herself, far from the room and from her lodgings, going whither her memories led her, to distant faces, to forgotten places, to pale and beloved countenances, lost in a solemn somnolence, which Germinie respected, saying:

"Mademoiselle is wrapt up in her reflections." One day, nevertheless, of every week, she went out. It had been on account of this excursion, and in order to be nearer the place to which she wished to go on this day, that she had left her apartments in the Rue Taitbout and had come to lodge in the Rue de Laval. One day in every week, nothing, not even sickness, being able to prevent her, she went to the cemetery of Montmartre, in which rested her father, her brother, the women whom she regretted, and all those whose pain had ended before her own. For the dead and for death she had an almost ancient reverence. The grave to her was sacred, dear, and a friend. She loved the earth of hope and deliverance in which her friends were sleeping, so that she looked for it and held her body in readiness.

On that day she used to set out early with her maid, who gave her an arm, and carried a folding-chair. Close to the cemetery, she entered the shop of a wreath-seller who had known her for long years, and who, in winter, used to bring her foot-warmer and place it under her feet. Here she would rest for a few moments; then, loading Germinie with wreaths of immortelles, she passed through the gate of the cemetery, took the walk on the left of the cedar at the entrance, and slowly made her pilgrimage from tomb to tomb. She threw away the withered flowers, swept up the dead leaves, fastened the wreaths, sat down upon her folding-chair, looked, dreamed, or with the end of her parasol abstractedly loosened a patch of mouldy moss on the flat-stone. Then she would get up, turn round as though to bid the grave that she was leaving good-bye, go some distance farther, stop again, talk in a whisper, as she had already been doing with that portion of her heart which slept beneath the stone; and, her visit being thus paid to all the dead of her affections, she would return slowly, religiously, enwrapping herself in silence, and as though afraid to speak.

III

IN her reverie, Mademoiselle de Varandeuil had closed her eyes. The maid's talk stopped, and the remainder of her life, which was that evening upon her lips, went back into her heart. The end of her story was this:

When little Germinie Lacerteux, not yet fifteen years old, had reached Paris, her sisters, eager to see her earning her own livelihood, and to put her in the way of getting her bread, had placed her in a little café on the Boulevard, where she acted both as lady's-maid to the mistress of the café and as assistant to the waiters in the heavy work of the establishment. The child, fresh from her village, and dropped here abruptly, felt strange and quite scared in this place, this service. She felt the first instinct of her modesty and her incipient womanhood quiver at the perpetual contact with the waiters, at the community of work, food, and existence with men; and every time that she was allowed out, and went to see her sisters, there were tears, and despair, and scenes in which, without complaining definitely of anything, she showed something like terror at going back, saying that she could not stay there any longer, that she did not like it, that she would rather go back home. She was answered that her coming had already cost money enough, that she was fanciful, that she was very well off where she was, and so she was sent back to the café in tears. She did not dare to tell all that she suffered from her association with these café waiters, brazen, jocular, and cynical as they were, fed on the leavings of debauchery, polluted by all the vices to which they ministered, and blending within them all the rottenness of the relics of orgy. At all hours she had to endure the cowardly jests, the cruel mystifications, and the unkindnesses of these men, who were happy at finding a little martyr in this shy, little lass with the oppressed and sickly look, who knew nothing, who was timorous and distrustful and thin, and pitiably clad in her sorry little country dresses. Bewildered, and as one overwhelmed beneath the un-intermittent torture, she became their butt. They played upon her ignorance, they deceived and deluded her with their tricks, they crushed her with fatigue, they dulled her with continual and pitiless mockeries that well-nigh drove her disconcerted understanding into imbecility. Then, again, they made her blush at things which they said to her, and of which she felt ashamed without understanding them. They played with filthy ambiguities upon the ingenuousness of her fourteen years. And they amused themselves by putting the eyes of her childish curiosity to the keyholes of the supper-rooms.

The girl wished to confide in her sisters, but she dared not. As with food a little flesh came upon her body, and a little color into her cheeks, their freedom increased and grew bolder. There were familiarities, gestures, approaches from which she escaped and rescued herself pure, but which impaired her candor by touching her innocence. Ill-treated, scolded, used brutally by the master of the establishment, who was accustomed to seduce his female servants, and who bore her ill-will because she was neither old enough nor fit to be his mistress, it was only from his wife that she met with a little support and humanity. She began to love this woman with a sort of animal devotion, and to obey her with dog-like docility. She performed all her commissions without either reflection or conscience. She carried her letters to her lovers, and was skilful in doing it. She became nimble, brisk, ingeniously subtle in order to pass, to slip, to glide among the awakened suspicions of her husband, and, without well knowing what she was doing, or what she was hiding, she took a wicked little mischievous and monkeyish joy in vaguely telling herself that she was working something of harm to the man and the house which wrought so much harm to her.

There was also among her comrades an old waiter of the name of Joseph, who protected her, warned her of the unkind tricks that were plotted against her, and, when she was present, checked too great freedom of conversation by the authority of his white hairs and with a paternal interest. Nevertheless, Germinie's horror of the house increased every day. One week her sisters were obliged to take her back to the café by force.

A few days afterwards there was a great review at the Champ de Mars, and the waiters had leave for the day. Only Germinie and old Joseph remained behind. Joseph was engaged in a little dark room putting away dirty linen. He told Germinie to come and help him. She went in, shrieked, fell, wept, entreated, struggled, called out despairingly — the empty house continued deaf.

When she came to herself, Germinie ran and shut herself up in her own room. She was not seen again during the day. On the morrow, when Joseph wished to speak to her, and advanced towards her, she recoiled in terror with a wild gesture and in mad fright. For a long time, whenever a man approached her she would involuntarily draw back with a first, abrupt movement, shuddering and nervous as though smitten with the fear of a distracted animal seeking some way of escape. Joseph, who had dreaded that she would denounce him, allowed her to keep him at a distance, and respected the frightful loathing which she displayed towards him.

She became pregnant. One Sunday she had been to spend the evening with her sister, the doorkeeper; after some vomitings she felt ill. A doctor who resided in the house was getting his key at the lodge; the two elder sisters learned from him the position of the youngest. The intractable, brutal revolts of pride characteristic of the honor of the people, and the implacable severities of religion, broke out on the part of the two women into indignant anger. Their shame turned to rage. Germinie recovered her senses beneath their blows, their abuse, the woundings of their hands, the outrages of their mouths. Her brother-in-law who was there and who could not forgive her the money that her journey had cost, looked at her in a jeering way, with the sly, fierce joy of an Auvergnat, with a laugh which brought to the young girl's cheeks even more color than the slaps of her sisters.

She accepted the blows; she did not repel the abuse. She did not seek either to defend or to excuse herself. She gave no account of how things had occurred, and of how little her own will entered into her misfortune. She remained dumb; she had a vague hope that they would kill her. On her eldest sister asking her whether there had not been violence, and telling her that there were commissaries of police and courts of law, she shut her eyes to the horrible thought of displaying her shame. For an instant only, when her mother's memory was flung in her teeth, she gave a look, a flash from her eyes which the two women could feel piercing their consciences; they remembered that it was they who had placed her in this situation, had kept her in it, had exposed and almost forced her to her shame.

The same evening Germinie's youngest sister took her to a cashmere-darner in the Rue Saint-Martin, with whom she lodged, and who, mad almost about religion, was banner-bearer in an association of the Virgin. She put her to sleep with herself on a mattress on the floor, and having her there within reach the whole night, she vented her ancient and venomous jealousies upon her, her resentment for the preferences and caresses given to Germinie by her father and mother. There were a thousand petty tortures, brutal or hypocritical unkindnesses, kicks with which she bruised her legs, shoves of her body with which in the cold of winter she gradually pushed her companion out of bed on to the tiled floor of the fireless room. During the day-time, the darner took possession of Germinie, catechised her, lectured her, and with her details of the tortures of the life to come, gave her a terrible and material fear of the hell whose flames she made her feel.

She lived there for four months shut up and not allowed to go out. At the end of four months she gave birth to a dead child. When she had recovered, she entered the service of a depilator in the Rue Laffitte, where during the first few days she experienced the joy of one released from prison.

Two or three times when going backwards and forwards she met old Joseph, who wished to marry her, and ran after her. She fled from him, and the old man never knew that he had been a father.

Nevertheless, Germinie pined away in her new place. The

house for which she had been engaged as maid-of-all-work was what servants call a "hole." Wasteful and a spendthrift, untidy and penniless, as is the case with women in the uncertain trades and problematic callings of Paris, the depilator, who was nearly always hovering between seizure for debt and going away, troubled herself but little about the manner in which her little maid was fed. She would frequently go out for the whole day without leaving her anything for dinner. The girl would satisfy herself as best she could with pickles, with salads and vinegared things such as beguile the appetite of young women, with charcoal even, which she would nibble with the depraved tastes and food caprices belonging to her age and sex.

This diet, following upon an accouchement, and adopted in a state of health that was weak and required tonics, emaciated, exhausted, and undermined the young girl. Her condition became alarming. Her complexion came to be of that whiteness which appears to turn green in the open light. Her swollen eyes were encircled with great, bluish shadows. Her discolored lips assumed a tint as of faded violets. She was rendered breathless by the slightest ascent, and people near her were annoyed by the incessant vibration coming from the arteries of her throat. With slow feet, and a sinking frame, she would drag herself along as though her weakness were extreme, and she were bending beneath the burden of life. With semi-dormant faculties and senses, she would swoon for a mere trifle, such as the fatigue of combing her mistress's hair.

She was quietly sinking into her grave when her sister found her another situation with a whilom actor, a retired comedian, living on the money which had been brought him by the laughter of all Paris. The worthy man was old, and had never had any children. He took pity on the wretched girl, thought about her, cared for her, nursed her. He took her to the country. He walked with her in the sunshine on the Boulevards, and felt himself revived on her arm. He was pleased to see her cheerful. Often to amuse her, he would take down a moth-eaten costume from his wardrobe, and try to recall a fragment of a part which he could no longer remember. The mere sight of the little maid in her white cap was a ray of youth coming back to him. The old age of the clown leaned upon her with the good fellowship and pleasure and childishness of a grandfather's heart.

But he died at the end of a few months; and Germinie fell back to waiting upon kept women, boarding-school mistresses, and shopkeepers in the arcades, when the sudden death of a servant-maid brought her into the service of Mademoiselle de Varandeuil, then residing in the Rue Taitbout, in the house in which Germinie's sister was concierge.

IV

THOSE who can see the end of the Catholic Religion in the time at which we find ourselves at present, do not know what powerful and infinite roots it still strikes into the depths of the people. They do not know the secret and delicate entwinings which it has for the woman of the people. They do not know what confession, what the confessor is for the poor souls of poor women. In the priest who listens to her, and whose voice comes softly to her, the woman of toil and pain sees not so much the minister of God, the judge of her sins, and the arbiter of her salvation, as the confidant of her sorrows and the friend of her miseries. However coarse she may be, there is always in her somewhat of the woman's inner nature, a feverish, quivering, sensitive wounded *something,* a restlessness and longing like that of a sick creature looking for the caresses of speech, just as a child's little troubles call for the crooning of a nurse.

She, no less than the woman of fashion, needs relief in expansiveness, confidence, effusion. For it is of the nature of her sex to wish to unbosom and to learn. There exist within her things which she needs to say, and upon which she would fain be questioned, pitied, comforted. She dreams of pitiful interest and of sympathy for hidden feelings of which she feels ashamed. Though her employers may be the best, the most familiar, the most friendly, even, with the woman who serves them, they will show her only those kindnesses which are thrown to a domestic animal. They will be anxious about the way in which she eats, or feels; they will care for the animal in her, and that will be all. They will never imagine that she can suffer in any other place than body, and they will never suppose in her the discomforts of soul, the immaterial melancholies and sorrows for which they themselves find relief by confiding in their equals.

To them the woman who sweeps and cooks has no ideas capable of rendering her sad or a dreamer, and they never speak to her of her thoughts. To whom, then, shall she carry them? To the priest, who awaits them, requests them and receives them, to the church-man who is a man of the world, a superior, a gentleman well bred, and learned, who speaks well, who is always gentle, accessible, patient, attentive, and who seems to despise nothing in the most humble soul, in the most poorly dressed penitent. The priest alone is the listener of the woman in the cap. He alone is troubled about her secret sufferings, about what disturbs her, and agitates her, and suddenly creates in maid, no less than in mistress, a longing to weep or the heaviness of a storm. He is the only one who seeks her outpourings, who draws from her what the irony of each day thrusts back, who busies himself about her moral health; the only one who lifts her higher than her material life, the only one who moves her with words of tenderness, charity, hope, — heavenly words such as she has never heard in the mouths of the men of her family-circle or the males of her own class.

After entering Mademoiselle de Varandeuil's service, Germinie lapsed into profound devotion, and ceased to love anything but the Church. She gradually gave herself up to the sweetness of confession, to the even, serene, low tones coming from the priest in the shade, to consultations which were like touchings with caressing words, and from which she went forth refreshed, light, delivered, happy, and with the pleasing sensation and comfort of a dressing in all the tender, painful and compressed parts of her being.

She did and could not unbosom herself anywhere but there. Her mistress had a certain masculine roughness which repelled expansiveness. There was a bluntness in her address and speech which drove back what Germinie would have been willing to confide in her. It was her nature to be brutal to all jeremiads which did not proceed from a pain or a sorrow. Her virile kindness was not compassionate to discomforts of the imagination, to the torments which thought creates for itself, to the cares which arise from woman's nerves and the disturbances of her organism. Germinie often found her callous, but the old woman had only been bronzed by her time and her life. The crust on her heart was as hard as her body. Never herself complaining, she did not like complaints around her. And in right of all the tears she had not shed she detested childish tears in grown people.

The confessional was soon a sort of delightful and sacred tryst-ing-place for Germinie's thoughts. Every day it had her first re-membrance and her last prayer. Throughout the day she knelt there in a dream, and while she worked it would come back to her eyes — its gold-filleted oak-wood, its pediment of an angel's winged head, its green curtain with the motionless folds, the shadowy mys-tery of its two sides. It seemed to her that now her whole life cen-tred in it, and that all her hours tended towards it. She lived through the week only to reach the desired, promised, called-for day. From Thursday, she was a prey to impatience; in the heightening of a delicious anguish she could feel, as it were, the material approach of the blissful Saturday evening, and when Saturday was come, her work hurried over, and mademoiselle's little dinner hastily served, she would make her escape and hasten to Notre Dame de Lorette, going to repentance as people go to love.

Having dipped her fingers in the holy water, and made a genu-flexion, she passed over the flagstones between the rows of chairs with the gliding movement of a cat stealing over a carpet. Stooping, almost creeping, she would advance noiselessly through the shad-ow of the aisle, as far as the veiled and mysterious confessional which she recognized and beside which she waited for her turn, lost in the emotion of waiting.

The young priest who confessed her lent himself to her frequent confessions. He grudged her neither time, nor attention, nor charity. He suffered her to talk at length, to relate in full to him all her little affairs. He was indulgent to her talkativeness, which was that of a troubled soul, and allowed her to pour out her most trifling griefs. He received the avowal of her anxieties, her longings, her troubles; he repelled and scorned nothing of the confidences of a servant who spoke to him of all the delicate and secret matters of her being, as they would be spoken of to a mother or to a physician.

This priest was young. He was good. He had lived the life of the world. A great sorrow had driven him, a crushed man, to the robe with which he wore the mourning of his heart. Something of the man remained within him, and he listened with sad pity to the unhappy heart of a servant maid. He comprehended that Germinie had need of him, that he was supporting her, strengthening her, saving her from herself, withdrawing her from the temptations of her nature. He felt a melancholy sympathy for this soul so fully formed of tenderness, for this young girl at once so ardent and so weak, for this unhappy creature so unconscious of herself, so given up to passion by her whole heart and body, and arguing so completely in her whole personality the destiny of temperament. Enlightened by the experience of his post, he was astonished, he was alarmed sometimes, at the flashes which came from her, the fire which showed in her eyes at the love-transport of a prayer, at the precipitation of her confessions, at her recurrences to that scene of violence, that scene in which her very sincere wish for resistance appeared to the priest to have been betrayed by a dizziness of the senses that was stronger than she.

This religious fever lasted for several years, during which Germinie lived concentrated, silent, radiant, devoted to God, — or at least she thought so. By degrees, however, her confessor had thought he could see that all her adorations turned towards himself. From glances, from blushes, from words which she no longer uttered to him, and others which she was growing bold enough to utter to him for the first time, he understood that the devotion of his penitent was going astray and becoming exalted by self-deception. She watched him when the service was over, followed him into the vestry, attached herself to him, and ran after his cassock in the church.

The confessor tried to warn Germinie, and to turn aside this amorous fervor from himself. He became more reserved, and armed himself with coldness. Distressed by this change, this indifference, Germinie, embittered and wounded, acknowledged to him one day at confession the feelings of hatred which came to her against two young girls, the penitents preferred by the Abbé. Then the priest, dismissing her without any explanation, sent her to another confessor. Germinie went two or three times to confess herself to this other confessor; then she went no more; then she even ceased to think of going; and of all her religion there remained in her thoughts but a certain far-off sweetness, like the flavorless odor of extinguished incense.

She had reached this point when mademoiselle fell ill. During the whole period of her sickness, Germinie, unwilling to leave her, did not go to mass. And the first Sunday on which mademoiselle, being completely recovered, had no further need of her attentions, she was astonished to see "her devotee" remain at home and not make her escape to the church.

"Ah," she said to her, "so you are not going to see your priests any more just now? What have they been doing to you, eh?"

"Nothing," said Germinie.

V

"THERE, mademoiselle! Look at me," said Germinie.

It was some months later. She had asked her mistress's permission to go that evening to the dance at the wedding of her grocer's sister, who had chosen her for a bridesmaid, and now she was coming to show herself fully arrayed in her low-necked muslin dress.

Mademoiselle raised her head from the old, large print volume in which she was reading, took off her spectacles, put them into the book to mark the page, and said:

"*You*, you pious creature, you at a dance! Do you know what it is, my girl, it seems to me perfectly absurd! You and the rigadoon — upon my word, the only thing you need now is the wish to get married! I warn you I will not keep you. I have no inclination to become a nurse to your brats. Come a little nearer. Oh ho! why, upon my word, Miss Show-all! We have been very coquettish, as I can see, for some time past."

"Oh no, mademoiselle," Germinie tried to say.

"Don't tell me," resumed Mademoiselle de Varandeuil following up her idea, "men are pretty fellows! They will take everything you have to give them ... not to mention the blows they give you. But marriage — I am sure that this idea of getting married runs in your brain when you see the others. I'll wager it's that that gives you such a face? Gracious goodness! now turn round a little and let yourself be seen," said Mademoiselle de Varandeuil in her tone of blunt caress; and, laying her thin hands on the arms of her easy chair, crossing her legs the one above the other, and shaking the tip of her foot, she began to inspect Germinie and her toilet.

"My word!" she said, after a few moments of mute attention, "What, is it you? Then I have never really looked at you properly. Good gracious, yes! Why — why! —" She mumbled some further vague exclamations between her teeth — "Where the mischief did you get that face of yours like the muzzle of a cat in love?" she said at last; and she began to gaze at her.

Germinie was ugly. Her hair, which was of dark chestnut, and appeared black, was frizzled and twisted into intractable waves, into little rough and rebellious locks, which had escaped and raised themselves upon her head in spite of the pomade upon her smoothened band. Her small, smooth, prominent forehead projected from the shadows of the deep sockets in which her eyes were almost unhealthily sunk and hollowed — small, watchful, twinkling eyes, which lessened and kindled with a twinkling like a little girl's, which softened and lit up their smile. These eyes did not look either brown or blue; they were of an indefinable and changeful grey, a grey which was not a color, but a light. Emotion showed in them in the fire of fever, pleasure in the lightning of a sort of intoxication, and passion in phosphorescence.

Her short, high, broadly-perforated nose, with open quivering nostrils, was one of those noses of which the people say that it is raining inside. A big blue vein swelled on one side of it at the corner of the eye. The breadth of face characteristic of the Lorraine stock appeared in her broad, strong, pronounced cheek-bones, which were covered with traces of small-pox. The greatest misfortune in her face was the excessive distance between the nose and mouth. This lack of proportion gave an almost simian character to the lower part of the countenance where a large mouth, with white teeth, and full, flat, and, as it were, crushed lips, smiled with a strange and vaguely irritating smile.

Her low dress showed her neck, the upper part of her breast, her shoulders, and the whiteness of her back, contrasting with her sunburnt face. It was a lymphatic whiteness, the sickly and, at the same time, angelic whiteness of flesh that does not live. She had allowed her arms to hang down by her side, round, smooth arms with pretty dimpled hollows at the elbow. Her wrists were delicate; her hands, which had no look of work, had a woman's nails. And gently, with lazy grace, she suffered her indolent waist to round and play, a waist that could be held within a garter, and that rendered still more refined to the eye the projection of the hips, and the rebound of the curves swelling the dress, an impossible waist, ridiculous in its slenderness, and delightful as is everything in woman which possesses the monstrosity of littleness.

From this ugly woman there was shed a harsh and mysterious seductiveness. Light and shade, conflicting with and shattering each other in her face with its abundant hollows and projections, imparted to it that radiance of voluptuousness which one who paints from love dashes into the rough sketch of his mistress's portrait. Everything about her, her mouth, her eyes, her very ugliness, was a provocation and solicitation. An aphrodisiac charm issued from her, attacking, and attaching itself to, the opposite sex. She released desire, and created the commotion that it brings. A sensual temptation sprang naturally and involuntarily from her, from her gestures, from her gait, from the slightest of her movements, from the air on which her body had left one of its undulations. Beside her, a man felt that he was near one of those disturbing and disquieted creatures, burning with the disease of love, and communicating it to others, whose faces recur to men at unsated hours, tormenting their heavy midnight thoughts, haunting their nights, and violating their dreams.

In the middle of Mademoiselle de Varandeuil's examination, Germinie stooped down, bent over her, and kissed her hand with eager kisses.

"Well — well — enough licking," said mademoiselle, "you would wear out the skin with your mode of kissing. Come, be off, amuse yourself, and try not to come in too late — don't wear yourself out."

Mademoiselle de Varandeuil was left alone. She put her elbows on her knees, gazed into the fire, and dealt some blows to the fuel with the tongs. Then, as she was wont to do when greatly pre-occupied, with the flat of her hand she gave the back of her neck two or three sharp little blows which made her black head-band all awry.

VI

IN talking matrimony to Germinie, Mademoiselle de Varandeuil touched the cause of Germinie's complaint. She laid her hand upon her trouble. The irregularity of her maid's temper, the vexation of her life, the languors, the emptiness, and the discontent of her nature, came from that disease which medicine calls "virgin's melancholy." The suffering of her four and twenty years was the ardent, exalted, poignant desire for marriage, for that thing too holily honorable for her, and to her apparently impossible in the face of the confession which her woman's probity must make of her fall, of her shame. Losses, family misfortunes, came to tear her from her thoughts.

Her brother-in-law, the husband to her sister the concierge, had had the dream of the Auvergnats: he had sought to unite the gains of a trade in *bric-à-brac* to the profits of his concierge's lodge. He had begun modestly with one of those street-stalls that hang about the doors of houses where sales on account of death are taking place, and on which, ranged on blue paper, may be seen plated candlesticks, ivory napkin rings, colored lithographs framed with gold lace upon a black ground, and three or four odd volumes by Buffon. What he made by the plated candlesticks intoxicated him. He hired a dark shop opposite an umbrella-mender's, in an arcade, and there began to trade in the curiosity which comes and goes in the lower halls of the Auction Rooms. He sold cock-patterned plates, pieces of the shoe belonging to Jean-Jacques Rousseau, and water-colored drawings by Ballue, signed Watteau. In this business he ran through what he had made, and then went into debt for some thousands of francs.

His wife, in order to assist the housekeeping a little, and to try to get out of debt, applied for, and obtained a situation as attendant at the Théâtre-Historique. She had her door looked after in the evening by her sister, the dressmaker, went to bed at one o'clock, and got up at five. After a few months she contracted pleurisy in the corridors of the theatre; it lingered and carried her off at the end of six weeks. The poor woman left a little three-year-old daughter ill of measles, which had assumed the most deadly form in the stench of the garret and in the air wherein the child had been breathing her mother's death for more than a month. The father had left for his native place to try to borrow money. There he married again, and nothing more was heard of him.

On leaving her sister's funeral, Germinie hastened to visit an old woman who lived by those curious industries, which in Paris prevent Misery from dying outright of hunger. The old woman followed several occupations. Sometimes she cut horse-hair into equal lengths for brushes, sometimes she divided pieces of ginger-bread. When this work was at a standstill, she would cook for petty itinerant traders, and wash the faces of their children. During Lent she rose at four o'clock in the morning, and went to Notre-Dame to procure a chair, which she retailed, when the people arrived, for ten or twelve sous. To warm herself in the hole in which she lived in the Rue Saint-Victor, she would go at dusk and secretly tear the bark off the trees at the Luxembourg. Germinie, who knew her from giving her the kitchen crusts every week, hired her a servant's room on the sixth floor of the house, and installed her in it with the little girl. She did this on a first impulse, and without reflection. Her sister's harshness at the time of her pregnancy she remembered no longer; she had not even found it necessary to forgive it.

Germinie had now but one thought: her niece. She wanted to revive her, and prevent her from dying by dint of taking care of her. She made her escape every moment from mademoiselle's house, climbed the stairs four at a time to the sixth floor, ran to kiss the child, gave it some tisane, settled it in its bed, looked at it, and went down again out of breath, her color heightened with pleasure.

Germinie lavished everything upon the little girl; attention, caresses, the heart-breath with which one reanimates a little creature ready to die away, consultations, doctor's visits, costly medicines, the remedies of the rich — she gave her all. Her wages went in this way. For nearly a year she made her take some broth every morning, and, given to sleep as she was, she used to get up at five o'clock to make it, awaking of her own accord like a mother.

At last the child was saved, when one morning Germinie received a visit from her sister, the dressmaker, who had married a mechanic two or three years before, and now came to bid goodbye: her husband was going with some comrades who had just been hired for Africa. She was leaving with him, and she proposed to Germinie to take the little girl and bring it up yonder with her own child. They would take charge of it, and Germinie would only have to pay for the journey. It was a separation which must in any case be faced on account of Germinie's mistress. Moreover she, too, was her aunt. And she added words upon words in order to obtain the child, by means of whom she and her husband expected, when once in Africa, to move Germinie's pity, to trick her out of her wages, to swindle her in heart and purse.

To separate from her niece was a sore trial to Germinie. She had set something of her own existence upon the child. She had bound herself to her by anxieties and sacrifices. She had wrestled with sickness for her, and had rescued her from it: the little girl's life was a miracle of her own working. Nevertheless, she understood that she could never take her into mademoiselle's house; that mademoiselle, at her age, with the weariness belonging to her years, and the need of quiet which old people feel, would never endure the constantly active noise of a child. Moreover, the little girl's presence in the house would be a pretext for gossip, and would make the whole street talk. People would say that she was her daughter. Germinie confided in her mistress. Mademoiselle de Varandeuil knew all. She knew that Germinie had taken her niece; but she had pretended ignorance of the fact; she had wished to shut her eyes and see nothing, that she might be able to permit everything. She advised Germinie to entrust her niece to her sister, showing her all the impossibility of keeping her, and giving her money to pay for the journey of the family.

The departure was an anguish to Germinie. She found herself isolated and unoccupied. Having lost the child, she had nothing left to love; her heart grew weary, and in the emptiness of soul which she experienced without her little one, she turned again to religion, and once more took her tenderness to the church.

At the end of three months she received the news of her sister's death. The husband, who belonged to the tribe of whining, blubbering workmen, gave her in his letter, amidst coarse, emotional phrases, and strings of endearments, a distressing picture of his position — the burial to be paid for, fever rendering him unable to work, two children of tender age, without counting the "little one," and a household with no woman in it to heat the soup. Germinie cried over the letter; then her thoughts began to live in that house, beside the poor man, among the poor children, in that frightful country of Africa; and a dim desire to devote herself began to awake within her. Other letters followed in which, while thanking her for her assistance, her brother-in-law gave his misery, his forsaken condition, his complete misfortunes, a still more dramatic coloring, the coloring which the people give to things with its recollections of the Boulevard du Crime, and its scraps of unwholesome reading. Once caught by the humbug of this misfortune, Germinie could not free herself from it. She thought that she could hear childish cries calling her from over yonder. She was buried, absorbed in a resolution and design to go. She was pursued by this idea, and by the word Africa, which she turned over and over secretly in her heart, without speaking a syllable. Mademoiselle de Varandeuil, seeing her so thoughtful and sad, asked her what was the matter, but in vain: Germinie would not speak.

She was teased and tortured between what seemed to her a duty, and what appeared to her an act of ingratitude, between her mistress and her sisters' blood. She thought that she could not leave mademoiselle. And then she told herself that God would not forsake her family. She looked at the rooms, saying to herself: "Still I must go!" And then she was afraid that mademoiselle might be ill when she was no longer there. Another servant! At the thought of this she was seized with jealousy, and imagined that she could already see some one robbing her of her mistress. At other times, her religious notions impelling her to notions of immolation, she was quite ready to sacrifice her own existence to that of her brother-in-law. She wished to go and live with a man whom she detested, with whom she had always been unfriendly, who had almost killed her sister with sorrow, whom she knew to be drunken and brutal; and all that she expected from him, all that she dreaded from him, the certainty and the fear of all that she would have to suffer, served but to exalt her, to inflame her, to incite her to the sacrifice with increased impatience and ardor.

Often it would all subside in an instant; at a word or a gesture from mademoiselle, Germinie would return to herself and be quite different again. She would feel herself wholly and for ever attached to her mistress, and experience a kind of horror at the mere thought of separating her life from her own. She struggled on in this way for two years. Then one fine day she heard by chance that her niece had died a few weeks after her sister: her brother-in-law had concealed the death from her in order to have a hold upon her, and to attract her with her little savings to Africa. At this revelation Germinie lost all her illusion, and was cured at a single stroke. She scarcely remembered that she had wished to go.

VII

ABOUT this time a small dairy with no custom at the end of the street changed hands in consequence of a sale of the business by a judicial decree. The shop was restored. It was repainted. The front windows were adorned with inscriptions in yellow letters. Pyramids of the Colonial Company's chocolate, and flowered bowls of coffee, with little liqueur glasses at intervals, furnished the shelves in the window. At the door shone the sign of a copper milk jug intersected in the middle.

The new dairy-woman, who was trying to revive the establishment in this way, was a person of fifty years of age, brimming over with corpulence and still preserving some remnant of the beauty that was half sunken beneath her fat. It was said in the neighborhood that she had set up with the money of an old gentleman, whose servant she had been until his death in her own part of the country near Langres — for it happened that she was Germinie's fellow-countrywoman, belonging not to the same village, but to a small place beside it, and without having ever met or seen each other, she and Mademoiselle de Varandeuil's maid knew each other by name, and were linked together by common acquaintances and by memories of the same place.

The big woman was complimentary, mealy-mouthed, caressing. She said: "My sweet" to everybody, spoke in a small voice, and played the child with the doleful languor characteristic of corpulent people. She detested big words, she blushed and was scared at a trifle. She loved secrets, made everything a matter of confidence, talked gossip, and always spoke in your ear. Her life was spent in tattling and lamentation. She pitied others, she pitied herself; she bewailed her misfortunes and her stomach. When she ate too much she would say dramatically: "I am going to die." Nothing could have been more pathetic than her fits of indigestion. Her nature was one that was perpetually moved and tearful; she wept indifferently for a beaten horse, for a deceased acquaintance, or for soured milk. She wept over the various items in the newspapers, and she wept to see the passengers go by.

Germinie was quickly beguiled and moved to pity by this wheedling, constantly-affected dairy-woman, who invited the expansiveness of others and who appeared so tender-hearted. At the end of three months scarcely anything went into mademoiselle's house that did not come from Mother Jupillon's establishment. Germinie provided herself with everything, or nearly everything, there. She spent hours in the shop. Once there, she found it difficult to go away, she would remain, and be unable to rise. A mechanical slackness detained her. She would go on talking at the door, so as not to be gone yet. She felt herself attached to the dairy-woman's house by the invisible charm possessed by places to which we constantly return, and which in the end clasp us like things that love us. Then the shop, for her, meant the three dogs, the three ugly dogs, that belonged to Madame Jupillon. She had them always on her knee; she scolded them, she kissed them, she spoke to them; and when she became warm from their heat, she would feel at the bottom of her heart satisfaction like that of an animal rubbing itself against its young. Further, the shop meant to her all the stories of the neighborhood, the meeting-place of gossip, the news of a bill left unpaid by one or the carriage full of flowers brought to another — a place that was watchful of everything, and into which everything entered, even to the lace wrapper going into town on the arm of a servant-maid.

In time, everything served to tie her there. Her intimacy with the dairy-woman became closer through all the mysterious ties belonging to the friendships of the women of the people, through the continual chattering, the daily exchange of the trifles of life, the conversations for the sake of talking, the recurrence of the same "Good-morning" and "Good-evening," the sharing of caresses among the same animals, the sleeping side by side and chair against chair. The shop finally became a captivating place to her, a place wherein her thoughts, her speech, her very limbs and body, found marvelous comfort. Happiness with her came to be that time in the evening when, seated drowsily in a straw arm-chair beside Mother Jupillon asleep with her spectacles on her nose, she nursed the dogs as they lay rolled into a ball in the skirt of her dress; and while the expiring lamp grew dim on the counter, she would remain there, suffering her gaze to lose itself and gently die away with her thoughts, in the back part of the shop, on the triumphal arch made of snails' shells bound together with old moss, beneath the arch of which there stood a little copper figure of Napoleon.

VIII

MADAME JUPILLON, who professed that she had been married, and signed herself "Widow Jupillon," had a son. He was then a child. She had placed him at Saint-Nicolas, that great establishment for religious education where for thirty francs a month rudimentary instruction and a trade are given to children of the people, and to many natural children among them. Germinie got into the habit of accompanying Madame Jupillon on Thursdays when she went to see Bibi. This visit came to be a recreation to her, and something to be looked forward to. She would hurry the mother, be the first to reach the omnibus, which she was well pleased to enter with a big basket of provisions, upon which she crossed her arms during the journey.

Thereupon Mother Jupillon came to have a sore on her leg, an anthrax, which prevented her from walking for nearly eighteen months. Germinie went to Saint-Nicolas alone, and as she was ready and quick to attach herself to others, she busied herself about the child as though he were in some way connected with her. She never missed a Thursday, and always came with her hands full of the leavings of the week, cakes, fruits and sweetmeats which she used to buy.

She would kiss the urchin, be anxious about his health, feel whether he had his knitted waistcoat under his blouse, think that he was too red from running, wipe his face with her handkerchief, and make him show her the soles of his shoes to see whether they had not holes in them. She would ask him whether he gave satisfaction, whether he did his tasks well, whether he had many good marks. She spoke to him of his mother, told him to love the Lord, and walked with him in the court until the two o'clock bell rang, the child giving her his arm and feeling quite proud of being with a woman better dressed than the majority of those who came there, a woman dressed in silk.

He wanted to learn the flageolet, and it cost only five francs a month. But his mother would not give them to him. Germinie secretly brought him the hundred sous every month. It was humiliating to him to wear the uniform of his little blouse when he went out to walk, and on the two or three occasions in the year when he came to see his mother. One year, on his birthday, Germinie opened up a big bundle before him. She had had a tunic made for him. In the whole school there were scarcely twenty of his companions whose families were sufficiently well off to allow them to wear one.

She spoiled him in this way for some years, never letting him suffer for the want of anything, flattering in a poor child the whims and vanities of a rich one, and softening for him the privations and

40

hardships of that professional school which trains for a workman's life, wears a blouse, eats from a plate of brown crockery-ware, and in its virile apprenticeship tempers the people for toil. Meanwhile the boy was growing up. Germinie did not perceive it; in her eyes he was still a child. From habit she always kissed him.

One day she was summoned before the Abbé who conducted the school. He spoke to her of sending young Jupillon away. It was a matter of some bad books which had been found in his hands. Germinie, trembling at the thought of the blows which awaited the child at his mother's house, prayed, entreated, implored, and finally obtained the offender's pardon from the Abbé. Going down again, she tried to scold Jupillon, but at the first word of her lecture Bibi suddenly gave her to her face a look and a smile in which remained nothing of the child that he had been yesterday. She cast down her eyes, and it was she who blushed. A fortnight passed without another visit from her to Saint-Nicolas.

IX

AT the time when young Jupillon left school, the maid-servant of a kept woman who lived below Mademoiselle used sometimes to come to spend the evening at Madame Jupillon's with Germinie. A native of that Grand Duchy of Luxembourg, which provides Paris with cab-drivers and waiting-maids for high class prostitutes, she was what is popularly called a "great trollop"; she had the look of a mare, the brows of a water-carrier, and wanton eyes. She soon began to come every evening. She paid for cakes and glasses of liqueurs for everybody, amused herself by making young Jupillon romp, indulged in horse-play with him, sat down upon him, twitted him with being handsome, treated him as a child, and joked him coarsely for not being yet a man. The young fellow, pleased and elated by these attentions from the first woman who ever took any notice of him, soon allowed his preference for Adèle, as the new comer was called, to be seen.

Germinie was passionately jealous. Jealousy was the foundation of her nature; it formed the dregs and bitterness of her tenderness. She wished to have those whom she loved all to herself — to

41

hold them in absolute possession. She required that they should love none but herself. She could not allow them to divert and give to others the smallest particle of their affection; from the time that she had merited it, this affection was no longer theirs; they were no longer masters of its disposal. She detested the people whom her mistress seemed to receive more warmly than the rest, and to welcome as intimates. By her ill-tempered demeanor and cross looks she had estranged and almost driven from the house two or three of mademoiselle's old friends whose visits distressed her, as though the old ladies were coming to steal something from the rooms — to take some portion of her mistress away from her. People whom she had loved had become odious to her: she had not found that they loved her enough, and she hated them for all the love that she would fain have had from them. Altogether, her heart was most exacting and despotic. Giving all, she asked for all. At the smallest sign of cooling, or of division on the part of those upon whom she had bestowed her affection, she would break out and prey upon herself, passing nights in tears, and holding the world in execration.

On seeing this woman establishing herself in the shop, and growing familiar with the young man, all Germinie's jealousies were roused and turned into rage. Her hatred rose and rebelled with her disgust against this abandoned, shameless woman, who might be seen at table with soldiers on Sundays on the outer Boulevards, and whose face on Mondays bore the signs of her dissipation on the previous day. She did everything to induce Madame Jupillon to banish her, but she was one of the best customers of the dairy, and the dairy-woman, with all gentleness, refused to drive her away. Germinie had recourse to the son, and told him she was an unfortunate. But this only served to attach the young man to this ugly woman, whose evil reputation flattered him. Moreover, he had the cruel mischievousness of youth, and increased his amiability towards her, merely to see "the mug" that Germinie made, and to enjoy distressing her. Soon, Germinie perceived that this woman had more serious intentions than she had at first imagined; she understood what she wanted with the child — for the young man, with his seventeen years, was still a child to her.

From that time she dogged their footsteps; she never quitted them, she never left them alone for a moment. She made one at their parties, at the theatre, and in the country, shared all their walks

— was always there, present and troublesome, striving to restrain the servant, and to restore her to modesty with a whispered word: "A child! are you not ashamed?" she would say to her. The other would give a great laugh, as though it were a good joke. When they left the play, animated, heated by the fever of the performance and the excitement of the theatre, or when they were returning from the country, charged with a whole day's sunshine, intoxicated by the sky and open air, lashed by the wine at dinner, and indulging in such playfulness and freedom as are encouraged at night by the exaltations of pleasure, by the feasted joyousness and the mirthful senses of the woman of the people, Germinie sought to be ever between Jupillon and the maid. She tried every moment to break their arm-linked amours, to untie them, to uncouple them. Unweariedly would she separate them, and withdraw them continually from each other. She would place her own person between those two who sought to be together. She would glide between the gestures which sought for mutual contact; she would glide between those presented lips and offered mouths.

But she was herself touched and stricken by all that she prevented. She could feel the brushing of the hands that she separated, of the caresses which she checked midway, and which were deluded in straying upon herself. The sigh and breathing of the kisses that she parted would pass across her cheek. Without wishing it, and disturbed by a certain horror, she mingled in embraces and partook of desires in the friction and struggle which were every day diminishing about her person the young man's respect and reserve.

It happened one day that she was not so strong against herself as she had hitherto been. This time she did not shrink so abruptly from his advances. Jupillon felt that she was hesitating. Germinie felt it better than he did; but she had exhausted effort and torment, and was worn out with suffering. The love that the other woman had felt, which she had turned away from Jupillon, had slowly entered into her own heart. Now it was buried there, and bleeding with jealousy, she found herself weakened, unresisting, swooning like one mortally wounded in presence of the happiness that was coming to her.

Nevertheless, she repelled the attempts, the liberties of the young man, without saying anything, without speaking. She did not dream of belonging to him in another fashion, or of surrendering herself more fully. She lived on the thoughts of love, believing that she would always do so, and in the rapture which uplifted her soul, she drove away her fall and repulsed her senses. She continued quivering and pure — absorbed and suspended in abysses of tenderness, tasting and desiring nothing of her lover but his caress, as though her heart had been formed only for the sweetness of kisses.

X

THIS happy and unsatisfied love produced a singular physiological phenomenon in Germinie's physical being. It appeared as though the passion circulating within her renewed and transformed her lymphatic temperament. She no longer seemed to draw life, as formerly, drop by drop, from a miserly spring; a full and generous force flowed in her veins; the fire of a rich blood coursed through her body. She felt herself filled with warm health, and the joys of existence swept through her, beating their wings within her breast like birds in the sunshine.

A marvellous animation had come to her. The miserable, nervous energy which had sustained her, had given place to a healthy activity, to a clamorous, moving, overflowing liveliness. She knew her former weaknesses no more, her depression, her prostration, her drowsiness, her nerveless indolence. Her mornings once so heavy and torpid were now brisk, bright awakenings opening up in an instant to the cheerfulness of the day. She dressed herself playfully, and in haste; her nimble fingers moved of their own accord, and she was astonished at being so brisk, so full of spirits during those fainting hours in the early morning, when she had formerly so often felt her heart upon her lips. And throughout the day there was with her the same bodily good-humor, the same cheerfulness of movement. She must be constantly going, walking, moving, working, spending herself. At times, what she had lived through appeared to her to be extinguished, the natural sensations which she had hitherto experienced shrank from her into the remoteness of a dream, or the depth of a slumbering recollection. The past was behind her, as though she had passed through it beneath the veil of a fainting-fit, and with the unconsciousness of a somnambulist. It was the first time that she experienced the feeling, the impression at once harsh and soft, violent and divine, of the play of life breaking forth in its plenitude, its regularity and its power.

She went up and down stairs for a trifle. At a word from Mademoiselle she would clatter down the five flights. When she was seated, her feet danced upon the floor. She scrubbed, cleaned, arranged, beat, shook, washed without rest or truce, and was always at work, filling the rooms with her coming and going, and the incessant bustle of her person.

"Good gracious!" said her mistress, when deafened as by the noise of a child, "Germinie! how you do turn things upside down, don't you?"

One day on going into Germinie's kitchen, Mademoiselle saw a little earth in a cigar-box standing in the sink.

"What is that?" she said to her.

"It is some grass that I have planted to look at," said Germinie.

"So you have grown fond of grass, have you? All you want now is to have some canaries!"

XI

AFTER a few months, Germinie's life, her entire life, belonged to the dairy-woman. Mademoiselle's service was not very restrictive and took up very little of her time. A whiting, a cutlet, and there was nothing further to cook. In the evening, Mademoiselle might have kept her with her for company, but she preferred to send her to walk, to turn her out, make her take a little air and recreation. She only required her to be back at ten o'clock to assist her when going to bed, and she would even undress herself and go to bed very well alone when Germinie was late. All the hours which her mistress left her, Germinie came to live through and spend in the shop. She used now to go down to the dairy in the morning at the taking down of the shutters, which most frequently she brought in herself, have her coffee and milk, remain until nine o'clock, go up again for Mademoiselle's chocolate, and find means to return two or three times between breakfast and dinner, lingering, and talking in the back-shop for the smallest errand.

"What a chatter-box you are!" Mademoiselle would say to her, with a scolding voice and a smiling look.

At half-past five, when the little dinner had been cleared away, she would go down the stairs four at a time, establish herself at Mother Jupillon's, wait there for ten o'clock, climb the five stories again, and in five minutes undress her mistress, who, while acquiescing, would be somewhat astonished at seeing her in such a hurry to go to bed. She could recall the time when Germinie had a passion for sleeping in one easy-chair after another, and was never willing to go up to her room. The extinguished candle on Mademoiselle's night-table was still smoking when Germinie again found herself at the dairy-woman's, this time to remain until twelve or one o'clock. Often she left only when a policeman, seeing the light, knocked at the shutters and obliged them to close.

That she might be always there, and have the right of being there, that she might incrust herself in this shop, and never take her eyes off the man of her love, but brood over him, and look after him and keep company with him, she became the servant of the house. She swept the shop, did the cooking for the mother, and made the porridge for the dogs. She waited on the son, she made his bed, she brushed his clothes, she polished his shoes, happy and proud to touch what he had touched, moved to lay her hand where he had laid his body, ready to kiss the mud that came from him on the leather of his boots!

She did the work, she kept shop, she served the customers, Madame Jupillon relying for everything upon her; and while the brave girl was working and sweating, the big woman, assuming majestic and lady-like leisure at her door, stranded on a chair across the pavement, and inhaling the freshness of the street, fingered the delicious money of her profits again and again in the shopkeeper's pocket beneath her apron, the money which comes from selling, and which sounds so sweet in the ear of the petty tradespeople of Paris that the retired shopkeeper is at first quite melancholy at no longer having it jingling and fidgeting beneath his fingers.

XII

WHEN the spring had come, Germinie would say almost every evening to Jupillon:

"Suppose we were to go to the beginning of the fields?"

Jupillon would put on his red and black checked flannel shirt, and his black velvet cap, and they would set out for what the people of the neighborhood called "the beginning of the fields."

They went up the Clignancourt Road, and with the tide of suburban Parisians hastening on their way to drink in a little air, walked towards that great stretch of sky which rose straight from the pavement between the two rows of houses on the top of the ascent, and showed quite clear when an omnibus was not passing out of it. The heat subsided, the houses had no longer any sun except on the ridges of the roofs and the chimneys. As from a great door opening upon the country, there came from the end of the street and from the sky a breath of space and freedom.

At the Château-Rouge they came across the first tree and the first leaves. Then, in the Rue du Château, the horizon opened up before them in dazzling sweetness. The country stretched gleaming and indefinite in the distance, lost in the golden dust of seven o'clock. Everything quivered in the powder of light, which the light leaves behind it on the verdure which it effaces, and on the houses which it colors rose.

They descended, following the pavement blackened with games of hop-scotch, past long walls over which a branch hung here and there, past lines of houses, broken and interspaced with gardens; to their left rose tree-tops filled with light, clusters of leaves pierced by the setting sun which traced stripes of fire on the bars of the iron gratings. After the gardens, they passed the palings, the enclosures for sale, the buildings raised by anticipation in the newly-planned streets and now presenting the toothing at the sides to empty space, the walls covered at foot with heaps of bottle-ends, the large smooth-plastered houses with windows encumbered by cages and linen, and with the Y of a plumb-line on every story, the entrances to plots of ground looking like farmyards, with little hillocks in them browsed over by goats.

Here and there they stopped and smelled the flowers, the scent of some sorry lilac growing in a narrow yard. Germinie would pluck a leaf as she passed, and nibble it.

The mad, merry, circular flight of swallows revolved and grew complicated over her head. The birds called to one another. The sky answered the cages. She could hear everything singing around her, and with happy eyes she watched the women at the windows in their dressing-jackets, the men in the little gardens in their shirt-sleeves, the mothers on the door-steps with little brats between their knees.

The descent came to an end, the pavement ceased, the street was succeeded by a broad, white, chalky, dusty road, formed of rubbish, fragments of plaster, and crumbled lime and brick, and broken up and furrowed by ruts with shining edges, made by the iron on big wheels, and the crushing of carts laden with free-stone. Then began that which comes when Paris ends, and which grows where grass will not grow, one of those arid landscapes which great towns create around them, that first zone of suburb *intra muros,* where nature is withered, the earth worn out, and the country strewn with oyster-shells. There was now nothing but half-enclosed plots, showing carts and drays with the shafts pointing skywards in the air, yards for the sawing of stone, planking works, workmen's houses in process of construction, full of gaps and openings and bearing the masons' flag, wastes of grey and white sand, and market-gardens marked out with the line, beyond the ditches towards which the embankment of the road sloped in streams of pebbles.

Soon came the last street lamp, hanging to a green post. People were constantly going and coming. The road was alive, and it amused the eye. Germinie met women carrying their husbands' sticks, girls of easy virtue in silk on the arms of their brothers in blouses, and old women in Madras handkerchiefs, resting after work, and walking with folded arms. There were working men drawing their children in little carriages, urchins, with their lines, coming back from fishing at Saint-Ouen, and people trailing branches of flowering acacia at the end of a stick.

Sometimes a pregnant woman would pass holding out her arms before her to a tiny child, and casting the shadow of her pregnancy upon the wall.

All walked quietly, happily, with steps that liked to linger, with the cheerful lounging and the happy laziness of a stroll. No one was in a hurry, and the groups of promenaders formed in the distance dark and nearly motionless spots on the perfectly level horizon, which every now and then was traversed by the white smoke of a railway train.

They would come to the back of Montmartre to the kind of large ditches, the sloping beds crossed by grey and trodden paths. There was a little grass there, frizzled and yellowed by the sun which all aflame might be seen setting between the houses. And Germinie loved to meet with the mattress-carders at work, the knacker's horses grazing on the bare ground, the madder trousers of the soldiers playing at bowls, or the children flying a dark kite in the clear sky. Then, in order to cross the railway bridge, they turned down through that evil encampment of rag-pickers, the stonemasons' district below Clignancourt. They passed quickly by the houses built of stolen materials, and reeking with the horrors that they concealed; these hovels — a cross between a cabin and a burrow — terrified Germinie vaguely; she could feel crouching within them all the horrors of Night.

But at the fortifications her pleasure returned. She hastened to sit down with Jupillon on the slope. Close to her were families in groups, workmen lying flat on their faces, middle-class folk scanning the horizon with telescopes, and philosophers in misery, leaning with both hands upon their knees, and wearing coats greasy with old age, and black hats as red as their beards. The air was filled with the sounds of organ-playing. Below her, in the moat, were parties playing at puss in the corner. Before her eyes she had a motley crowd — white blouses, blue aprons on children running about, a revolving ring game, cafés, wine-shops, stalls for fried fish, games for macaroons, shooting-galleries half hidden in a cluster of verdure from which rose masts with tri-colored pendants; while further off, in a vapor, in a bluish mist, a line of tree-tops marked the course of a road. On the right she could see Saint-Denis and the great structure of its basilica; on the left, above a line of vanishing houses, the disc of the sun setting over Saint-Ouen was of cherry-colored fire, letting fall to the lower part of the sky as it were red pillars which upbore him trembling. And often this splendor was crossed for a moment by the ball of a child at play.

They would go down through the gate, pass the shops for Lorraine sausages, the cake-sellers, the boarded wine-shops, the green-less arbors of wood that was still white wherein a medley of men, women, and children were eating fried potatoes, mussels, and shrimps, and so would come to the first field and the first living grass. At the edge of the grass stood a hand-cart laden with ginger-bread and peppermint lozenges; and a woman sold licorice-water on a table in the furrow. A strange landscape in which there was a complete mixture — the smoke of frying and the evening mist, the noise of games and the silence shed from heaven, the odor of powdered dung and the smell of the green corn, the barrier and the idyll, the Fair and Nature! Germinie enjoyed it nevertheless; and urging Jupillon to go further, she would walk on the very edge of the road, thrusting her legs into the corn as she went, in order to feel its tickling freshness upon her stockings.

When they were returning she liked to re-ascend the slope. The sunshine was gone. The sky was grey below, pink in the middle, and bluish overhead. The horizon was growing black, the green-ness was deepening and darkening, the zinc roofs of the wine-shops were reflecting the moonlight, fires were beginning to dot the shadow, the crowd was becoming greyish, and the whiteness of linen blue. Everything was being gradually obliterated, blurred, and lost in a colorless and expiring residue of daylight, and thicken-ing shadows began to creep up amid the din of rattles, the noise of a crowd growing animated by the night, and of wine prompting to sing. The tops of the tall grass on the slope were swaying and bend-ing in the breeze. Then Germinie made up her mind to leave. She would return, filled with the falling night, giving herself up to the uncertain vision of things half-seen, passing the unlighted houses, again seeing everything on her way as though it were grown pale, weaned by the road that was hard to her feet, content to be weary, slow, tired, half-fainting, and feeling full of satisfaction.

At the first lighted lamps in the Rue du Château, she fell to the pavement from a dream.

XIII

MADAME JUPILLON wore a look full of happiness when she saw Germinie, and kissed her with effusiveness, and spoke to her with endearments of voice, and looked at her with sweetness of expres-sion. The huge woman's kindness seemed, in her case, to find vent in emotion, and tenderness, and confidence of a maternal description. To Germinie she confided her shop accounts, her woman's secrets, the most intimate recesses of her life. She seemed to devote herself to her as to a person of her own blood in process of initiation into family interests. When she spoke of the future, Germinie was always mentioned as some one from whom she was never to be separated, and who formed part of the household. Often she would let certain discreet and mysterious smiles escape her, smiles seeming to indicate that everything was seen and without displeasure. Sometimes, also, when her son was seated beside Germinie, she would suddenly fasten moistening, motherly eyes upon them, and embrace the couple in a look which seemed to bring together and bless the heads of her two children. Without ever speaking, without uttering a word that might constitute an engagement, without opening her mind and binding herself, and while continuing to repeat that her son was still very young to enter upon housekeeping, she encouraged Germinie's hopes and illusions by the attitude of her entire person, by her airs of secret indulgence and complicity of heart, and by those intervals of silence in which she seemed to open to her a mother-in-law's arms. And displaying all her talents for falseness, employing her mines of sentiment, her ingenuous artfulness, and that easy, intricate deceit which is characteristic of fat people, the big woman succeeded through the assurance, the tacit promise of marriage, in overcoming all resistance on the part of Germinie, who finally suffered the young man's ardor to snatch from her what she believed she was giving in advance to her husband's love.

Throughout this game the dairy-woman had been desirous of only one thing: of attaching to herself and keeping a servant who cost her nothing.

XIV

AS Germinie was going one day down the back staircase, she heard a voice calling over the banisters, and Adèle shouting to her to bring her up two sous' worth of butter and ten of absinthe.

"Now indeed you shall sit down for a minute," said Adèle to her when she brought her back the absinthe and the butter. "And you have given up coming in here, you are never to be seen now. Come! you have plenty of time for being with your old woman. *I* could not live with such a figure-head of antichrist as that! Do stay. There's no work to be done here to-day. There's no money, and Madame is in bed. Whenever there's no money she goes to bed, does Madame, and she stays there reading novels the whole day. Will you have some?" and she offered her the glass of absinthe. "No? Oh, of course, you don't drink. It's funny not to drink. You are wrong. Look here: it would be very kind of you to write me a line to my sweetheart, Labourieux, you know; I have spoken to you about him. See, here is Madame's pen and some of her paper; it's got a nice scent. D'ye take me? He's a trump, my dear, is that man! He's in the butchery, as I have told you. My word, it doesn't do to contradict him! When he has just drunk a glass of blood after kill-ing his beasts, he's like a madman, and if you make him obstinate — well, he *does* hit out. But what would you have? It's because he's strong that he's like that. You ought to see him hitting himself blows on the chest hard enough to kill an ox, and saying to you: 'This is a wall!' Ah, he is a fine fellow, he is! Take pains with his letter, won't you? Make it fetch him. Say nice things to him, you know, and rather sad. He delights in that. At the theatre he likes nothing but what makes everybody cry. See! imagine that it's your-self writing to a lover."

Germinie began to write.

"I say, Germinie! Don't you know? It's a queer notion Madame has taken into her head. How curious it is in women like that, who can go in for the grandest things, and can have everything, and marry kings if it suits them! And there's no mistake about it when one is like Madame, with a face and figure like hers. And then with the nick-nacks that they cover themselves with, and all their para-phernalia of dresses, and lace everywhere, and everything, how can anybody be expected to resist them? And if it's not a gentleman, but some one like ourselves, you may imagine how that turns his head all the more. A woman in velvet is what'll upset his brain.

Yes, my dear, just think if Madame hasn't gone cracked about that boy Jupillon! That's all was wanted to make us die of starva-tion here!"

Germinie, with her pen raised above the letter which she had begun, was looking at Adèle and devouring her with her eyes.

"That's a staggerer, isn't it?" said Adèle, smacking her lips and sipping the absinthe in small mouthfuls, her eyes lit up with joy at seeing Germinie's wry face. "Ah! the fact is, it's funny; but as for truth, I'll guarantee it's being true. She noticed the fellow on the door-step of the shop the other day as she was coming back from the races. She has gone in two or three times under pretence of buying something. She is to have some perfumery brought to her, to-morrow, I believe. But no matter; that's their own lookout, isn't it? Now then, my letter? You're annoyed at what I have told you? You used to do the prude, so I didn't know. Oh-h-h! so, that's it — now I understand what you were telling me about the youngster. I can quite believe now that you didn't want him touched! Sly creature!"

And at a gesture of denial from Germinie:

"Tut! tut!" Adèle went on. "What is it to me? A child fresh from his mother's milk? Thanks! that's not my sort. However, that's your own business. Now let's see about my letter, eh?"

Germinie bent over the sheet of paper. But she was in a fever; her nervous fingers made the pen splutter.

"Look here," she said, throwing it down, after a few moments: "I don't know what's wrong with me to-day. I'll write it for you another time."

"Just as you like, my girl, but I rely upon you. Come to-morrow then, and I'll tell you about Madame's fooleries. We'll have a good laugh!"

And when the door was shut, Adèle burst out laughing; it had cost her nothing but a little humbug to get hold of Germinie's secret.

XV

WITH young Jupillon, love had been nothing but the satisfaction of a certain curiosity in evil which sought in the knowledge and possession of a woman for the right and pleasure of despising her. This man, on emerging from childhood, had brought no ardor or fire to his first *liaison,* but the cold, blackguardly instincts which are awakened in children by bad books, the confidences of companions, the conversations of a boarding-school, the first breath of impurity deflowering desire. All that a young man throws around the woman who yields to him, all that he veils her with, caresses, loving words, imaginings of tenderness, these had no existence whatever for Jupillon. Woman was to him nothing but an obscene image; and a woman's passion appeared to him merely to be something forbidden, illicit, coarse, indecent, funny, something excellent for disillusion and irony.

Irony — the base, cowardly, wicked irony which belongs to the lowest of the people — was this fellow's entire nature. He embodied the type of those Parisians who wear on their faces the chaffing skepticism of that great city of humbug in which they were born. Smiles — the wit and malice of the Parisian physiognomy — were with him always mocking and impertinent. Jupillon had the mirthfulness of a wicked mouth with what was a most cruelty at the two corners of upturned lips that quivered with nervous movement. On his face, which was pale with such paleness as is imparted to the complexion by the biting of *aqua fortis* on copper, on his small, sharp, decided, impudent features were mingled bluster, energy, heedlessness, intelligence, impudence — all kinds of rascally expressions which in him were softened down at certain times by a look of feline cunning

His trade as a glove-cutter — he had kept to glove-making after two or three unfortunate attempts in various apprenticeships — his habit of working in the shop-window and of being a spectacle for passers-by had imparted to his whole person the self-possession and elegance of an attitudinizer. In the workshop looking upon the street, dressed in his white shirt, his little black "Colin" tie, and his tight waisted trousers, he had learnt the affectations, the pretensions in dress, and the "mob" graces of the workman who is an object of attention. And his doubtful elegancies — the parting down the middle, the hair over the temples, the low shirt-collars disclosing the entire neck, the straining after feminine appearances and affectations — gave him an uncertain figure which was rendered more ambiguous by his beardless face with its merest shading of two little pencils of moustache, and his sexless features, to which passion and anger imparted all that is bad in the wicked little face of a woman. But to Germinie all these airs and this style on the part of Jupillon implied distinction.

Constituted in this way, having nothing within him that could love, and incapable of being attached even through his senses, Jupillon found himself quite embarrassed and wearied by a worship which grew intoxicated with itself and whose frenzy went on continually increasing. Germinie was overwhelming him. He thought her ridiculous in humiliation, and comical in devotion. He was tired, disgusted, sick of her. He had had enough of her love, enough of her person. He fled from her. He made his escape to meet his friends. He alleged accidents, business to be gone about, work that was pressing. In the evening, she waited and he did not come; she thought that he was busy, and he was in some obscure billiard room, or at some barrier ball.

XVI

THERE was a ball one Thursday at the "Boule Noire," and dancing was going on. The room had the modern character of the pleasure resorts of the people. It glittered with false riches and poor luxury. There were the sort of paintings and tables which one sees in wine-shops, gilded gas-apparatus and glasses for drinking a quartern of brandy, velvet and wooden benches, the wretchedness and rustic-ity of a country inn amid the embellishments of a palace of card-board.

Crimson velvet valances with a gold-lace stripe hung at the win-dows, and were economically repeated in paint under the looking-glasses, which were lit up by triple-branched sconces. On the walls, in large white panels, pastorals by Boucher, surrounded by painted frames, alternated with Prud'hon's "Seasons," astonished to find themselves there; and over the windows and doors dropsical loves played among fine roses that had been taken off the pomatum-pot of some suburban hair dresser. Square posts, spotted with sorry ara-besques, supported the middle of the room in the centre of which was a small octagonal gallery for the orchestra. An oaken barrier, breast-high and serving as a back to a red, meagre bench, enclosed the dancers. And against this barrier on the outside, green-painted tables with wooden benches were crowded together in two rows, thus surrounding the ball with a café.

In the space reserved for dancing, beneath the sharp fire and darting flames of the gas, were all sorts of women clad in dark, worn, faded woollen-stuffs, women in black tulle caps, women in black paletots, women in jackets worn out and frayed at the seams, women cramped in the fur tippets of open-air dealers and side-street shops. Amidst all this, there was not a collar to frame the youthfulness of the faces, not a scrap of a light petticoat fluttering out of the whirlwind of the dance, not a touch of white among these women, sad-colored to the toes of their dull boots, and wholly clad in the hues of wretchedness. This absence of linen gave an appearance of poverty-stricken mourning to the ball; it imparted something sad, and dirty, deadened and earthy, to all these forms, a kind of vague, sinister aspect wherein the return from the hospital was mingled with the return from the pawnshop!

An old woman, bare-headed and with her hair parted on the side of her head, was handing round the tables a basket filled with pieces of Savoy cake and red-cheeked apples.

From time to time the dance, in its swinging and whirling, would display a dirty stocking, the Jewish type of a street sponge-seller, red fingers at the end of black mittens, a brown, moustached face, an under-petticoat spotted with dirt two days old, a second-hand crinoline strained and quite bent, flowered village calico, or a piece of a kept woman's cast-off garments.

The men wore overcoats, limp caps turned down behind, and woollen comforters, unfastened and hanging down their backs. They invited the women by pulling the cap-ribbons that streamed behind them. A few in hats, surtouts, and colored shirts, had a look like that of the insolent domestics and stablemen of some great household.

Everywhere there was hopping and movement. The women dancers threw themselves about and capered, animated, clumsy, and riotous beneath the lash of bestial joy. And during the second figure might be heard the giving of such addresses as Impasse du Dépotoir.

Here it was that Germinie walked in just as the quadrille was ending with the air of "Daddy Bugeaud's Cap," in which the cymbals, bells, and drum had imparted to the dance the giddiness and madness of their noise. At a glance Germinie took in the room, with all the men bringing back their partners to the places marked by their caps. She had been deceived; *he* was not there; she did not see him. Nevertheless she waited. She entered the dancing enclosure and sat down on the edge of a bench, trying not to look too uncomfortable. From their linen caps, she had concluded that the women seated in a row beside her were servants like herself. Fellow-servants intimidated her less than the dancing-lasses, with their hair in a net, their hands in the pockets of their paletots, impudent eyes, and humming lips.

But, even on her bench, she soon attracted malevolent attention. Her bonnet — only a dozen women at the ball wore bonnets — her scalloped petticoat the white of which showed beneath her dress, the gold brooch in her shawl, created hostile curiosity around her. They cast ill-natured glances and smiles at her. All the women seemed to be asking themselves whence this new-comer came, and to be telling themselves that she had come to take the lovers of the rest. Friends walking through the room, clasped together as though for a waltz, with their hands slipped about each other's waists, made her cast down her eyes as they passed before her, and then moved off shrugging their shoulders and turning back their heads.

She changed her position and again encountered the same smiles, the same hostility, the same whisperings. She went to the end of the room, and all these women's eyes followed her; she felt herself enwrapped in looks of malice and envy from the hem of her dress to the flowers in her bonnet. She was red in the face; at times, she feared that she would weep. She wished to go away, but courage to cross the room wholly failed her.

She began to look mechanically at an old woman walking slowly round the room with a silent step like a night-bird's circling flight. A black bonnet of the color of burnt paper confined the bands of her whitening hair. From her square, high, manlike shoulders hung a lead-colored Scotch tartan. On reaching the door she cast a last look into the room, and took it all in with the eye of a vulture seeking meat and finding none.

Suddenly there was a shout: it was a policeman turning out a slight youth who was trying to bite the man's hands, and was clinging to the tables against which, as he fell, he made a sharp, breaking noise.

As Germinie turned away her head she perceived Jupillon: he was there, in the recess of a window, smoking at a green table between two women. One was a tall blonde with scanty, frizzled, hemp-like hair, a flat, stupid face, and round eyes. A red flannel chemise was wrinkled up her back, and with her hands she was dancing about the two pockets of a black apron that covered her maroon-colored skirt. The other, who was small and dark, with a face that was quite red from being washed with soap, was muffled, with all the coquetry of a fish-wife, in a white knitted hood with a blue border.

Jupillon had recognized Germinie. When he saw her getting up and coming to him with a fixed look, he leaned over to the ear of the woman in the hood, and squaring himself as he sat, waited with both elbows on the table.

"Hello! is that you?" he said, when Germinie was in front of him motionless, erect, mute. "This is a surprise! Waiter, another bowl."

And emptying the bowl of mulled wine into the glasses of the two women, he exclaimed:

"Look here, don't be a fool. Sit down there."

And as Germinie did not stir:

"Tut! these are ladies who belong to friends of mine — ask them!"

"Mélie," said the woman in the hood to the other, in rasping tones, "don't you see? It's the gentleman's mother! Make room for the lady since she's kind enough to drink with us."

Germinie cast a murderous glance at the woman.

"Eh! what?" resumed the latter, "that annoys you, madame, does it? Excuse me! you ought to have told me. What age does she think herself, eh, Mélie? By Jove! you choose'em young, you do; you're not particular!"

Jupillon was covertly smiling, lounging at ease, and inwardly sneering. His whole person betrayed the cowardly joy which bad men take in seeing the sufferings of those who suffer because they love them.

"I want to speak to you — to yourself — not here — outside," said Germinie to him.

"I hope you'll enjoy yourselves! Are you coming, Mélie?" said the woman in the cape, relighting an extinguished cigar-end forgotten by Jupillon on the table beside a slice of lemon.

"What do you want?" asked Jupillon, moved in spite of himself by the tone of Germinie's voice.

"Come!"

And she began to walk in front of them. There was crowding and laughing as she went. She could hear voices and phrases, and muttered hootings.

XVII

JUPILLON promised Germinie that he would return to the ball no more. But the young man was beginning to have the reputation of a Brididi at these tavern-hops of the barrier, at the "Boule Noire," the "Reine Blanche," and the "Ermitage." He had become a dancer who brings the consumers at the table to their feet, a dancer who has a whole hall hanging on the sole of his boot as he flings it two inches higher than his head, a dancer whom the women of the place invite, and to whom they frequently offer refreshments to dance with them. The ball was not to him merely a ball, it was a theatre, a public popularity, applause, the flattering murmurs of his name in the various groups, the ovation of a cancan-dancer's glory beneath the fire of the lamps.

On the Sunday he did not go to the "Boule Noire," but on the Thursday following he returned; and Germinie, seeing clearly that she was unable to prevent his going, determined to follow him and to stay there as long as he stayed. Seated at a table in the background, in the worst-lighted corner of the room, she followed him and watched him with her eyes during the whole of the quadrille; and if he lingered when it was over, she would go and take him away, withdrawing him almost by force from the hands and endearments of the women, who, in malicious sport, would persist in pulling and detaining him.

As she quickly became known, the insults around her ceased to be vague, subdued, and distant as at the first ball. Words assailed her to her face, and laughter spoke to her aloud. She was obliged to spend her three hours amid mockings which pointed at her, indicated her with the finger, named her, fastened her age upon her face. Every moment she was obliged to endure the expression, "old woman," which the young hussies would spit at her over their shoulders. Still, these women simply looked at her; but often partners invited to drink by Jupillon, brought by him to the table where Germinie was, and drinking the bowl of mulled wine for which she paid, would remain leaning on their elbows, with their cheeks upon their hands, appearing not to see that there was a woman there, moving towards her place as though it were empty, and making no reply, when she spoke to them. Germinie could have killed these women whom Jupillon made her entertain and who despised her so much that they did not so much as notice her presence.

It came to pass that, worn out by her sufferings, and revolted by all the humiliation which she was obliged to suffer in this place, she conceived the idea that she too would dance. She could see no other means of keeping her lover from others, of having him the whole evening, perhaps of attracting him by her success should she chance to succeed. For a whole month she worked in secret in order to learn how to dance. She went over the figures, and the steps. She strained her body, toiled to acquire the flinging of the waist and whirl of the petticoat which she saw applauded. After doing this she ventured; but everything baffled her and added to her awkwardness — the hostility by which she felt herself surrounded, the smiles of astonishment and pity which had traversed the lips when she took her place within the dancing enclosure. She was so ridiculous and so much laughed at that she had not the courage to try again. She once more buried herself gloomily in her dark corner, leaving it only to seek Jupillon and lead him away with the mute violence of a woman who tears her husband from the public-house and carries him off by the arm.

It was soon rumored through the street that Germinie went to these balls, and that she never missed one. The fruiterer, at whose shop Adèle had already been gossiping, sent her son "to see"; he came back saying that it was true, and he related all the annoyances to which Germinie was subjected, but which were nevertheless ineffectual to prevent her from returning. Then there was no longer any doubt in the neighborhood as to the relations between mademoiselle's servant and Jupillon, relations which a few charitable souls disputed still. The scandal was discovered, and in one week the poor girl, dragged through all the slanders of the neighborhood, christened and greeted with the foulest names in the language of the street, fell at a single stroke from the most highly expressed esteem into the most brutally published contempt.

Hitherto her pride — and it was great — had enjoyed that respect and consideration which, in a district of women of easy virtue, surrounds the servant who serves a respectable person honestly. People had accustomed her to consideration, deference, attention. She was excepted from among her companions. Her honesty, which was beyond suspicion, her conduct, which gave rise to no remarks, the confidential position which she held in her mistress's house and which reflected a portion of her mistress's repute upon herself, caused the tradespeople to treat her on a different footing from that of other servants. People spoke to her cap in hand, and always said "Mademoiselle Germinie" to her. They hastened to serve her; they pushed forward the only chair in the shop to have her wait. Even when she bargained, they were still polite with her, and did not call her "a haggler." Jests that were rather too lively were checked in her presence. She was invited to big entertainments, to family gatherings, and was consulted about things.

All was changed as soon as her relations with Jupillon and her regular attendance at the "Boule Noire" became known. The neighborhood took its revenge for having respected her. The shameless servants of the house approached as though she were an equal. One, whose lover was at Mazas, said "My dear" to her. Men addressed her familiarly, and showed freedom by look, tone, gesture, hand. Even the children on the pavement, who had formerly drawn themselves up to give her a curtsy, fled from her as from one whom they had been told to fear. She felt that she was being treated in an underhand way, that she was being served abominably ill. She could not take a step without walking into the midst of contempt, and receiving her shame upon the cheek.

This was to her a terrible forfeiture of herself. She suffered as though her honor were being torn piece by piece from her in the kennel. But in proportion to her sufferings she pressed herself against her love and cleaved to it. She was not angry with it, she uttered no reproach against it. She clung to it by all the tears that it brought her pride to shed. And, thrown back and riveted upon her shame, she might be seen in the street through which lately she had passed proudly and with head carried high, advancing furtively and fearfully, with bent back, and oblique glance, anxious to avoid recognition, and hastening her steps in front of the shops which swept out their slanders upon her heels.

XVIII

JUPILLON used to complain unceasingly of the annoyance of working for others, of not being "in quarters of his own," of not being able to find fifteen or eighteen hundred francs in his mother's purse. He asked for no bigger sum in order to rent two rooms on a ground-floor, and start a little glove-business. And already he had his plans and his dreams: he would set up in the neighborhood, which was an excellent one for his trade, full of purchasers and extravagant ladies who think nothing of kids at five francs a pair. To gloves he would soon unite perfumery and ties; then with his big profits, and the money obtained in selling the business again, he would move into a shop in the Rue Richelieu.

Whenever he spoke of this, Germinie asked him for a thousand explanations. She wanted to know all that was necessary for setting up the business. She asked for the names of the tools and accessories, with their prices and the dealers in them. She questioned him about his trade and his work so inquisitively and at such length that finally Jupillon, being out of patience, ended by saying to her:

"What is all that to you? The work bothers me enough as it is; don't talk to me about it!"

One Sunday she was walking up towards Montmartre with him. Instead of going by the Rue Trochot she went by the Rue Pigalle.

"But it's not that way," said Jupillon to her.

"I know that," she said, "but come, nevertheless."

She had taken his arm, and as she walked she turned a little away from him that he might not see what was passing on her face. In the middle of the Rue Fontaine-Saint-Georges, she stopped him abruptly in front of two ground-floor windows, and said to him:

"Look there!"

She was trembling with joy.

Jupillon looked: between the two windows, he saw on a plate in bright copper letters:

GLOVE WAREHOUSE JUPILLON

He saw white curtains in the first window. Through the panes in the second he perceived pigeon-holes, cardboard boxes, and, in the foreground, the little work-table of his trade, with the large scissors, the jar for the pieces, and the pointed knife for trimming the skins.

"Your key is at the doorkeeper's," she said to him.

They went into the first room of the shop.

She became eager to show him everything. She opened the cardboard boxes and laughed. Then pushing open the door of the other room:

"See, you won't be stifled there as in your mother's garret. Does it please you? Oh! it's not handsome but it's clean. I should have liked mahogany for you. Does this please you, this hearth-rug? And the paper — I was forgetting."

She placed in his hand a receipt for rent.

"Here! it's for six months. Ah! you'll have to set to work immediately to make money. There are my pence in the savings bank gone at a stroke. Ah! here, let me sit down. You look so pleased — it has such an effect upon me — it makes me giddy — I have lost my legs."

And she let herself slide on to a chair. Jupillon bent over her to kiss her.

"Ah! yes, they are gone," she said to him, seeing his eyes looking for her earrings. "They're like my rings. Look, do you see, all gone."

And she showed him her hands stripped of the poor jewels she had worked so long to buy.

"That was for the arm-chair, all that, see, but it's all horse-hair."

And as Jupillon stood before her with the look of a man embarrassed, and seeking for words of thanks:

"Why, you are quite funny. What is the matter with you? Ah! it is for that?" And she indicated the room. "You're foolish! I love you, don't I? Well?"

Germinie said this simply, in the way that the heart says sublime things.

XIX

SHE became pregnant. At first she doubted, and dared not believe it. Then, when she was certain of it, an immense joy filled her, a joy which steeped her soul. Her happiness was so great and so strong that it instantly stifled the anguish, the dread, the trembling thoughts, which commonly enter into the maternity of unmarried women and embitter the expectation of delivery, the divine hope living and stirring within them. The thought of the scandal caused by her detected *liaison,* of the exposure of her guilt in the neighborhood, the thought of that abominable thing which had made her think constantly of suicide; the disgrace, even the fear of seeing herself found out by mademoiselle and driven away by her, could in no degree affect her bliss. As though she had already lifted it in her arms before her, the child that she was awaiting suffered her to see nothing but itself; and with but scanty concealment she bore her woman's shame almost proudly beneath the gaze of the street in the pride and radiancy of the mother that she was going to be. She was distressed only at having spent all her savings, at being without money and indebted to her mistress for several months' wages in advance. She bitterly regretted her poverty for the reception of her child. Often when passing through the Rue Saint-Lazare she would stop in front of a linen warehouse, in the windows of which were displayed layettes for rich children. Her eyes would devour all the prettily worked and coquettish linen, the quilted bibs, the long, short-waisted robe trimmed with English embroideries, the whole toilet of cherub and doll. A terrible longing, the longing of a pregnant woman, seized her to break through the glass and steal it all, and behind the display of the window the shopmen, who had become used to seeing her standing there, would point her out to one another and laugh.

Then again, amid the happiness which overwhelmed her, amid the rapturous joy which uplifted her entire being, an anxiety would at times pass through her. She asked herself how the father would accept the child. Two or three times she had wanted to announce her pregnancy to him and had not dared to do so. At last one day, seeing him with the face for which she had been waiting so long in order to tell him everything, a face in which there was a touch of tenderness, she confessed to him, with blushes, and as though asking his pardon for it, what was making her so happy.

"What an idea!" said Jupillon.

Then, when she had assured him that it was not an idea and that her pregnancy was positively five months old:

"What luck!" returned the young man. "Much obliged to you!"

And he swore. "Just you tell me who's to give this sparrow his beakful?"

"Oh, be easy! he won't suffer, that's my business. And then it will be so nice! Don't be afraid; no one will know anything about it. I'll manage. See! during the last days I'll walk like this, with my head back — I'll wear no more petticoats — I'll squeeze myself, you'll see! — No one will notice anything, I tell you — A little child of our own, just think!"

"In short, since it's so it's so, isn't it?" said the young man.

"I say," ventured Germinie timidly, "suppose you were to tell your mother?"

"Mammy? — No, indeed. You must be confined and after that we'll bring the brat to the house — that'll touch her up, and perhaps she'll give us her consent."

XX

TWELFTH NIGHT came. It was the occasion of a great dinner-party given regularly every year by Mademoiselle de Varandeuil. On this day she used to invite all the children, big and little, belonging to her relations and her friends. The little dwelling could scarcely hold them. It was necessary to put part of the furniture upon the landing. And a table was laid in each of the two rooms which formed the whole of mademoiselle's abode.

For the children this day was a great treat to which they used to look forward a week beforehand. They ran up the staircase behind the pastry-cook waiters. At table they overate themselves without being scolded. In the evening they would not go to bed, climbed upon the chairs, and made a din which always gave Mademoiselle de Varandeuil a headache next day; but she was not vexed with them, for she had the happiness of a grandmother's birthday in hearing them, in seeing them, in fastening behind them the white napkins which made them look so rosy. And for nothing in the world would she have failed to give this dinner-party, which filled an old maid's rooms with all those little fair, mischievous heads, and gave them in one noisy day, youth and laughter for a year.

Germinie was engaged in cooking this dinner. She was whipping cream in a basin on her knees when suddenly she felt her first pains. She looked at herself in the bit of broken glass which she had over her dresser, and she saw that she was pale. She went down to Adèle: "Give me your mistress's rouge," she said to her. And she put some on her cheeks. Then she went upstairs again, and, unwilling to indulge her pain, finished the dinner. It had to be served, and she served it. At dessert, when handing plates, she leaned against the furniture, and held to the backs of the chairs, hiding her torture with the horrible, shrivelled smile of those whose bowels are being wrung.

"Ah! you are ill?" asked her mistress, looking at her.

"Yes, mademoiselle, a little — perhaps it's the fire, the kitchen — "

"Well, go to bed. You are not wanted any more, and you can clear away to-morrow."

She went down again to Adèle.

"It's come," she said to her, "quick — a cab. Isn't it in the Rue de la Hutchette that you told me your midwife is, opposite a copper-planisher's? You haven't a pen and some paper, have you?"

And she began to write a line for her mistress. She told her that she was suffering excessively and was going to a hospital, that she did not say where because mademoiselle would tire herself coming to see her, and that she would be back again in a week.

"There!" said Adèle, out of breath, and giving her the number of the cab.

"I may remain there," said Germinie to her, "but not a word to mademoiselle. That's all. Swear it to me, not a word!"

She was going down the stairs when she met Jupillon.

"Hello!" he said, "where are you going — out?"

"I am going to be confined. The pains came on during the day. There was a large dinner-party. Ah! it was hard! Why do you come here? I told you never to come, I won't have it!"

"The fact is — I must tell you — I'm just now in absolute need of forty francs. There, truly, in absolute need."

"Forty francs! why, I have only just enough for the midwife."

"It's a nuisance — there! It can't be helped," and he gave her his arm to assist her downstairs. "By Jove! I shall have a job to get them, all the same."

He had opened the door of the vehicle: "Where is he to take you?"

66

"To La Bourbe," said Germinie. And she slipped the forty francs into his hand.

"Don't," said Jupillon.

"Ah! nonsense — there or anywhere else! Besides, I've seven francs left."

The cab started.

Jupillon stood for a moment motionless on the pavement, looking at the two napoleons in his hand. Then he began to run after the cab, and, stopping it, said to Germinie through the window:

"At least, let me see you to the place?"

"No, I'm in too much pain. I'd rather be alone," answered Germinie, writhing on the cushions of the cab.

At the end of an eternal half-hour the cab stopped in the Rue de Port-Royal, in front of a black door surmounted by a violet lantern which announced to medical students passing in the street that, on that night and at that very moment, there was the curiosity and interest of a painful delivery at the Maternity.

The driver got down from his box and rang. The porter, assisted by a maid, took Germinie under the arms and brought her up to one of the four beds in the delivery ward. Once in bed her pains became a little easier. She looked round her, saw the other empty beds, and at the end of the immense apartment, a large hearth such as is found in the country, blazing with a great fire in front of which swaddling-clothes, sheets, and under-covers were hanging to dry.

Half an hour afterwards Germinie was delivered; she brought a little girl into the world.

Her bed was wheeled into another ward. She had been there for several hours, lost in the sweet weakness of deliverance which follows the frightful pangs of child-birth, perfectly happy and astonished at being still alive, bathed in ease and profoundly affected by the vague happiness of having created. Suddenly a cry of "I'm dying!" made her look to one side: she saw one of her neighbors throw her arms round the neck of a nursing student midwife, fall back again almost immediately, stir for a moment beneath the sheets, and then move no more. Almost at the same instant there rose from an adjacent bed another horrible, piercing, terrified cry, the cry of one who looks on death; it was a woman calling with despairing hands on the young pupil; the latter hastened to her, stooped down, and fell stiff and fainting to the ground.

Then silence returned; but Germinie and the other women in the room that were still alive remained between the two dead women and the half dead woman — who was not brought to herself by the coldness of the floor for more than an hour — without even venturing to pull the bell hung in each bed for the purpose of summoning assistance.

At that time there was at the Maternity one of those terrible puerperal epidemics which breathe death upon human fruitfulness, one of those poisonings of the air which simply empty in whole rows the beds of women in travail and which once used to shut up La Clinique: it was like the passing of the plague, a plague which blackens the countenance in a few hours, carries off everyone, sweeps away the strongest and the youngest, a plague which issues from the cradle, the Black Death of mothers!

Every hour, and especially at night, there were round about Germinie corpses such as are the handiwork of milk fever, corpses which seemed to be a violation of nature, tortured corpses, frenzied with shriekings and troubled with hallucination and delirium, death-struggles which rendered the strait-waistcoat of madness a necessity, death-struggles which would suddenly spring from the bed, carrying the sheets with them, and causing the whole ward to shudder at the thought of seeing the corpses of the amphitheatre return! Life departed there as though wrenched from the body. The sickness itself assumed shapes of horror, and monstrous appearance. In the beds beneath the lamp-light, the sheets rose in the centre dim and horrible with the swellings of peritonitis.

For five days Germinie, curling and gathering herself up in her bed, and closing eyes and ears as best she might, was strong enough to strive against all these terrors and to yield only occasionally to them. She wanted to live, and her strength was stimulated by the thought of her child and by the recollection of mademoiselle. But on the sixth day her energy was exhausted, and her courage forsook her. A chill entered into her soul; she told herself that all was over. The hand that death lays upon your shoulder, the presentiment that you are about to die, was already touching her. She was sensible of the first attack of the epidemic, the belief that she belonged to it, and the impression that she was already half possessed by it. Without being resigned, she abandoned herself. Her life, vanquished in anticipation, scarcely continued the effort to struggle. She was in this condition when a head bent like a light over her bed.

It was the head of the youngest of the pupils, a fair head with long golden hair, and blue eyes of such sweetness that dying women could see heaven opening up within them. When women in delirium saw her they used to say: "See! it is the Holy Virgin!"

"My child," she said to Germinie, "you must ask for your discharge at once. You must leave. Dress yourself very warmly, and protect yourself well. As soon as you are in bed at home, you must take something hot, tisane, or an infusion of lime-flowers. Try to perspire. In this way you will be none the worse. But go. Here, tonight," she said, casting her eyes over the beds, "it would not be good for you. Don't say that it is I who am making you leave: you would have me turned out."

XXI

GERMINIE recovered in a few days. The joy and pride of having given birth to a little creature in whom her own flesh was blended with that of the man she loved, the happiness of being a mother, saved her from the consequences of a badly nursed confinement. She was restored to health, and she wore a look of gratification with life that her mistress had never before seen with her.

Every Sunday, whatever the weather, she set off at about eleven o'clock. Mademoiselle thought that she went to see a friend in the country, and was delighted with the benefit which her maid derived from these days in the open air. Germinie used to take Jupillon, who allowed himself to be carried off without overmuch grumbling, and they would leave for Pommeuse where the child was, and where a good luncheon, ordered by the mother, awaited them. Once in the carriage on the Mulhouse railway, Germinie could no longer speak, could no longer reply. Leaning towards the window she seemed to have all her thoughts in front of her. She gazed as though her longing would fain have outstripped steam.

Scarcely had the train stopped, when she sprang out, threw her ticket to the collector, and hastened into the Pommeuse road, leaving Jupillon behind. She approached, she arrived, she was come; there it was! She would rush upon her child, take it out of the nurse's arms with jealous hands — mother's hands! — press it, clasp it, embrace it, devour it with kisses, and looks, and laughter! She would admire it for a moment, and then distracted, blissful, mad with love, would cover it with lip-tenderness to the tips of its little naked feet.

They used to lunch. She sat down to table with the child on her knees, and could eat nothing. She had been kissing it so much that she had not yet seen it, and she would begin to seek to detail the little one's resemblance to them both. One feature was his, another her own.

"That is your nose — these are my eyes. In time she will have hair like yours — it will curl! Look, these are your hands — it's your own self — "

And for hours she indulged in the exhaustless and delightful dotage of a woman who wants to give a man a share in their daughter. Jupillon acquiesced in it all without too much impatience, thanks to the three-sou cigars which Germinie used to take out of her pocket and give him one by one. Moreover, he had discovered a means of diversion: the Morin flowed past the end of the garden. Jupillon was a Parisian, and he was fond of angling.

When the summer had come they stayed the whole day by the water's edge at the end of the garden, Jupillon on a spring-board thrown over two stakes, Germinie, with the child in her lap, seated on the ground beneath the medlar which bent over the river. The day was perhaps a brilliant one, the sun burning the great flaming water-sheet which threw off the flashings like a mirror. It was like a bonfire of sky and river, in the midst of which Germinie would hold up her daughter and make her trample upon her, naked and rosy, with her short vest, her skin quivering with sun-light here and there, her flesh struck with rays like the angel-flesh which Germinie had seen in pictures.

She experienced divine delights when the little thing, with the meddling hands of a child as yet unable to speak, would touch her on the chin and mouth and cheeks, would persist in putting her fingers into her eyes, would check them, in her play, at a look, and would cover her whole face with the tickling torment of those dear little hands which seem to be groping about for a mother's face: it was as though her child's life and warmth were straying over her features. From time to time she would send half her smile to Jupillon over the baby's head, and cry to him:

"Now, just look at her!"

Then the child used to fall asleep with those parted lips which smile in slumber. Germinie bent down to her breathing, listening to her rest; and by degrees, lulled by the child's respiration, she forgot herself deliciously as she gazed at the poor locality of her happiness, the country garden, the apple-trees with leaves covered with little yellow snails, the rosy apples on the south side, the stick at the foot of which twined the pea-stems, twisted and parched, the cabbage-bed, the four sunflowers in the little circular bed in the middle of the walk; and, quite close to her, on the river's bank, the plots of grass filled with mercury plants, the white nettle-tops against the wall, the washerwomen's boxes, the bottles of lye, and the truss of straw scattered by the frolics of a puppy in coming out of the water. She gazed and mused. She dreamed of the past, having her future on her knees. With the grass, the trees, and the river, which were there before her, she formed again, in memory, the rustic garden of her rustic childhood. She could once more see the two stones going down into the water, where her mother, before putting her to bed, used to wash her feet in summer when she was quite a child.

"I say, Daddy Remalard," said Jupillon from his position on his plank to the goodman who was watching him, on one of the hottest days of August, "do you know the hook's not worth a rap with the red worm on it?"

"It 'ud want a gentle!" said the peasant, sententiously.

"Well, we'll have it! Daddy Remalard, you must get a calf's lights on Thursday, and hang 'em up for me on this tree, and next Sunday we'll see."

On Sunday Jupillon had miraculous luck, and Germinie heard the first syllable coming from her daughter's lips.

XXII

ON Wednesday morning Germinie found a letter for her when she went downstairs. In this letter, which was written on the back of a laundress's receipt, Mother Remalard told her that her child had fallen ill almost as soon as she had left: that since then she had been growing worse, that she had consulted the doctor, that he had spoken of a noxious fly which had bitten the child, that she had brought her to him the second time, that she was at her wits' end, that she had had pilgrimages made for her. The letter concluded thus:

"If you could see what trouble I have with your little one, and if you could see how bonny she is when she is not enduring pain!"

This letter had upon Germinie an effect like that of a great blow impelling her forward. She went out and proceeded mechanically in the direction of the railway that brought her to her child. She was bareheaded and in slippers, but she paid no heed to this. She must see her child, and see her immediately; after that she would return. She gave a moment's thought to mademoiselle's breakfast, and then forgot it. Suddenly, when half way, she saw the time by a clock on a cab-office — she recollected that there was no train at that hour. She retraced her steps, saying to herself that she would hurry over the breakfast, and then find some pretext for being free for the rest of the day. But when breakfast had been served she could find none: her head was so full of her child that she was unable to invent a lie; her imagination was dull. And then, if she had spoken and asked, she would have burst out with it, and she was conscious of having the words, "'Tis to see my baby," on her lips. At nightfall she dared not make her escape; mademoiselle had had a little pain the previous night, and she was afraid she might be wanted.

The next day when she went in to mademoiselle with a story imagined during the night, and prepared to ask permission to go out, mademoiselle said to her, as she read the letter which Germinie had brought up from the lodge:

"Ah, it's my old friend, Madame de Belleuse, who wants you for the whole day to help her with her preserves. Come, my two eggs, post-haste, and be off with you. Why, what now! that ruffles you? What is the matter?"

"I — oh! not at all," Germinie found strength to say.

All that long day she spent amid the heat of pans and the tying up of pots in such torture as is suffered by those who are fast bound by their lives far from the sickness of those they love. She endured the anguish of those unfortunates who cannot follow their anxieties, and, sinking into the depths of despair at their remoteness and uncertainty, imagine every moment that death is about to take place without them.

Finding that there was no letter on Thursday evening, no letter on Friday morning, she was reassured. If the little one had been worse, the nurse would have written to her. The child was getting better, and she imagined it to herself saved and cured. They are constantly at death's door, are children, and they recover so quickly. And then, hers was so strong. She resolved to wait, to have patience until Sunday, which was only forty-eight hours distant, beguiling the remnant of her fears with the superstitions which say yes to hope, persuading herself that her daughter had "escaped," because the first person that she had met in the morning had been a man, because she had seen a red horse in the street, because she had guessed that a foot passenger would go down such a turning, because she had ascended a story in so many strides.

On Saturday morning, going in to see Mother Jupillon, she found her engaged in shedding big tears over a print of butter which she was covering up with a wet cloth.

"Ah! it's you," said Mother Jupillon. "That poor coal-woman! I can't help crying for her — there! She's just left here. Perhaps you don't know, but in her trade they can only clean their faces with butter — and now her love of a little girl, she's at the point of death — you know the darling child. Dear, dear! such is life. Ah, Lord, yes. Well, just now she said to her, 'Mammy, I want you to clean my face with butter, immediately, to get ready for God!' Ah, ah!"

And Mother Jupillon began to sob.

Germinie made her escape. She could not remain quiet during the whole day. Every moment she went up to her room to prepare the little things which she wished to take to her child next day in order to make her "tidy," and to prepare a little toilet for her, as for one risen from the dead. As she was going down in the evening to put mademoiselle to bed, Adèle handed her a letter which she had found lying for her below.

XXIII

MADEMOISELLE had begun to undress when Germinie entered the room, took a few steps, dropped upon a chair, and almost immediately after giving two or three long, deep sighs, heart-heaving

ournful, mademoiselle saw her fall writhing back, roll off the
r, and sink upon the ground. She tried to raise her, but Germinie
s shaken by convulsive movements of such violence that the old
oman was obliged to let the frenzied body fall again to the floor
with its limbs contracting and concentrating for a moment and then
flying out at random right and left, launching forth with the click of
a released spring, and throwing down everything with which they
came in contact.

At mademoiselle's cries from the landing, a servant ran to the
house of a neighboring doctor, whom she did not find; four other
women belonging to the house assisted mademoiselle to take up
Germinie and carry her to the bed in her mistress's room, on which
she was laid, after her stay-laces had been cut.

The terrible shocks, the nervous slackenings of the limbs, and
the cracking of the tendons had ceased, but across the neck and the
breast, which was uncovered by the loosening of the dress, there
passed undulating movements which were like waves raised beneath
the skin, and which could be perceived by the quivering of the skirt
to run down to the feet. With head thrown back, heightened color,
eyes full of sad tenderness — of that gentle anguish to be observed
in the eyes of the wounded — and big veins tracing themselves beneath her skin, Germinie, panting and giving no reply to the ques-
tions addressed to her, kept putting up both hands to her throat and
neck, and scratching them; she seemed to be trying to pluck thence
the sensation of something rising and falling within her.

It was in vain that they made her inhale ether and drink orange-
flower water: the waves of pain passing through her body continued
to traverse her, and in her countenance there remained persistently
that same expression of melancholy gentleness and sentimental
anxiety which seemed to add a soul-suffering to the flesh-suffering
of all her features. For a long time everything appeared to wound
her senses and to affect them painfully — the shining of the light,
the sound of voices, and the perfume of things. At last, suddenly,
at the end of an hour, tears, a deluge springing from her eyes, re-
moved the terrible crisis. Then there was only a shuddering at long
intervals through her exhausted frame, which was soon quieted by
weariness, by a general collapse. It was necessary to carry Germinie to her own room. The letter which Adèle had handed to her
contained the tidings of her daughter's death.

XXIV

AFTER this crisis Germinie lapsed into a stupor of grief. For months she remained insensible to everything; for months she was completely invaded and filled by the thought of the little creature which was no more, and she bore her child's death in her bosom as she had borne its life. Every evening when she went up to her room, she took her poor darling's cap and vest out of the trunk which stood at the foot of the bed. She looked at them and touched them! she spread them out upon the bedclothes; she remained for hours weeping over them, kissing them, speaking to them, uttering to them the words which afford a mother's sorrow speech with the shade of a little daughter.

Weeping for her child, the unhappy mother wept for herself. A voice whispered to her that with the child living, she was saved; that with the child to love, she had a Providence; that all that she dreaded in herself — her tenderness, her transports, her ardors, all the fires of her nature — would centre upon the head of the child and there be sanctified. By anticipation, she seemed to feel the heart of the mother soothe and purify the heart of the woman. In her daughter she could discern something celestial that would redeem and cure her, like a little angel of deliverance issuing from her faults to strive for her and rescue her from the evil influences which pursued her, and by which she sometimes believed herself possessed.

When she began to emerge from this first annihilation of despair, when, with the returning perception of life and sensation of things, she looked around her with eyes that could see, she was roused from her grief by a bitterness that was keener still.

Having become too big and heavy for the work of her dairy, and finding that, in spite of all that Germinie did, she had still too much to do, Madame Jupillon had sent for a niece from her own district to assist her. There was the youthfulness of the country in this girl; she was a woman in whom there was still something of the child, lively and vivacious, with dark eyes that were full of sunshine, and lips full, round, and red, like the pulp of a cherry, with the summer of her native countryside in her complexion, and the warmth of health in her blood.

Ardent and ingenuous, the young girl, during the first days after her coming, had approached her cousin naturally and simply from that inclination of like years which prompts youth to seek out youth. She had thrown herself in his way with the shamelessness of innocence, with candid boldness, with the freedom taught by the fields, with the happy foolishness of a rich nature, with all sorts of temerities, ignorances, bold franknesses, and rustic coquetries, against which her cousin's vanity had been quite unable to defend itself.

By the side of this child, Germinie had no rest. The young girl wounded her every minute by her presence, her contact, her caresses, by everything which acknowledged love in her amorous person. Her engrossment of Jupillon, the work which brought her close to him, the countrified amazement which she displayed before him, the semi-confidences which she allowed to come to her lips when the young man was out, her merriment, her jokes, her healthy good-humor, all exasperated Germinie, all raised secret wrath within her; all wounded that obstinate heart whose jealousy was such that the very animals made her suffer when they seemed to love some one whom she loved.

She dared not speak to Mother Jupillon and denounce the girl to her for fear of betraying herself; but whenever she found herself alone with Jupillon, she broke forth into recriminations, complaints, and quarrels. She would remind him of a circumstance, a word, something that he had done, said, replied, some trifle forgotten by him, but still sore within her.

"Are you mad?" said Jupillon to her; "a young thing like that!"

"A young thing, is she? Go along! and she has such eyes that all the men look at her in the street. The other day I went out with her, and I was ashamed. I don't know how she contrived it, but we were followed by a gentleman the whole time."

"Well! what of that? She's pretty, that's all!"

Pretty! Pretty! And at this word, Germinie flung herself upon the young girl's face, and tore it with savage words as with claws.

Often she ended by saying to Jupillon:

"There! you love her!"

"Well, what then?" Jupillon would reply, not displeased by these disputes, by the sight and sport afforded by the anger which he used to tease and goad, by the amusement given him by this woman, whom, beneath her sarcasm and indifference, he could see half-losing her reason, growing distracted, stumbling into incipient madness, running her head against a wall.

As a sequel to such scenes which recurred and were repeated every day, a revolution was wrought in this variable, extreme, extravagant temperament, in this soul wherein violence jostled violence. Slowly poisoned, love decomposed and turned to hate. Germinie began to detest her lover, and to seek for everything that could make him more detested. And as her thoughts reverted to her daughter, to the loss of her child, to the cause of its death, she persuaded herself that it was he who had killed it. She conceived a horror of him, shrank from him, fled from him as from the curse of her life, with the terror that is felt of one who is your Misfortune!

XXV

ONE morning, after a night in which she had been revolving within her all her thoughts of grief and hate, Germinie, on entering the dairy to fetch her four sous' worth of milk, found two or three servants in the back-shop taking an early dram. Seated at table, they were sipping gossip and liquor.

"Hello!" said Adèle, striking her glass upon the table, "is that you already, Mademoiselle de Varandeuil?"

"What's this?" said Germinie, taking Adèle's glass. "I want some."

"You're as thirsty as that, this morning, are you? Brandy and absinthe, that's all. It's my Tommy's mixture — the soldier, don't you know? He never drank anything else. Stiff, isn't it?"

"Yes, indeed," said Germinie, with the lip-motion and eye-wrinkling of a child who is given a glass of liquor at dessert at a large dinner-party.

"It's good, all the same." Her courage was rising. "Madame Jupillon — the bottle this way — I'll pay for it."

And she threw the money upon the table. After three glasses:

"I'm tight!" she cried, and burst into a fit of laughter.

Mademoiselle de Varandeuil had gone that morning to receive the half-yearly payment of her dividends. When she came back at eleven o'clock she rang once, twice, but nothing came of it.

"Ah!" she said to herself, "she's gone downstairs."

She opened the door with her key, went to her room and entered it: the mattresses and sheets of her bed, which was in course of making, were thrown back over two chairs; and Germinie was stretched across the palliasse, sleeping, and inert like a mass of matter, in the listlessness of sudden lethargy.

At the sound of mademoiselle, Germinie sprang up, and drew her hand across her eyes:

"Eh?" she said, as though someone were calling her. Her looks were dreamy.

"What is the matter?" said Mademoiselle de Varandeuil, in alarm. "Did you fall? Are you unwell?"

"I! no," replied Germinie. "I was asleep — what o'clock is it? It's nothing — ah! how stupid — "

And she began to beat the mattress, turning her back towards her mistress to hide the color that the drink had brought into her face.

XXVI

ONE Sunday morning, Jupillon was dressing in the room that Germinie had furnished for him. His mother sat and watched him with that wondering pride which is to be observed in the eyes of the mothers of the people when in the presence of a son who is got up like a "gentleman."

"You're dressed like the young man on the first floor!" she said to him. "One would think it was his coat — it's not right to say it, but you look quite the swell, you do."

Jupillon, engaged in tying his cravat, did not reply.

"What a lot of hearts you'll break!" resumed Mother Jupillon, giving her voice a tone of caressing insinuation. "Listen to what I say to you, Bibi, you big, bad boy: if the lasses make slips, why, so much the worse for them: it's their own lookout and their own business. You're a man, ain't you, in age, and constitution and everything? I can't always keep you tied up, and so I said to myself as well one as another — so go in for her — and I acted as though I saw nothing. Well, yes, I mean Germinie. As she pleased you, and it kept you from wasting your money with bad women — and then I saw nothing inconvenient about the girl until now. But it's come to be different. They're making remarks in the neighborhood — telling a lot of horrible things about us — the vipers! We're above all that, I know — when one's been honest all one's life, thank God! But one never knows what may happen: Mademoiselle would only have to pry into her maid's affairs. For my part, the bare idea of a court of justice makes me dizzy. What do you say to that, Bibi, eh?"

"Faith! mother — just as you like."

"Ah! I knew you loved your dear, darling mammy!" said the monstrous woman, kissing him. "Well, invite her to dinner this evening. Bring up two bottles of our Lunel, the two-franc sort that gets into the head, and make sure of her coming. Be sweet with her, and make her believe that it's to be a great occasion — Put on your best gloves: you'll make much more of an impression — "

About seven o'clock in the evening, Germinie arrived, full of happiness, cheerfulness and hope, her head filled with dreams and the air of mystery which Jupillon had imparted owing to his mother's invitation. They dined, drank, and laughed. Mother Jupillon began to cast moved, moist, swimming glances at the couple seated in front of her. When at their coffee, she said, as though wishing to be alone with Germinie:

"Bibi, you know you've something to do this evening."

Jupillon went out. Madame Jupillon, sipping her coffee, then turned towards Germinie with the countenance of a mother asking for her daughter's secret, and shrouding her confession beforehand in the forgiveness of her indulgence. For a moment the two women remained thus in silence, the one waiting for the other to speak, and the other having the cry of her heart on the tip of her tongue. Suddenly, Germinie sprang from her chair, and rushed into the big woman's arms:

"If you only knew, Madame Jupillon!"

She spoke, and wept, and kissed.

"Oh! you will not be angry with me! Well, yes; I do love him — I have had a child by him — it's true, I love him — for three years — "

At each word, Madame Jupillon's face had grown more chill and icy. She put Germinie from her coldly, and in her most doleful voice, in tones of lamentation and despairing grief, she began to say, like one choking:

"Oh, heavens! — you — to tell such things as that to me — his mother! — to my face. Heavens, is it possible! My son! — a child — an innocent child! You have been shameless enough to debauch him! And you even tell me that it was you! No, it is not possible! I, who had such confidence — it's enough to kill me. There is no security left in this world! Ah! mademoiselle, I would not have believed it of you all the same! Well! these things do make my head swim. I tell you, it's a revelation to me — I know what I am, and I'm likely to be ill after it!"

"Madame Jupillon! Madame Jupillon!" Germinie murmured in a tone of entreaty, ready to die of shame and grief on the chair upon which she had fallen back. "I ask your forgiveness. It was stronger than I. And then I thought — I believed — "

"You believed! Good gracious, you believed! What did you believe? You, my son's wife, eh? Oh, Lord! is it possible, my poor child?"

And constantly assuming a more plaintive and mournful voice as she continued to cast these wounding words at Germinie, Mother Jupillon resumed:

"But, come, my poor girl, people must be rational. What was it I always said? That it might be done if you were ten years younger. You were born in 1820, as you have told me, and we're now in 1849. You see you're going on thirty, my good girl. Look here, it hurts me to tell you this — I should be so unwilling to give you pain — but one has only to look at you, my poor lass — What can you expect? It's age — Your hair — you might lay your finger in the parting — "

"But," said Germinie, within whom there was beginning a murmuring of sullen wrath, "what about the money your son owes me — my money? The money I drew out of the savings bank, the money I borrowed for him, the money I — "

"Ah! he owes you money? Why, yes, what you lent him to begin his trade. Well, you needn't make such a fuss. Do you think that you've got thieves to deal with? Do you suppose we mean to deny having had your money from you, even though there's no receipt if you want a proof. I remember now — the honest, childlike fellow wanted to write one out, in case he should die — but, all at once, people are made pickpockets without more ado. Ah, goodness! life's not worth the having in such times as these. Ah! I am well punished for becoming attached to you. But, I tell you, I can see it all now clearly enough. Oh! you are shrewd, you are. You wanted to buy my son for yourself and for life. Thank you, I'd rather not. It's cheaper to pay you back your money. The leavings of a café waiter — my poor, dear child! — God keep him from such a thing!"

Germinie had snatched her bonnet and shawl from the peg, and was outside.

XXVII

MADEMOISELLE was seated in her large easy-chair at the corner of the fire place in which a few embers always slumbered beneath the ashes. Her black head-band, lowered upon the wrinkles of her forehead, fell almost to her eyes. Her black dress, which was shaped like a frock and allowed her bones to project through it, lay in meagre folds over the meagreness of her person, and fell straight down from her knees. A small black shawl was crossed and fastened behind her back after the fashion of little girls. She had laid her upward-turned and half-opened hands upon her thighs, poor, old woman's hands, awkward and stiff, and swollen at the joints and knuckles by the gout.

Sunk in the bent, broken-down attitude which obliges old people to raise their heads in order to see you and speak to you, she lay in a heap, buried, as it were, in the darkness whence there emerged nothing but her face, yellowed by biliousness to the tone of old ivory, and the warm flame of her brown eyes. Looking at her, at the living, cheerful eyes, the miserable frame, the poverty-stricken dress, the nobility with which she bore her years and all her sorrows, she might have been taken for a fairy at the Petits-Ménages.

Germinie was beside her. The old maid said:

"The cushion is under the door, Germinie, eh?"

"Yes, mademoiselle."

"Do you know, my girl," Mademoiselle de Varandeuil resumed after a pause, "do you know that when one has been born in one of the handsomest mansions of the Rue Royale, and ought to have been the possessor of the Grand and the Petit-Charolais, and ought to have had the château of Clichy-la-Garenne for a country seat; and when it took two servants to carry the silver dish on which the joint was served in your grandmother's house — do you know, it requires a good deal of philosophy," and mademoiselle placed a hand upon her shoulders with difficulty — "to see oneself meeting one's end here, in this abominably rheumatic hovel where, in spite of all the cushions in the world, you get these miserable draughts. That's right, stir up the fire a little."

And stretching out her feet towards Germinie, who was on her knees before the fire place, and laughingly putting them under her nose she went on:

"Do you know one wants a great deal of that philosophy to be able to wear stockings in holes! Foolish creature! I don't say it to scold you; I know very well that you can't do everything. You might get a woman to come and do the mending. That's not very difficult. Why don't you tell the girl who came last year? She had a face that pleased me."

"Oh, she was as black as a mole, mademoiselle."

"There now! I was sure — To begin with, you never think well of anybody. That's so, isn't it? But wasn't she Mother Jupillon's niece? We might have her for a day or two in the week —"

"That strumpet shall never set foot in here again. "

"Come, more difficulties! You are wonderful at worshipping people, and then being unable to bear the sight of them. What has she done to you?"

"She is an unfortunate, I tell you!"

"Tut! what has that to do with my linen?"

"But, mademoiselle —"

"Well! find me another — I don't insist upon her. But find one for me. "

"Oh, the women who are brought in do no work. I will do your mending myself. There's no need for anyone. "

"You? Oh, if we are to reckon upon your needle!" said mademoiselle, gaily; "and besides, Mother Jupillon will never leave you the time —"

"Mademoiselle Jupillon? Ah! yes she will, for all the dust that I shall make in her house now!"

"What? She, too? is *she* thrown aside? Oh, ho! Make haste make another acquaintance, or else, good gracious! there wi bad times in store for us!"

XXVIII

THE winter of that year ought to have ensured a portion in Paradise to Mademoiselle de Varandeuil. She had to endure all the reaction of her servant's grief, the torment from her nerves, the vengeance of her provoked and sour temper, to which the approach of spring was soon to impart that kind of wicked madness which accrues to sickly sensibilities from the critical season, the birth-time of nature, the restless, irritating fecundation of summer.

Germinie began to have dried eyes, eyes which had been weeping though they had ceased to weep. She uttered an everlasting: "There's nothing the matter with me, mademoiselle," spoken in that hollow tone which stifles a secret. She assumed mute and grief-stricken postures, funeral attitudes, and airs of the kind with which a woman's person will set forth sadness and make her shadow a trouble. With her face, her looks, her mouth, the folds of her dress, her presence, with the noise that she made when walking in the adjoining apartment, with her very silence, she enwrapped mademoiselle in the despair of her person. At the least word she would bristle up.

Mademoiselle could not make a remark to her, ask her for the slightest thing, or express a wish, a desire: she took everything as a reproach. Thereupon she would indulge in ferocious outbursts. She would grumble and weep:

"Ah! I am very unfortunate! I can see quite well that mademoiselle does not like me any more."

Her fancies against people found vent in sublime grumblings. "She always comes when it's wet," she would say on finding a little mud left on the carpet by Madame de Belleuse. During the first week of the New Year, the week when all who were left of Madcmoiselle de Varandeuil's relations and connections, without exception, rich and poor, ascended to her fifth story and waited on the landing at the door to relieve one another in the six chairs in her room, Germinie's ill temper, impertinent remarks, and sullen complaints were increased. She would continually imagine injuries on her mistress's part, and punish her by a dumbness which nothing could break. Then would come fits of weakness. All round her, mademoiselle could hear through the partitions furious strokes of broom and feather-brush, scrubbings, jerky flappings, and all the nervous work of a servant who, by abusing the furniture, seems to say:

"Well, you're getting your work done, at any rate!"

Old people are patient with old servants. Habit, slackened will-power, horror of change, dread of new faces, everything inclines them to weakness, concession, cowardice. In spite of her quickness, her readiness to become angry, to break out, to rage and fume, mademoiselle said nothing. She appeared to see nothing. She made a pretence of reading when Germinie entered. Ensconced in her chair, she would wait until her maid's temper passed off or burst forth. She stooped beneath the storm; she had neither word nor thought of bitterness against her maid. She only pitied her so great-ly that she herself suffered as much.

In Mademoiselle de Varandeuil's view Germinie was, in fact, not a servant; she was Devotion, and, as such, must necessarily cause her to close her eyes. This isolated old woman whom death had for-gotten, and who, at the end of her life, found herself alone, and drag-ging her affections from grave to grave, had found her last friend in her servant. She had bestowed her heart upon her, as upon an adopted daughter, and she was especially unhappy at being unable to comfort her. Moreover, Germinie would, at times, come back to her out of the depths of her gloomy melancholy and evil temper, and throw herself upon her knees before her kindness. Suddenly a ray of sunshine, a beggar's song, a trifle such as will pass through the air, and unbend the soul, would cause her to melt into tears and en-dearments; she would indulge in burning effusiveness, in delighted kissing, as in an all-effacing joy at being alive once more. At other times it was over some small ailment of mademoiselle's; and the old servant immediately recovered her smiling face and gentle hands.

Sometimes on these occasions, mademoiselle used to say to her:

"Come, my girl, there is something the matter with you. Come, tell me?" And Germinie would reply: "No, mademoiselle, it is the weather."

"The weather!" mademoiselle would repeat with a doubtful air, "the weather!"

XXIX

ONE evening in March, Mother Jupillon and her son were talking at the corner of their stove in the back-shop.

Jupillon had just been drawn for the army. The money which his mother had set aside for buying him off had been consumed by six months of bad trade, by credits given to girls living in the same street who one fine morning had put their key under the door-mat. He himself was in a bad way and had an execution in his place. During the day he had gone to a former employer to ask him to make him an advance in order to procure a man in his place. But the old perfumer had not forgiven him for having left him and set up for himself, and he had refused point-blank. Mother Jupillon was in grief and was giving way to tearful lamentations. She kept repeating the number drawn by her son:

"Twenty-two! twenty-two!" — And she said: "Yet I sewed a black, velvety spider and its web into your coat. Ah! I ought rather to have done as I was told, and put on you the cap you were baptized in. Ah! the good God is not just. And to think of the fruit-seller's son getting a good one. So much for being honest! And the two baggages at number 18 who have just taken to their heels with my money. They might well give me their hand-shakings. Do you know that they are in my debt for more than seven hundred francs? And the blackamoor over the way — and that little fright who had the face to eat pots of raspberries at twenty francs each — what they have robbed me of besides! But there, you're not gone yet, all the same. I'll sell the dairy first. I'll go back to service, I'll be a cook, I'll be a charwoman, I'll be anything at all. Why, I'd draw money from a stone for *you*!"

Jupillon smoked and let his mother talk. When she had finished:

"Enough said, mother — all that's nothing but words," he remarked. "You're plaguing your digestion and it's not worth while. There's no need for you to sell anything. There's no need for you to put yourself about. What will you bet that I buy myself off without its costing you a sou?"

"Lord!" said Madame Jupillon. "I've a notion of my own." And after a pause, Jupillon went on: "I didn't want to thwart you about

Germinie — at the time of the gossip, you know — you thought it was time for me to break with her — that she would get us into a scrape — and you turned her out, straight. That wasn't my plan — I didn't think her so bad as all that for the butter in the place. But after all you thought you were doing right. And perhaps, in fact, you did do right; instead of quieting her you have kindled her for me — just kindled. I've met her once or twice — and she's changed — Ay, she's pining away!"

"But you know quite well she hasn't another sou — "

"Of her own, I daresay. But what of that? she'll get some — she's good still for two thousand three hundred francs, there!"

"And if you are compromised?"

"Oh, she won't steal them — "

"Goodness knows!"

"Well! it will only be from her mistress. Do you think her mademoiselle will have her run in for that? She'll discharge her, and the thing will go no further. We'll advise her to take a change of air in another neighborhood, and we'll see no more of her. But it would be too stupid of her to steal. She'll make arrangements, and search, and manage — I don't know how, indeed, but, you know, that's her own lookout. It's a time for showing off one's talents. In fact, you don't know, but they say her old woman is ill. If the worthy damsel were to go off and leave her all her nick-nacks, as people are saying in the neighborhood — what then? It would be pretty foolish to have sent her to the right about then, eh, mammy? You have to go a little carefully, you see, when you're dealing with people who may fall into four or five thousand francs a year."

"Goodness! — what's that you're telling me! But after the scene I had with her — Oh, no! she'll never be willing to come back here again."

"Well! I'll bring her back — and not later than this evening," said Jupillon, getting up and rolling a cigarette between his fingers.

"No excuses, you understand," he said to his mother, "it would be useless. And coldness — seem to receive her only from weakness, on my account. One doesn't know what may happen."

XXX

JUPILLON was walking backwards and forwards on the pavement in front of Germinie's house, when Germinie came out.

"Good-evening, Germinie," he said, just behind her.

She turned round as though she had been struck, and, without answering him, instinctively took two or three steps forward, and away from him.

"Germinie!"

Jupillon said only this to her, without stirring, without following her. She came back to him, as an animal is brought back to the hand by drawing in its cord.

"What?" she said. "Money again? or some of your mother's follies that you have to tell me?"

"No, it's to tell you that I am going away," said Jupillon to her with a grave air. "I've been drawn for the army, and I'm leaving."

"You are leaving?" she said. Her ideas seemed to be not yet awake.

"Look here, Germinie," returned Jupillon, " I've given you pain. I've not been kind to you, I know. It was partly cousin. What could I do?"

"You are leaving?" returned Germinie, taking hold of his arm. "Do not lie, you are leaving?"

"I tell you, yes, and it's true. I am only waiting for my orders. They want more than two thousand francs for a man this year. It is said that there's going to be a war; in short, it's a chance."

While he was speaking he was making Germinie walk down the street.

"Where are you taking me?" she said to him.

"To mother's — to have you both friends again, and put an end to all this fuss — "

"After what she said to me? Never!" And Germinie pushed away Jupillon's arm.

"Then if that's so, good-bye — "

And Jupillon raised his cap.

"Am I to write to you from the regiment?"

For an instant Germinie was silent, for a moment she hesitated. Then she said abruptly:

"Come on," and signing to Jupillon to walk beside her, she went up the street again.

They both began to walk beside each other without speaking. They reached a paved road, which retreated and extended eternally between two lines of lamps, between two rows of twisted trees that threw up handfuls of dry branches towards heaven, and overlaid large, smooth walls with their lean and motionless shadows. There beneath a sky that was keen and cold with a reflection of snow, they walked for a long time, diving into the vagueness, and infinity, and strangeness that belong to a street which ever follows the same line of wall, the same lamps, which ever leads towards the same night. The dark and heavy air which they were breathing savored of sugar, and sweat, and carrion. Now and then a kind of flaming light passed before their eyes: it was a cart, the lantern of which shone on disemboweled beasts, and pieces of bleeding meat thrown over the crupper of a white horse: the light on the flesh streamed through the darkness like a conflagration of purple, like a furnace of blood.

"Well? have you finished your reflections?" said Jupillon. "This little Avenue Trudaine of yours is not particularly cheerful, do you know?"

"Come on," said Germinie.

And, without speaking, she again began to walk in the same abrupt and violent fashion which showed the agitation of all the tumults in her soul. Her thoughts passed into her gestures. Distraction visited her footsteps, and madness her hands. Now and then she had the shadow of a woman belonging to the Salpêtrière behind her. Two or three passers-by stopped for a moment and looked at her; then, being Parisians, they passed on.

Suddenly she stopped with a gesture of despairing resolve.

"Ah dear!" she said, "one pin more in the pincushion. Come!"

And she took Jupillon's arm.

"Oh! I know very well," said Jupillon to her, when they were close to the dairy, "my mother has not been fair to you. You see, she's always been too respectable a woman all her life; she doesn't know, she doesn't understand. And then, look here, I'll tell you what's at the bottom of the whole thing: she's so fond of me herself that she's jealous of the women who like me. Just go in there!"

And he pushed her into the arms of Madame Jupillon, who kissed her, muttered some words of regret, and hastened to cry in order to relieve her embarrassment and to render the scene more affecting.

The whole of that evening Germinie kept her eyes fixed on Jupillon, almost frightening him with her look.

"Come," he said to her as he was taking her home, "don't be such a wet-blanket as all that. People need philosophy in this world. Why, I'm a soldier, that's all! They don't always come back, it's true, but after all — Look here! I'd like us to amuse ourselves for the fortnight that I've got left, because it will be so much gained, and if I don't come back, well! I'll at least have left you with a pleasant recollection of me."

Germinie made no reply.

XXXI

FOR a week Germinie did not set foot again in the shop. The Jupillons, not seeing her come back, were beginning to despair. At last, about half-past ten one evening, she pushed open the door, walked in without salutation of any kind, went up to the little table at which mother and son were sitting half asleep, and laid down an old piece of linen, with her hand closed upon it in a claw-like grip. "There!" she said.

Letting go the corners of the piece of linen she poured out what was inside of it, and there streamed upon the table greasy bank-notes pasted together behind or fastened with pins, old louis d'or that had grown green, hundred-sou pieces that were perfectly black, forty-sou pieces, ten-sou pieces — money of poverty, of labor, of the money-box, money soiled by dirty hands, chafed in the leathern purse, worn among the sous that filled the till — money that savored of sweat. For a moment she looked at all that was spread out before her as though to convince her own eyes; then in a sad and gentle voice, the voice of her sacrifice, she said simply to Madame Jupillon, "There it is. That's the two thousand three hundred francs to buy himself off with."

"Ah, my good Germinie!" said the big woman, choking with a first rush of emotion; and she threw herself upon Germinie's neck, who allowed herself to be kissed. "Oh! you will take something with us, a cup of coffee — "

"No, thank you," said Germinie, "I'm worn out, and I've had to run about, upon my word, to get them. I'm going to bed. Another time." And she went out.

She had had to "run about" as she said to collect such a sum, to realize this impossible thing, to find two thousand three hundred francs whereof she had not the first five! She had searched for them, begged them, picked them up piece by piece, almost sou by sou. She had gathered them, scraped them up here and there, one after another, by loans of two francs, of a hundred francs, of fifty francs, of twenty francs, of whatever people would give. She had borrowed from her porter, her grocer, her fruiterer, her poulterer, her laundress; she had borrowed from the tradesmen of the neighborhood, and from the tradesmen of the neighborhoods in which she had at first lived with mademoiselle. She had swept every kind of money into the sum down to the miserable pittance of her water-carrier. She had begged everywhere, extorted humbly, prayed, entreated, invented stories, swallowed her shame at lying and seeing that she was not believed. The humiliation of confessing that she had no money invested, as people had believed, and as she, in her pride, had allowed them to believe, the commiseration of persons whom she despised, refusals, alms — she had submitted to all these, had endured what she would not have endured to find herself bread, and not once and with a single individual, but with thirty or forty, with all who had ever given her anything, or from whom she had expected anything.

At last she had got the money together, but it was her master, and possessed her for ever. She belonged to the obligations which existed between her and others, to the service which her tradesmen, well aware of what they were doing, had rendered her. She belonged to her debts, to what she would have to pay every year. She knew it; she knew that all her wages would be absorbed in this way, that with the usurious arrangements left by her to the will of her creditors, and the acknowledgments that they had required, mademoiselle's three hundred francs would do little more than pay the interest of her loan of two thousand three hundred francs. She knew that she would be a debtor, that she would always be a debtor, that she would be bound for ever to privations, to embarrassment, to every possible retrenchment in dress and toilet.

She entertained scarcely more illusions respecting the Jupil-

lons than she did about her future. Her money with them was lc.
— of this she had a presentiment. She had not even calculated that
the sacrifice would touch the young man. She had acted on a first
impulse. If she had been told to die in order to prevent his departure, she would have died. The thought of seeing him a soldier, the
thought of the battlefield, of the cannon, of the wounded, at which
a woman closes her eyes in terror, had induced her to do more than
die; to sell her life for this man, and, for his sake, to sign her own
everlasting misery!

XXXII

IT is an ordinary result of nervous disturbances in the organism
to disorder human joys and sorrows, to deprive them of proportion and equilibrium, and to push them to the extreme of excess.
It would seem that under the influence of this disease of impress-
ibility, the senses become quickened, refined, spiritualized, they
exceed their natural measure and limit, pass beyond themselves,
and impart a sort of infinitude to the enjoyment and suffering of the
creature. The infrequent joys which Germinie still had were now
mad joys, joys from which she emerged intoxicated and with the
physical characteristics of intoxication.

"Why, my girl," mademoiselle could not help saying to her,
"one would think you were drunk."

And when she relapsed into her troubles, and sorrows, and anxieties, her affliction would be still more intense, more frenzied and
delirious than her mirth.

The time had come when the terrible truth, of which she had
caught a glimpse, but which had then been veiled by later illusions,
finally appeared to Germinie. She saw that she had not been able to
attach Jupillon to her by the devotion of her love, by the spoliation
of all that she possessed, by all these money sacrifices which were
involving her life in the embarrassment and agony of a debt that it
was impossible to pay. She felt that he brought her his love with
reluctance, a love to which he imparted the humiliation of a charity.
When she informed him that she was pregnant for a second time,
this man, whom she was about to make a father, had said to her:

"Well! women like you are a good joke! always full or ready to begin again!"

Thoughts came to her, suspicions such as come to genuine love when it is deceived, forebodings of the heart which tell women that they are no longer in sole possession of their lovers, and that there is another because there must be another.

She had ceased to complain, to weep, to recriminate. She gave up striving with this man who was armed with coldness, and who so well knew how to outrage her passion, her unreason, her tender follies, with his icy, blackguard ironies. And she set herself to wait in resigned anguish for — what? She did not know; perhaps, until he would have no more of her!

Heart-broken and silent she spied upon Jupillon; she dogged him and watched him; she tried to make him speak by throwing in a word when he was inattentive. She revolved about him, seeing, apprehending, surprising nothing, but remaining nevertheless persuaded that there was something and that what she dreaded was true; she scented a woman in the air.

One morning, having come down earlier than usual, she saw him on the pavement a few steps in front of her. He was dressed, and kept looking at himself as he walked. From time to time he raised the edge of his trousers a little, to see the polish on his boots. She began to follow him. He went straight on without turning. She reached the Place Bréda behind him; on the Place, beside the cabstand, a woman was walking up and down. Germinie could see only her back. Jupillon went up to her, and the woman turned: it was his cousin.

They began to walk to and fro beside each other on the Place; then they proceeded through the Rue Bréda towards the Rue de Navarin. There the young girl took Jupillon's arm, not leaning on it at first, but afterwards, as they walked on, stooping gradually with the movement of a bending bough, and leaning upon him. They walked slowly, so slowly that Germinie was sometimes obliged to stop in order not to be too close to them. They went up the Rue des Martyrs, crossed the Rue de la Tour-d'Auvergne, and went down the Rue Montholon. Jupillon was speaking; the cousin was saying nothing, was listening to Jupillon, and, absent as a woman inhaling a bouquet, was casting vague little side-looks from time to time, little glances like those of a frightened child.

On reaching the Rue Lamartine in front of the Passage des Deux-Sœurs, they turned back; Germinie had only just time to spring into an entry. They passed without seeing her. The girl was grave, and slow in walking. Jupillon was talking close to her neck. For a moment they stopped, Jupillon making great gestures, and the young girl looking fixedly on the pavement. Germinie thought that they were going to part; but they again began to walk together and took four or five turns, passing and repassing in front of the Passage.

At last they entered it. Germinie darted from her hiding-place, and leaped after them. From the grating of the Passage she could see part of a dress disappearing within the doorway of a small private house, next door to the shop of a liquor-dealer. She hastened to the doorway, looked at the staircase, could see nothing more. Then all her blood mounted to her head with a thought, a single thought which her idiotic lips kept repeating: "Vitriol! — Vitriol! — Vitriol!" And her thought becoming instantly the very action of her thought, her frenzy transporting her suddenly into her crime, she was ascending the stairs with the bottle well hidden beneath her shawl; she was knocking continuously and very loudly at the door. Some one came at last; he half opened the door. She passed without paying any attention to him. She was capable of killing him! — and she was going up to the bed, to *her!* She was taking her by the arm, and saying to her: "Yes, 'tis I — this will last you your life!" And over her face, her breast, her skin, over all that was young in her, and proud, and beautiful for love, Germinie could see the vitriol marking, burning, hollowing, bubbling, making something that was horrible and that flooded her with joy. The bottle was empty and she was laughing.

And in her frightful dream, her body also dreaming, her feet began to walk. Her steps went on before her, passed down the Passage, entered the street, and took her to the grocer's. For ten minutes she stood by the counter with eyes that saw nothing, the vacant, bewildered eyes of one bent on murder.

"Come, what do you want?" said the shop-woman to her, out of patience, and almost frightened at this motionless woman.

"What do I want?" said Germinie. She was so full of and so possessed by what she desired, that she thought she had asked for the vitriol. "What do I want?" And she drew her hand across her forehead. "Ah! I have forgotten."

And she went stumbling out of the shop.

XXXIII

AMID the torture of a life in which she suffered death and passion, Germinie, seeking to deaden the horrors of her thoughts, had gone back to the glass which she had taken from Adèle's hands one morning, and which had given her a whole day of forgetfulness. From that day she had begun to drink. She had drunk little morning "sips," like the maids of kept women. She had drunk with one and drunk with another. She had drunk with men who came to breakfast at the dairy. She had drunk with Adèle, who drank like a man, and who took a vile pleasure in seeing this honest woman's maid sinking as low as herself.

At first, in order to be able to drink, she had required temptation, society, the clinking of glasses, the excitement of language, the warmth of a challenge; soon afterwards, she came to drink when alone. Then it was that she had drunk from the half-filled glass brought upstairs under her apron and hidden in a corner of the kitchen; that in solitude and despair she had drunk those mixtures of white wine and brandy which she swallowed continuously, until she had found in them that for which she was thirsting — sleep. For what she desired was not the heady fever, the happy confusion, the living madness, the waking and delirious dream of intoxication; what she desired, what she asked for, was the dark happiness of sleep, of unremembering and dreamless sleep, of leaden sleep falling upon her like a bludgeon on the head of an ox: and she found it in those blended liquors which crushed her and brought her head to lie upon the cloth of her kitchen table.

To sleep such overwhelming sleep, to sink in the daytime into such a night, had come to be with her a truce to, and a deliverance from, a manner of life which she had lost courage either to continue or to end. A boundless yearning for non-existence was all that she felt in her wakefulness. Such hours of her life as she lived collectedly, under self-inspection, looking into her conscience, a spectator of all her shamefulness, seemed so abominable to her! She preferred to be dead to them. Nothing in the world but sleep was left to her that would give her complete forgetfulness, the congested sleep of Drunkenness which cradles in the arms of Death.

Here, in the glass which she forced herself to drink, and which she emptied with frenzy, her sufferings, her griefs, the whole of her horrible present would drown and disappear. Within half-an-hour her thought ceased to think, her life to be; all that she was had, to her, no further existence, and even time was no longer with her. "I am drowning my troubles," she had replied to a woman who had told her that she would ruin her health by drinking. And as during the re-actions which followed her periods of intoxication, there returned to her a more painful self-consciousness, a greater grieving and detestation for her faults and her misfortunes, she sought out stronger alcohol, rawer brandy, she even drank absinthe pure in order to lapse into a duller lethargy, and to render her insensibility to all things still more complete.

Finally she succeeded in inducing periods of annihilation which lasted half a day, and from which she emerged only partially awake, with stupefied intellect, blunted perceptions, hands which did things simply from habit, gestures like those of a somnambulist, a body and soul in which thought, will, and memory seemed to be still slumbering and dim as in the hazy hours of morning.

XXXIV

HALF-AN-HOUR after the frightful occasion when, touching crime in thought as though with fingers, she had wished to disfigure her rival with vitriol and had fancied that she had done so, Germinie re-entered the Rue de Laval bringing up a bottle of brandy with her from the grocer's.

For two weeks she had been mistress of the apartments, free to indulge in her drunkenness and brutishness. Mademoiselle de Varandeuil, who, as a rule, hardly ever stirred from home, had most exceptionally gone to spend six weeks in the country with one of her old friends; and she had been unwilling to take Germinie with her through fear of allowing the other servants to see her bad example, and to become jealous of a maid accustomed to her easy service, and treated on a footing other than their own.

On entering mademoiselle's room, Germinie gave herself only time to throw her bonnet and shawl upon the ground before she began to drink in hurried mouthfuls, with the neck of the brandy-bottle between her teeth, until everything in the room was spinning around her, and the whole of the day had vanished from her brain. Then, staggering, feeling that she was falling, she tried to lie down on her mistress's bed in order to sleep, but her intoxication flung her aside upon the night-table. From there she rolled to the floor and moved no more: she was snoring.

But the shock had been so violent that during the night she had a miscarriage, followed by one of those fluxes wherein life ebbs away. She tried to raise herself to go and call on the landing, she tried to get upon her feet, but could not. She felt herself slipping towards death, entering it, descending into it with lingering slow-ness. At last, putting forth a final effort, she dragged herself as far as the door opening on the staircase; but when there she found it impossible to lift herself as high as the lock, impossible to cry out. And she would have died at last, had not Adèle, uneasy at hearing a moaning sound as she passed in the morning, sent for a locksmith to open the door, and a midwife to deliver the dying woman.

When mademoiselle returned at the end of a month, she found Germinie up, but so weak that she was obliged to sit down every minute, and so pale that she no longer seemed to have any blood in her body. They told her that Germinie had had a flux of which she had nearly died, and mademoiselle suspected nothing.

XXXV

GERMINIE greeted mademoiselle's return with feeling caresses, moistened with tears. Her tenderness was like a sick child's; it had the same lingering gentleness, the same beseeching air, the same timorous and startled sadness of suffering. She sought to touch her mistress with her pale, blue-veined hands. She approached her with a sort of trembling and reverent humility. Most frequently, seated opposite to her on a footstool, and looking up at her with the eyes of a dog, she would get up at intervals to kiss her on some part of her dress, return to her seat, and then, a moment later, perform the same action over again.

There was anguish and entreaty in these caresses and kisses of Germinie's. The death that she had heard approaching her like a person, with somebody's footsteps, those hours of exhaustion when, in bed and alone with herself, she had reviewed her life, and retraced her past, the remembrance and the shame of all that she had concealed from Mademoiselle de Varandeuil, the terror of a judgment from God uprising from the heart of her old religious ideas, all the reproaches and all the fears which haunt those who are about to die, had created a supreme terror in her conscience; and remorse — remorse which she had never been able to kill within her — was now living and crying out in the weakened, shaken being, which was still but imperfectly linked back to life, was still scarcely attached once more to a belief in existence.

Germinie was not one of those happy natures who do evil and leave the memory of it behind them, reverting to it no more in regretful thought. Unlike Adèle, she had not one of those gross material organisms which can be penetrated only by animal impressions. She had not such a conscience as will escape from suffering through brutishness, and through that dense stupidity in which a woman vegetates, ingenuously faulty. In her a morbid sensitiveness, a sort of *cerebral erethism,* a tendency of her head to be always working and disquieting itself in bitterness, anxiety, and self-discontent, a moral sense which had erected itself, as it were, within her after every fall, all the gifts of nicety, choiceness, and misfortune, united to torture her, and every day thrust back further and more cruelly into despair the torment of what would scarcely have caused such lengthened sorrows to many of her kind.

Germinie yielded to the rush of passion, but she had no sooner done so than she despised herself for it. Even during her pleasure she could not forget herself entirely and lose herself. Amid her self-distraction there rose constantly before her the image of mademoiselle with her austere, maternal face. Germinie did not feel shamelessness come to her in proportion as she sank beneath the level of her virtue. The degradations into which she plunged strengthened her in no degree against disgust and horror of herself. Habit did not bring *her* callousness. Her polluted conscience rejected its pollutions, struggled amidst its shame, was torn asunder in its repentance, and did not for one moment permit to her the full enjoyment of vice, the entire deadness of degradation.

Thus, when mademoiselle, forgetting the servant that she was, bent over her with one of those abrupt familiarities of voice and

nich brought her close to her heart, Germinie, in con-
nd a sudden prey to blushing timidity, would become mute
ot-like beneath the horrible pain of seeing all her unworthi-
She would fly, she would make an excuse for tearing herself
 y from this affection, which had been so odiously deceived,
and which as it touched her, stirred and thrilled all her remorse.

XXXVI

A MIRACULOUS feature in this life of disorder and anguish, this
shameful and broken life, was that it did not break out. Germinie
suffered none of it to start forth, she suffered none of it to rise to her
lips, she suffered none of it to be seen in her countenance, none of it
to appear in her demeanor, and the accursed depths of her existence
ever remained hidden from her mistress.

It had, indeed, sometimes befallen Mademoiselle de Varandeuil
to be vaguely sensible of some secret on the part of her maid, of
something that she was hiding from her, of some obscure spot in
her life; she had had moments of doubt and mistrust, and instinctive anxiety, beginnings of confused perception, the scent of a trail
that was constantly sinking and losing itself in gloom. At times she
had thought that she had come close in this girl to things secret and
cold, to mystery, to shadow. At other times, again, it had seemed
to her that her maid's eyes did not express the utterance of her
lips. Without intending it, she had retained in her memory a phrase
which Germinie used often to repeat: "A sin hidden is a sin half
forgiven."

But what especially engaged her thoughts was her astonishment
at seeing that, in spite of an increase in her wages, in spite of the
little daily presents which she gave her, Germinie bought nothing
new for her toilet, had no new dresses, no new linen. Where did her
money go? She had almost acknowledged to her the withdrawal of
her eighteen hundred francs from the savings bank. Mademoiselle
thought over this, and then said to herself that here was the whole
of her maid's mystery; it was money embarrassments, obligations
which, doubtless, she had formerly contracted on account of her
relations, and perhaps fresh sendings "to her rascally brother-in-

law." She had so good a heart and so little method! She had so little knowledge of the value of a hundred-sou piece! That was all: mademoiselle was sure of it; and as she knew her maid's obstinate nature, and had no hopes of changing her, she said nothing to her.

When this explanation did not completely satisfy mademoiselle, she attributed whatever she found strange and mysterious in her maid to a somewhat secret-loving feminine nature, which preserved the disposition and distrustfulness of the peasant-woman, jealous of her own little concerns, and delighting to bury a fragment of her life deep within her, just as, in villages, people heap up sous in a woollen stocking. Or else she persuaded herself that it was sickness, her continual state of suffering, that gave her these whims and this secretiveness. And her thoughts, in their investigation and their curiosity, stopped here with the indolence and also with something of the egoism of the thoughts of old persons, who, with an instinctive dread of the ends of things and of the hearts of people, are unwilling to be too anxious, or to know too much. Who could tell? Perhaps all this mysteriousness was only some trifle undeserving of her anxiety or interest, some feminine squabble or quarrel. She was reassured and lulled by this thought, and ceased her inquiry.

And how could mademoiselle have guessed Germinie's degradations and the horror of her secret! In her most poignant griefs, in her wildest intoxications, the unhappy woman maintained the incredible strength requisite for restraining and burying all. From her passionate, extravagant nature, so ready to pour itself out in expansiveness, there never escaped a phrase, a word that might have been a lightning-flash, a gleam. Vexations, scornings, sorrows, sacrifices — the death of her child, the treachery of her lover, the death struggle of her love, all remained silent, stifled within her as though she were straining both hands upon her heart. The occasional swoonings which came upon her, and in which she seemed to be struggling with the griefs that were strangling her, the feverish, frenzied caresses given to Mademoiselle de Varandeuil, the sudden outpouring which resembled crises seeking to give birth to something, ended always without speech and took refuge in tears.

Even sickness with its weakness and nervelessness drew nothing from her. It could not impair the heroic will to be silent to the end. Her nerve-crises wrung from her cries and nothing more. When a young girl she used to dream aloud; she forced her dreams

ak no more; she closed the lips of her sleep. As mademoiselle
it have perceived from her breath that she drank, she ate garlic
scallions, and in the stench of them concealed the odor of her
drunkenness. Even her intoxications, her drunken lethargies, she
trained to rouse at her mistress's step, and to remain awake in her
presence.

She thus led as it were two lives. She was like two women,
and by her energy, adroitness, and feminine diplomacy, with the
self-possession that was always present with her even in the confusion of drink, she succeeded in separating these two lives, in living them both without mingling them, in refraining from confusing
the two women who were in her, in remaining to Mademoiselle
de Varandeuil's eyes the honest and steady girl that she had been,
in emerging from a debauch without taking the flavor of it with
her, in displaying, when she had just left her own lover, a sort of
shamefacedness like that of an old maid disgusted by the scandal-
ous behavior of the other servant-women. No utterance or manner
of dress was ever such as might rouse a suspicion of her clandes-
tine life; nothing about her savored of her nights. When she set her
foot upon the matting in Mademoiselle de Varandeuil's apartment,
when she approached her and found herself face to face with her,
she would assume the language, the attitude, even certain folds of
the dress which keep from a woman the very thought of a man's
approaches.

She spoke freely of everything, as though she had to blush at
nothing. She was bitter against the faults and shame of others, as
is a person who is without reproach. She jested about love with
her mistress in a gay, unembarrassed, offhand manner; she had the
appearance of talking about an old acquaintance that she had lost
sight of. And to all those who saw her only as Mademoiselle de
Varandeuil saw her, and in her mistress's house, there was about
her thirty-five years a certain atmosphere of peculiar chastity, a perfume of severe and not to be suspected honesty, which is characteristic of old servants and ugly women.

Nevertheless, all this falsity of appearance was not hypocrisy
with Germinie. It was not the outcome of perverse duplicity, of depraved calculation: it was her affection for mademoiselle that made
her what she was in her mistress's house. She wanted at all costs to
save her the sorrow of seeing her and of piercing her inmost nature.

She deceived her solely to keep her affection, and with a sort of respect; into the horrible comedy that she was acting there crept a pious, religious feeling, like the feeling of a young girl who lies to her mother's eyes that she may not grieve her heart.

XXXVII

LIE! she had lost the power of doing anything else. She felt it to be a kind of impossibility to draw back from her position; she did not so much as entertain the idea of an effort to get out of it, so craven, so overwhelmed, so vanquished was she, so completely did she still feel herself bound to this man by all sorts of base chains and degrading ties, by the very contempt which he no longer concealed from her!

Sometimes she was frightened as she reflected upon herself. Village ideas, village fears recurred to her, and her youthful superstitions whispered to her that this man had thrown a spell over her, that he had made her eat "unleavened bread." Without this would she have been as she was? Would she have had that emotion throughout her being at the mere sight of him, that almost animal sensation of a master's approach? Would she have felt her whole person, her mouth, her arms, the love and caressing of her gestures going out involuntarily to him? Would she have belonged to him thus completely? Long and bitterly did she recall all that ought to have cured her, to have saved her — the disdain of the man, his insults, the depravity of the pleasures which he had required from her — and she was compelled to acknowledge to herself that she had found no sacrifice too dear for him, and that for him she had swallowed the uttermost dregs of disgust. She strove to imagine a degree of degradation to which her love would refuse to descend, and she could find none. He might do what he would with her, insult her, beat her, and she would still be his, and beneath his heel! She could not see herself as no longer belonging to him. She could not see herself without him. To have this man to love was a necessity with her; she warmed herself in him and lived in him, and breathed in him. Nothing similar seemed to exist round about her among the women of her rank. None of the companions to whom she had access experienced in a *liaison* the violence, the bitterness, the torture, the happiness in suffering which she found in her own. None experienced that which was killing her, and which she could not forego.

To herself, she appeared extraordinary and of an exceptional disposition, of the temperament of animals that are rendered faithful by evil treatment. There were days on which she no longer knew herself, and on which she asked herself whether she was still the same woman. In reviewing all the baseness to which Jupillon had bent her, she could not believe that it was she who had undergone it all. She, who knew herself to be violent, fiery, full of bad passions, revolts and storms, she had resigned herself to all this submissiveness and docility! She had repressed her anger, had driven back the thoughts of blood which had so often risen to her brain! She had been always obedient, always patient, always with bowed head! She had made her temper, her instincts, her pride, her vanity, and more than all, her jealousy, the ragings of her heart, crawl at this man's feet! To keep him, she had gone so far as to share him, to allow him mistresses, to receive him from the hands of others, to search his cheek for a place on which his cousin had not kissed him!

And now, after exhausting the many concessions with which she had wearied him, she retained him by a more disgusting sacrifice, she drew him by presents, she opened her purse to bring him to the place of meeting, she purchased his amiability by satisfying his whims and caprices, she paid this man who trafficked in his kisses, and asked gratuities from love! And she lived on from one day to the next in terror of what the wretch might require of her on the morrow.

XXXVIII

"HE wants twenty francs." Germinie repeated this several times to herself, but her thought did not pass beyond the words that she uttered. Her walk, and the ascent of the five stories had dazed her. She dropped into a seat on the greasy settle in her kitchen, bent her head, and laid her arms upon the table. Her head was singing. Her thoughts would go from her, and then return as in a crowd, and stifle one another within her, while of them all there remained to her but one, ever keener and more fixed:

"He wants twenty francs!—twenty francs!—twenty francs!— "

And she looked around her as though she would find them there in the fireplace, in the dust-basket, or beneath the stove. Then she thought of the people who were in her debt, of a German maid, who had promised to repay her a year ago. She got up and fastened on her cap. She no longer said: "He wants twenty francs;" she said: "I shall get them."

She went down to Adèle:

"You haven't twenty francs for a bill that's been brought? Mademoiselle is out."

"No such luck," said Adèle: "I gave my last twenty francs to madame yesterday evening to go out to supper. The jade hasn't come in again yet. Will you have thirty sous?"

She hastened to the grocer's. It was Sunday, and three o'clock; the grocer had just closed his shop.

There were some people at the fruit-woman's; she asked for four sous' worth of herbs.

"I have no money," she said. She hoped that the fruit-woman would say to her: "Do you want some?" The fruit-woman said: "What a piece of affectation! as though people were afraid about that!" There were other servants there, so she went out without speaking.

"There's nothing for us?" she said to the concierge. "Ah! by the way, you haven't got twenty francs, my Pipelet, have you? It would save my going up again."

"Forty if you like."

She drew her breath. The concierge went up to a cupboard in the back part of his lodge.

"Ah! by jove! my wife has taken the key. But how pale you are!"

"It's nothing," and she escaped into the courtyard towards the back staircase.

As she went up again this is what she was thinking:

"There are people who find twenty-franc pieces. It's to-day that he wants them, so he told me. Mademoiselle gave me my money not five days ago, and I can't ask her. For that matter what are twenty francs more or less to her? The grocer would have lent them to me without doubt. There's that other that I used to deal with in the Rue Taitbout; he didn't close until the evening on Sundays —"

She was on her own story and in front of the door. She leaned over the balustrade of the front staircase, and looked to see whether any one was coming up, entered, went straight to mademoiselle's room, opened the window, and took a deep breath, resting both elbows on the crossbar. Some sparrows hastened thither from the chimneys round about, thinking that she was going to throw them some bread. She shut the window and looked into the room at the top of the chest of drawers, first at a marble vein, then at a little money-box of West Indian wood, then at the key, a small steel key, which had been forgotten in the lock. Suddenly, her ears tingled; she thought that some one was ringing; she went to open the door, but there was no one there. She came back with the feeling that she was alone, went to the kitchen for a cloth, and turning her back to the chest of drawers, began to rub the mahogany of an armchair; but she could still see the box, she could see it open, she could see the righthand corner in which mademoiselle put her gold, the little papers in which she wrapped up the francs hundred by hundred; her twenty francs were there! She shut her eyes as though they were dazzled. She was sensible of a vertigo in her conscience; but immediately it rose in its entirety against itself, and it seemed to her as if her indignant heart were mounting up within her breast.

In an instant the honor of her whole life had reared itself between her hand and the key. Her past of probity, disinterestedness, devotion, twenty years of resistance to the evil counsels of that corrupt district, twenty years of contempt for theft, twenty years in which her pocket had not contained a farthing belonging to her employers, twenty years of indifference to lucre, twenty years in which temptation had not approached her, her lengthened and natural honesty, the confidence of mademoiselle — all these came back to her at a stroke. The years of her youth embraced her and took her back. From her family even, from the recollection of her parents, from the pure memory of her wretched name, from the dead from whom she sprang, there arose as it were a murmuring of guardian shadows around her. For a second she was saved.

Then by insensible degrees evil thoughts crept one by one into her head. She sought for matters of bitterness, for reasons for ingratitude towards her mistress. She compared her own wages with the amount of which the other maids of the house used in vanity to boast. She considered that mademoiselle was very well off, that she ought to have given a greater increase since she had been with her. And then, she suddenly asked herself, why does she leave the key in the box? And then she began to think that the money which was there was not money for living on, but savings of mademoiselle's to buy a velvet dress for a god-daughter; money which was lying idle — she said to herself again. She hurried her reasons as though to prevent herself from discussing her excuses. "And then, it is only for once — she would lend them to me if I asked her — and I will pay them back —"

She put out her hand, and turned the key. She paused; it seemed as though the great silence around her were looking at her and listening to her. She raised her eyes, and the glass threw her back her features. At the sight of this countenance of her own, she was afraid; she recoiled in terror and shame as though before the face of her crime; it was a thief's head that she had upon her shoulders.

She had fled into the corridor. Suddenly she turned upon her heels, went straight to the box, gave the key a turn, thrust in her hand, searched through hair-lockets and keepsake trinkets, blindly took a coin from a little pile of five louis pieces, shut the box, and escaped into the kitchen. She held the little coin in her hand and did not dare to look at it.

XXXIX

IT was then that Germinie's debasement and degradation began to appear in her whole person, to make her dull and dirty. A sort of sleep overtook her ideas. She was no longer quick and prompt to think; what she had read and learnt seemed to escape her. Her memory, which formerly had retained everything, became confused and forgetful. The wit of the Parisian servant gradually forsook her conversation, her replies, her laughter. Her physiognomy, which lately had been so lively, had lost all its lightning-glances. Her whole person seemed to betoken the return of the stupid peasant that she had been when she arrived from the country and went to a stationer's to buy ginger-bread. She seemed to have lost the power of comprehension. Mademoiselle saw her look with a face of an idiot, when she spoke to her. She was obliged to explain to her, and repeat to her twice or thrice, what, hitherto, Germinie had caught from a hint. Seeing her in this condition, slow and drowsy, she asked herself whether some one had not changed her maid.

"Really you are becoming a stupid fool!" she said to her sometimes in her impatience.

She remembered the time when Germinie had been so useful to her in recalling a date, in addressing a card, in telling the day when the wood had come in or the cask of wine had been begun, all these being things which escaped her own old brain. *Germinie could now remember nothing.* When she was reckoning up with mademoiselle in the evening she could not recall what she had bought in the morning. "Wait!" she would say, and after a vague gesture nothing recurred to her. To spare her eyes, mademoiselle had grown accustomed to have the newspaper read to her by her maid; but Germinie came to hesitate in such a fashion, and to read with so little intelligence, that mademoiselle was obliged to decline the service.

While her intellect thus grew constantly weaker, her body also was abandoned and neglected. She renounced the toilet, and even cleanliness. In her heedlessness she preserved nothing of a woman's care; she no longer dressed herself. She wore dresses spotted with grease and rent under the arms, aprons in tatters, stockings in holes, with misshapen old shoes. She allowed the kitchen smoke, coal, blacking, to soil her, to be wiped up by her as by a dishcloth. Formerly she had indulged in the coquetry and luxury of poor women — the love of linen. No one in the house wore fresher caps. Her little collars, which were quite simple and plain, had always that whiteness which lights up the skin so prettily and makes the whole person tidy. Now she wore caps that were worn and crumpled, and that looked as though she had slept in them. She did without cuffs, her collar allowed a strip of dirt to be seen against the skin of her neck, and one felt she was even filthier below than above. A rank and stagnant odor of wretchedness came from her. Sometimes it was so strong that Mademoiselle de Varandeuil could not help saying to her:

"Go and change, my girl; you smell of poverty." In the street she no longer looked as though she belonged to any decent person. She no longer seemed to be a respectable person's servant. She was losing the aspect of a maid who, careful and respectful of herself in her very dress, bears about her the reflection of her house, and the pride of her employers. From day to day she was becoming that abject, bare-breasted creature whose dress sweeps the kennel — a *sloven*.

Neglecting herself, she neglected everything around her. She no longer tidied, or cleaned, or washed. She allowed disorder and dirt to find their way into the apartments, to invade mademoiselle's home, that little home whose cleanliness had formerly made mademoiselle so content and proud. The dust collected, spiders spun their webs behind the picture-frames, the mirrors grew dull, the marble chimney-pieces and mahogany furniture became tarnished; moths flew from the no longer shaken rugs, worms established themselves in places unswept by brush or broom; forgetfulness everywhere scattered dust upon the slumbering and neglected things which formerly were awaked and revived by the energy of every morning.

Ten times over had mademoiselle tried to pique Germinie's pride in the matter; but then, the whole day long, there was a cleaning so furious and accompanied by such fits of temper, that mademoiselle resolved never to do so again. One day, nevertheless, she was bold enough to write Germinie's name with her finger in the dust on the looking-glass; it was a week before Germinie forgave her. Mademoiselle at last resigned herself to it. She did no more than say very gently, when she saw her maid in a momentary good humor:

"Confess, my girl, that the dust has a good time with us!"

To the astonishment and remarks of the friends who still came to see her and whom Germinie was obliged to admit, mademoiselle would reply in a tone of pity and compassion:

"Yes, it is dirty, I know. But what of it? Germinie is ill, and I would rather that she did not kill herself."

Sometimes when Germinie had gone out she ventured with gouty hands to give a wipe with a napkin to the chest of drawers, a stroke with a feather brush to a picture-frame. She used to make haste, dreading lest she should be scolded, lest she should have a scene, if her maid came in and saw her.

Germinie did scarcely any more work; she hardly served the meals. She had reduced her mistress's lunch and dinner to the simplest dishes, the quickest and easiest to cook. She made her bed without raising the mattresses in the English fashion. The servant that she had once been was recovered and revived within her only on the days on which mademoiselle gave a little dinner, when the number of covers was always sufficiently large owing to the band of children invited. On such days Germinie would emerge as though by magic from her laziness and apathy, and drawing strength from a sort of fever, would recover all her old activity in front of her stoves and lengthened table. And mademoiselle would be astounded to see her, all-sufficing, alone and unwilling to receive assistance, cooking a dinner for ten people in a few hours, serving it, and clearing it away with the hands and all the quick adroitness of her youth.

XL

"NO — this time, no," said Germinie, getting up from the foot of Jupillon's bed, on which she had been seated. "There is no means. So you don't know that I haven't got another sou, nothing that is called a sou. You haven't seen the stockings I wear!"

And raising her petticoat, she showed him stockings that were all in holes and fastened with selvages.

"I haven't what will get me a change of anything. Money? why, on mademoiselle's birthday, I hadn't enough just to give her some flowers. I bought her a bunch of violets for a sou, so! Money, indeed! Do you know how I got your last twenty francs? By taking them out of mademoiselle's cash-box. I have replaced them, but that's all over. I'll have no more of that kind of thing. It's all very well for once. Where would you have me find them now, just tell me that? People can't pawn their skins, and there's no other way that I know of. But another thing like that I'll never do in my life again! Anything you like, but not that, not stealing! I'll do it no more. Oh, I know well enough what will happen to me with you — but so much the worse!"

"Well, have you done exciting yourself?" said Jupillon. "If you had told me that about the twenty francs, do you imagine that I'd have wanted them? I didn't think you were such a beggar as that. I saw you always getting along. I fancied it wouldn't put you out to lend me a twenty-franc piece that I'd have paid you back in a week or two with the rest. But you don't say anything. Well, that's all about it; I'll ask you no more. It's no reason why we should get angry, is it?"

And casting an indefinable glance upon Germinie:

"Till Thursday, eh?"

"Till Thursday!" said Germinie, desperately.

She longed to throw herself into Jupillon's arms, to ask his forgiveness for her wretchedness, to say to him:

"You see, I cannot!"

"Till Thursday!" she repeated, and went away.

When she knocked at the door of Jupillon's ground-floor lodgings on Thursday, she thought that she could hear the footsteps of a man retreating into the back part. The door opened; before her stood the cousin in a hair-net, an ample red jacket, slippers, and the toilet and face of a woman who is at home in a man's home. Her things were lying about here and there. Germinie could see them on the furniture for which she had paid.

"What does madame want?" asked the cousin, impudently.

"Monsieur Jupillon."

"He is out."

"I will wait for him," said Germinie, as she tried to enter the other room.

"At the concierge's, then." And the cousin barred her passage.

"When will he be back?"

"When hens have teeth," said the young girl, gravely; and she shut the door in her face.

"Well, it's just what I expected from him," said Germinie, as she walked along the street. The paving-stones seemed to be giving way beneath her nerveless legs.

XLI

COMING in that evening from a baptismal dinner party which she had been unable to decline, mademoiselle heard talking in her room. She thought that there was some one with Germinie, and pushed open the door in astonishment. By the light of a black smoky candle she could at first see nobody; then, looking carefully, she perceived her maid lying curled up on the foot of her bed.

Germinie was asleep and was speaking. She spoke in a strange tone, and one which inspired emotion and almost fear. The vague solemnity of supernatural things, a breath from beyond the limits of life was in the room with this involuntary, escaping, throbbing, suspended speech of sleep which was like a disembodied soul straying upon dead lips. It was a slow, deep, distant voice, with long breathing pauses and words exhaled like sighs, crossed by vibrating and poignant tones which penetrated the heart, a voice full of the mystery and trembling of the night in which the sleeper seemed to be groping after memories, and to be passing her hand over faces. These words were audible:

"Oh! she loved me well. And he, if he were not dead — we'd be happy now, wouldn't we? No, no! But it's done — so much the worse — I won't tell — "

And then came a nervous shrinking as though Germinie wished to thrust back her secret, and bring it back from the edge of her lips.

Mademoiselle had leaned with a sort of terror over this abandoned, self-alienated body, to which the past was returning like a ghost to a forsaken house. She listened to these confessions ready to spring forth and mechanically arrested, to this unknowing thought which was speaking wholly of itself, to this voice which could not hear itself. A feeling of horror came upon her; she felt as if she were beside a corpse possessed by a dream.

After an interval of silence, of a sort of pulling to and fro amid what she appeared to be seeing again, Germinie seemed to allow the present period of her life to come to her. What escaped her, what she poured forth in detached and inconsequent words, consisted, so far as mademoiselle could understand, in reproaches addressed to some one. And as she went on speaking her language became as unrecognizable as her words, as her voice transposed into the notes of the dream. It soared above the woman, above her daily toil and expressions. It was like a people's language purified and transfigured in passion. Germinie was accenting her words with their orthography; she was uttering them with their eloquence. The phrases came forth from her mouth with their rhythm, their anguish, and their tears, as from the mouth of an admirable actress. There were impulses of tenderness broken by cries; then came revolts, outbursts, and marvellous, strident, merciless irony ever stifled in a fit of nervous laughter that repeated and prolonged the same insult to the echo.

Mademoiselle was bewildered, astounded, listening as in a theatre. Never had she heard disdain falling from such a height, contempt being shattered in such a manner and springing into laughter, a woman's utterance containing so much of vengeance against a man. She searched her memory; such acting, such intonations, a voice so dramatic and lacerating as this consumptive, heart-breaking one, she could recollect only with Mademoiselle Rachel.

At last Germinie awoke abruptly, her eyes filled with the tears of her sleep, and she sprang off the bed on seeing that her mistress had come back.

"Thanks," said the latter to her, "don't trouble. Sprawl away on my bed, as you are doing!"

"Oh! mademoiselle," said Germinie, "I was not where you lay your head. There, that will warm your feet!"

"Well, just tell me what you were dreaming about. There was a man in it, and you were arguing."

"I?" said Germinie, "I have forgotten." And seeking after her dreams she began to silently undress her mistress. When she had put her into bed:

"Ah! mademoiselle," she said to her as she tucked in the clothes, "won't you give me a fortnight, just for once, to go home? I remember now — "

XLII

SOON afterwards mademoiselle was astonished by an entire change in the manner of life and habits of her maid. Germinie lost her sullenness, her wild tempers, her rebelliousness, her word-mutterings wherein scolded her discontent. She suddenly emerged from her laziness, and recovered zeal in her work. She no longer took whole hours to do her shopping; she seemed to shun the street. She went out no more in the evening; she scarcely stirred from mademoiselle's side, encompassing her, tending her from her rising to her bedtime, taking continuous, incessant, almost irritating care of her, never allowing her to get up, or even to stretch out her hand to take anything, serving her, watching over her as over a child. At times, wearied of this eternal occupation about her person, mademoiselle would open her mouth to say to her:

"Well now! are you going to decamp from here soon!"

But Germinie would turn her smile upon her, a smile so sad and so sweet that it checked the impatience on the old maid's lips. And Germinie would continue to remain near her with a sort of charmed and divinely stupid look, in the immobility of profound adoration, the absorption of almost idiotic contemplation.

The reason was that at this juncture all the poor girl's affection was returning towards mademoiselle. Her voice, her gestures, her eyes, her silence, her thoughts went out to her mistress's person with a fervor of an expiation, the contrition of a prayer, the transport of a religion. She loved her with all the tender violence of her nature. She loved her with all the betrayals of her passion. She would fain have rendered to her all that she had not given her, all that others had taken from her. Every day her love embraced her mistress more closely, more religiously, so that the old maiden lady felt herself pressed, enwrapped, gently warmed by the glow of two arms that were thrown about her old age.

XLIII

BUT the past and her debts were always with her, and every hour repeating to her: "If mademoiselle knew!"

She lived in a criminal's agony, in trembling pain from which no instant was free. Not a ring came to the door that she did not say to herself, "There it is!" Letters in a strange handwriting filled her with anxiety. She tortured the wax with her fingers, she thrust them into her pocket, she hesitated about giving them, and the moment at which mademoiselle opened the terrible paper, and ran over it with an old woman's indifferent eye, cost her the emotion that is caused by an expected sentence of death. She felt her secret and her falsehood to be in everyone's keeping. The house had seen it and could speak. The neighborhood knew it. Her mistress was the only person left of those round about her whose good opinion she could steal.

Going up and down stairs she encountered the concierge's glance, a glance which smiled and said to her: "I know!" She no longer ventured to call him familiarly: "My Pipelet." When she came in, he used to look into her basket. "Ah, I am so fond of that!" his wife would say when there was something good. In the evening she would bring them down what was left. She could no longer eat. In the end she fed them.

The whole street alarmed her like the staircase and the concierge's lodge. In every shop there was a face that reflected her shame and speculated upon her guilt. At every step she was forced to purchase silence at the cost of humility and submissiveness. The tradespeople whom she had been unable to repay had a hold upon her. If she considered anything too dear, some jeering woman would remind her that they were masters and that she must pay if she did not wish to be exposed. A jest, an allusion would make her turn pale. She was tied to the place, obliged to deal there, to allow her pockets to be ransacked as though by accomplices.

The new dairy-woman, successor to Madame Jupillon, who had left to keep a grocer's shop at Bar-sur-Aube, would palm off her bad milk upon her, and when she told her that mademoiselle complained about it and scolded her every morning:

"Your mademoiselle! " replied the dairy-woman, "don't tell me she bothers you!"

When she smelt a fish at the fishmonger's and said to her:

"It's been on the ice."

"Nonsense!" the woman would return, "say at once that I put the influence of the moon into its gills to make it look fresh! And so, my dear, people are hard to please to-day!"

Mademoiselle wished her to go to the central market on account of a dinner-party; she spoke of this in presence of the fruiterer:

"Ah! yes, indeed, to the market! I should like to see you going to the market!"

And she cast a glance at Germinie in which the latter could see the bill she owed sent up to her mistress.

The grocer sold her his snuffy coffee, his damaged prunes, his spoilt rice, his old biscuits. When she took courage to make some remark:

"Tut!" he would say, "surely an old customer like you wouldn't find fault. When I tell you that what I give you is good —"

And he would cynically weigh for her with false weights what she asked for and what he made her ask for.

XLIV

IT was a great trial to Germinie — a trial which she sought, nevertheless — to pass through a street in which there was a school for little girls, on her way back after getting mademoiselle's evening paper before dinner. She frequently found herself in front of the door at the hour when school was over; she wished to escape, and she would stand still.

There was first the sound of a swarm, a humming, a great joyousness of children such as fills the Parisian street with prattling. From the dark and narrow passage running beside the schoolroom, the little ones escaped as from an open cage, ran off pell-mell, hastened onwards, frolicking in the sun. They pushed and hustled one another, tossing their empty baskets over their heads. Then the groups called to one another and formed; little hands went out to other little hands; friends gave their arms to one another; couples took each other round the waist or held each other round the neck, and began to walk, eating the same slice of bread and butter. The troop soon advanced, and all loitering went slowly up the dirty street. The tallest, who were ten years old, would stop to talk, like little women, at the gate-ways. Others would halt to drink from their luncheon bottles. The smallest amused themselves by wetting the soles of their shoes in the gutter. And there were some who would put a cabbage-leaf that they had picked up from the ground on their heads, a green cap from the good God beneath which laughed their fresh little faces.

Germinie would watch them all and walk with them. She joined their ranks that she might feel the rustling of their pinafores. She could not take her eyes off the little arms with the satchels jogging beneath them, the little brown-spotted dresses, the little black drawers, the little legs in their little woollen stockings. To her there seemed to be a kind of divine light on all these fair little heads, with their soft tresses like those of the infant Jesus. A playful little lock on a little neck, a trifle of childish flesh above the edge of a

114

chemise, or below a sleeve, this was, at times, all that she saw: to her it was the whole sunshine of the street, — and Heaven!

Meanwhile the troop was diminishing. Every street drew off the children of the neighboring streets. The school was dispersing on the roadway. The gaiety of all these little footsteps was gradually dying away. The little dresses were disappearing one by one. Germinie followed the last; she attached herself to those who went the farthest.

On one occasion, when walking in this way, and feeding her eyes upon the memory of her daughter, she was suddenly seized with a passion for kissing and darted upon one of the children, grasping it by the arm with the gesture of a child-stealer.

"Mamma! mamma!" the little one called and wept, as she made her escape.

Germinie fled.

XLV

WITH Germinie the days followed one another alike, equally sorrowful and dark. She had finally ceased to expect anything from chance and to ask anything from the unforeseen. Her life seemed to her to have been shut up for ever in its despair: it was still to be always the same merciless thing, the same smooth, straight road of misfortune, the same pathway of shadow with death at the end. In time there ceased to be a future for her. And yet, amid the hopelessness in which she cowered, there passed through her at times thoughts which made her raise her head and look out before her and beyond her present. At times the illusion of a lost hope smiled upon her. It seemed to her that she might still be happy, and that, if certain things took place, she would be so. Then she imagined these things to herself. She arranged accidents and catastrophes. She linked the impossible to the impossible. She renewed all the chances of her life. And her fevered hope, setting itself to create on the horizon the events of her desire, soon grew intoxicated with the mad vision of its hypothesis.

Then by degrees this delirium of hope departed from Germinie. She told herself that it was impossible, that nothing of what she dreamed could come to pass, and she used to remain absorbed in reflections, and sunk upon her chair. Soon, after a few moments, she would get up, go in a slow and uncertain fashion to the fire-place, groping on the chimney-piece for the coffee-pot, and make up her mind to take it; she was going to learn the remainder of her life. Her weal and her woe, all that was to happen to her was there, in the fortune of this woman of the People, on the plate upon which she had just poured the dregs of the coffee.

She drained off the liquid from the dregs, waited for a few minutes, breathed upon it with the religious breath with which her childish lips used to touch the paten at the church in her village. Then, bending down, she kept her head advanced, dreadful in its immobility, with fixed, absorbed eyes bent upon the black trail scattered in spots on the plate. She sought for what she had seen fortunetellers find in the granulations and almost imperceptible dottings left by the residue of the coffee on being poured off. She exhausted her sight upon these thousands of little spots, discovering in them shapes, letters, signs. She separated some of the grains with her finger in order to have a clearer and plainer view of them. She turned and revolved the plate slowly in her hands, questioned her mystery on all sides, and pursued in to its circle of appearances, images, name-rudiments, shadows of initials, likenesses of somebody, outlines of something, embryos of omens, figurations of nothing, which announced to her that she would be "victorious." She wanted to see, and she compelled herself to guess. Beneath the intensity of her gaze, the china became animate with her waking visions; her griefs, her hatreds, the faces that she detested, rose up little by little from the magic plate and the designs of chance. Beside her, the candle, which she forgot to snuff, cast its intermittent and expiring gleam; the light sank into silence, the hour passed into night, and Germinie, as though petrified in arrested anguish, remained still riveted there, alone, and face to face with the terror of the future, seeking to distinguish the confused features of her destiny in the specks of the coffee, until she believed that she could see a cross by the side of a woman, who looked like Jupillon's cousin, a cross, that is to say *an approaching death.*

XLVI

THE love which she lacked, and which she wished to deny herself, then became the torture of her life, an incessant and abominable anguish. She had to defend herself against the feverishness of her body, and stimulations from without against the ready emotions, and weak cowardliness of her flesh, against all the natural solicitations that assailed her. She had to wrestle with the heat of the daytime, with the suggestions of the night, with the moist warmth of the hours of storm, with the breath of her past and of her recollections, with the things suddenly depicted within her, with the voices that whispered kisses in her ear, with the quiverings that gave fondness to every limb.

For weeks and months and years her temptation lasted, and she did not yield to it, did not take another lover. Dreading herself, she shunned man and fled from his sight. She continued to be unsociable and a recluse shut up with mademoiselle, or else upstairs in her own room; and she no longer went out on Sundays. She had given up seeing the servants belonging to the house, and, to ensure occupation and self-forgetfulness, she plunged into extensive sewing-tasks, or buried herself in sleep. When musicians came into the courtyard she used to shut her windows that she might not hear them, for the voluptuousness of music melted her soul.

In spite of it all she could not grow either calm or cold. Her evil thoughts kindled spontaneously, lived and struggled of themselves. At all times the fixed idea of desire uprose from her entire being, became throughout her whole person that wild unending torment, that delirium of the senses in the brain: obsession, — obsession which nothing can drive away and which always returns, shameless, desperate, image-swarming obsession which introduces love through all a woman's sense, communicates it to her shut eyes, rolls it reeking through her head, drives it hot through her arteries!

In time, the nervous shock of these continual assaults, the irritation of this painful continence, began to confuse Germinie's powers of perception. Her eyes seemed to rest on her temptations; a frightful hallucination brought close to her senses the reality of their dreams. It came to pass that at certain times, whatever she saw, whatever was before her, the chandeliers, the legs of the furniture, the arms of the easy chairs, everything about her assumed appearances and forms of impurity. Obscenity sprang up from all that was before her eyes, and came to her. Then, looking at the time by the cuckoo-clock in her kitchen, like a condemned criminal no longer in possession of her own person, she would say:

"In five minutes I shall go down into the street."

And when the five minutes were over, she remained where she was and did not go down.

XLVII

THERE came a time in this life when Germinie resigned the struggle. Her conscience yielded, her will bent, and she bowed to the fate of her life. All that was left to her of resolution, energy and courage departed before her sense, her despairing conviction, of her powerlessness to save herself from herself. She felt that she was in the current of something which was ever moving, and which it was useless, almost impious, to attempt to stay. That great world-force which imposes suffering, that evil power, Fatality, which on the marble of ancient tragedies bears the name of a god, and on the tattooed brow of the galleys is called *No Luck,* was crushing her, and Germinie bowed her head beneath its foot.

When in her hours of discouragement she again experienced in memory the bitterness of her past, when she traced from childhood the links in her mournful existence, that file of sorrows which had accompanied her years and grown with them, the whole sequence of her life which had been like a conjunction and adjustment of wretchedness wherein she had never distinguished the hand of that Providence of whom she had heard so much — she told herself that she was one of those unfortunates devoted at their birth to an eternity of misery, one of those for whom happiness was not intended, and who are acquainted with it only by envying it in others. She fed and feasted on this thought, and from searching into the despair that it caused her, from sifting within herself the continuity of her misfortunes and the sequence of her griefs, she came to see the persecution of her ill-luck in the pettiest mischances of her life and work.

A little money lent by her, and not repaid, a bad coin giv
in a shop, a commission which she executed badly, a purchase ⸱
which she had been deceived, all these things never resulted with
her from her own fault or from accident. It was the sequel to the
rest. Life was in a conspiracy against her, and persecuted her in everything, everywhere, in small things as well as in great, from her
daughter's death to the badness of the grocery. There were days on
which she broke everything that she touched, and she then imagined that she was cursed to the very finger tips. Cursed! ay, damned
almost, as she persuaded herself when she questioned her body,
when she sounded her senses. Did she not feel stirring in the fire
of her blood, in the appetite of her organs, in her burning weakness, the Fatality of Love, the mystery and domination of a disease
which was stronger than her modesty or her reason, which had already delivered her over to the shamefulness of passion, and which
— she knew by presentiment — was to do so again.

Thus she had now only a single utterance upon her lips, an utterance which was the refrain of her thoughts:

"What can you expect? I am unfortunate: I have no luck. Nothing succeeds with me."

She used to say this like a woman who has resigned hope. With
the thought which every day became more rooted, that she had been
born under an unfavorable star, that she belonged to hatreds and
vengeances higher than herself, a terror came to her of everything
that happens in life. She lived in that cowardly anxiety in which the
unforeseen is dreaded like a calamity about to make its appearance,
in which a ring at the bell alarms, in which we turn a letter over and
over, weighing its mystery, and not daring to open it, in which the
news that you are going to hear, the lips that are parted to speak to
you, bring the perspiration to your temples. She had come to be in
that state of mistrust, of nervousness, of trembling at destiny, in
which misfortune sees only misfortune, and in which one would
fain stay his life that it may pause, and cease to advance yonder,
whither all the desires and expectations of others are impelling it.

At last she arrived through tears at that supreme disdain, that pin-
nacle of suffering, where the excess of pain is like irony, where sorrow, passing beyond the bounds of the strength of the human creature, passes beyond its sensitiveness, and where the heart stricken
and no longer sensible to blows says defiantly to Heaven: "Again!"

XLVIII

"WHERE are you going in that style?" said Germinie one Sunday morning to Adèle, who, dressed all in her best, was passing before the open doorway of her room on the corridor of the sixth floor.

"I'm off to a proper jollification. There's a lot of us — big Marie, you know, the big dare-devil — Elisa from 41, both the Badiniers, tall and short — ay, and men too. First of all, I shall have my 'dealer in sudden death.' Well — ah, you don't know who that is? — my last, the fencing-master of the 24th; and then there's one of his friends, a painter and a regular jolly fellow. We're going to Vincennes. Everybody's taking something and we're to have dinner on the grass. The gentlemen will pay for the drink, and we'll have some fun, I promise you."

"I'll go," said Germinie.

"You? Nonsense! why, you have done with parties."

"I tell you I'll go, and I will," said Germinie, with abrupt decision. "Just give me time to let mademoiselle know, and to put on a dress. Wait for me and I'll get half a lobster at the pork-butcher's."

Half an hour afterwards the two women set out, went along by the boundary wall, and found the rest of the company at table outside a café on the Boulevard de la Chopinette. After having some black currant ratafia all round, they got into two large cabs and rolled away. On reaching Vincennes they alighted in front of the fort, and the whole band began to walk in a troop along the slope of the trench. As they passed in front of the wall of the fort the fencing-master's friend, the painter, called out to an artillery-man on duty beside a cannon:

"I say, old boy, you'd rather drink one than mount guard over it." *

"How funny he is," said Adèle to Germinie, giving her a great nudge with her elbow.

Soon they were quite in the Bois de Vincennes.

Narrow beaten tracks, full of footprints, crossed one another in all directions over the trampled and hardened earth. In the spaces

---

* "Cannon" (cannon) is a slang term for a glass of wine drunk at the bar of a wine-shop.

between these little paths, there stretched patches of grass, but grass that was crushed, dried up, yellow and dead, scattered about like litter, the straw-colored blades of which were entangled on all sides with brushwood amid the dull greenery of nettles. Here might be recognized one of those rural spots to which the great suburbs go to lounge on Sundays, and which remain like turf trampled by a crowd after a display of fireworks. Twisted, ill-grown trees stood at intervals, small elms with grey trunks, spotted with yellow leprosy, and lopped to the height of a man, sickly oaks eaten by caterpillars, and with only the lace-work of their leaves remaining. The verdure was paltry, wasted and scanty; the leafage in the air looked thin; the stunted, worn, and scorched foliation, merely speckled the sky with green. The flying dust of high roads covered the ground with grey. The whole had the wretchedness and leanness of a trampled and choked vegetation, the sorry look of verdure on the outskirts of a city, where nature seemed to be issuing from the pavement. No song in the branches, no insect on the beaten soil; the noise of the carts bewildered the birds; the organ suppressed the silence and quivering of the wood; the street passed humming through the landscape.

On the trees hung women's hats fastened into handkerchiefs with four pins; an artilleryman's tuft shone red every moment through openings in the leaves; cake-sellers rose amid the thickets; on the bare turf, bloused children were cutting sticks, workmen's families were trifling away the time and eating cake, urchin's caps were catching butterflies. It was one of the woods modelled on the old Bois de Boulogne, dusty and broiling, a vulgar and tawdry prom- enade, one of those places of niggardly shade, where the people go for an outing at the gates of capitals, parodies of forests, full of corks, where bits of melon rind and suicides are to be found in the underwood.

The heat that day was stifling; there was a faint and cloud- wrapped sun, a strong, veiled and diffused light which almost blinded the gaze. The air had a dull heaviness; nothing moved; the greenery with its hard shadows did not stir, the wood was weary and as though crushed beneath the heavy sky. Now and then only, a breath of air would arise, trailing and skimming the ground. A south wind would pass, one of those enervating winds, fallow and flat which blow upon the senses, and inflame the breath of desire.

Without knowing whence the sensation came, Germinie felt, passing over her whole body, something that was akin to the tickling caused by the down of a ripe peach upon the skin.

They went on merrily, with that somewhat intoxicated activity which the country causes in those who are of the people. The men ran, and the women skipped after them and caught them. They played at rolling about. There was eagerness to dance among them, and desire to climb the trees; while the painter amused himself by throwing pebbles from a distance into the loopholes in the gates of the fortress, which he always succeeded in doing.

At last they all sat down in a sort of glade, at the foot of a clump of oaks, the shadow of which was lengthening in the light of the setting sun. The men, lighting matches on the drill of their trousers, began to smoke. The women chattered, laughed, threw themselves back every minute in loud fits of silly hilarity, and shrill bursts of joy. Germinie alone remained without speaking or laughing. She did not listen, she did not look. Her eyes, beneath her lowered eyelids, were fixed steadily upon the toes of her boots. Absorbed in herself, she seemed to be absent from the actual place and hour. Lying stretched at full length on the grass, with her head somewhat raised by a clod of earth, the only movement that she made was to lay the palms of her hands flat on the grass beside her; then after a short time she would turn them upon their backs and rest them in the same way, repeating this constantly that she might get the freshness of the earth to allay the burning of her skin.

"There's a lazy hussy! are you snoring?" said Adèle to her.

Germinie opened wide her burning eyes without answering her, and until dinner-time she preserved the same attitude, the same silence, the same lethargy, feeling around her for the places upon which she had not yet laid the fever of her hands.

"Adèle!" said a woman's voice, "sing us something."

"Ah!" replied Adèle, "I haven't wind enough before eating."

Suddenly a big paving stone, hurled through the air, fell beside Germinie close to her head; at the same moment she heard the painter's voice calling to her:

"Don't be frightened. It's your chair."

Each one put his handkerchief on the ground by way of tablecloth. The eatables were untwisted from the greasy papers. Some quart bottles being uncorked, the wine went round, foaming in glasses wedged between tufts of grass, and all began to eat pork-butcher's meat on slices of bread and butter which served as plates. The painter carved, made paper boats to hold the salt, imitated the orders of the café waiters, calling out:

"Bourn! The Pavilion! Serve!"

By degrees the party became animated. The atmosphere, the wine and the food stimulated the merriment of the open-air repast. Hands grew neighborly, lips met, free expressions were whispered in the ear, shirt sleeves encircled waists for a moment, and from time to time greedy kisses echoed amid unrestrained embraces.

Germinie said nothing and drank. The painter, who had placed himself beside her, felt himself becoming stiff and embarrassed with this singular neighbor who amused herself "so internally." Suddenly with his knife, he began to beat a tattoo on his glass which sounded above the noise of the party and raising himself on both knees:

"Ladies!" he said in a voice, like that of a parrot which has been talking too much, "To the health of a man in misfortune: to mine! Perhaps, that will bring me good luck. Jilted, yes, ladies; well, yes, I've been jilted. I'm a widower, an out and out widower — clean! I'm as bewildered as a bell-founder. It's not that I cared particularly about it, but habit, that old rascal, habit's the cause of it. In fact I'm bothered as much as a bug in a watch-spring. For the last fortnight, life has with me been like a cup of coffee without a drop of brandy in it. I who love love as if it had made me. No woman! That's a weaning for a man of years! Since I've known what it is, I've had respect for the priests; I quite feel for them, I do, on my word of honor. No longer a woman, and there are so many of them! But I can't walk about with a placard: *A man to let. Apply now to so and so.* First, it would be necessary to be licensed by the prefect, and then people are so foolish that it would create crowds. All of which, ladies, is for the purpose of informing you that, if there were any one among the persons you know, who would like to form an ac-quaintance — an honorable acquaintance — a nice little fictitious marriage, there need be no trouble; here I am — Victor Médéric Gautruche, a stay-at-home fellow, a regular house ivy-plant for sentiment. You've only to ask at my old lodgings, at the 'Safety-Key.' And as merry as a hunchback who has just drowned his wife. Gautruche! *alias* Gogo-la-Gaieté, there you are. A nice easygoing young man that doesn't manufacture botherations; a good chap that takes things easy and that's not going to give himself the stomach-ache with this Adam's ale."

As he said this he sent a bottle of water that was beside him flying twenty paces off.

"Hurrah for the walls! They are to this child what heaven is to God! Gogo-la-Gaieté paints them all the week, Gogo-la-Gaieté stumbles against them on Monday! With all this, not jealous, not naughty, not inclined to kick over the traces; a regular ducky who has never left his mark on any of the other sex. As for appearance, well, I'm your man!"

He rose to his feet, and drawing up his great, ill-formed figure in his old blue coat with its gold buttons, lifting his grey hat to display his bald, smooth, and perspiring skull, and raising his head which was like that of an unfeathered old bird, he went on:

"You see what it is. It's not an ornamental property, it's not a flattering one to show off. But it's productive, somewhat unfurnished, but well built. Well, there are forty-nine years, as much hair as there is on a billiard-ball, a dog's-grass beard that you might make tisane with, foundations that are still pretty firm, feet as long as La Villette, and, with all that, leanness enough to take a bath in a gunbarrel. That's the lot. Pass the prospectus. If there's a woman who'll have the whole in a lump — some one that's steady, and not too young, and that won't amuse herself by stroking me too much the wrong way — You understand, I don't ask for a princess from Batignolles — Very well, then, it's a case!" Germinie seized Gautruche's glass, half-emptied it at a draught, and held it out to him on the side at which she herself had drunk.

As evening was falling, the party returned on foot. At the wall of the fortifications, Gautruche drew a large heart on the stone with cuts of his knife, within which everyone's name was placed beneath the date.

When night had come Gautruche and Germinie were on the outer boulevards, up as far as the Rochechouart Gate. Beside a low house bearing a plaster panel whereon might be read: *Madame Merlin. Dresses cut out and tried on, two francs,* they stopped before a little stone staircase which, after the first three steps, led into darkness at the very back of which was the blood-red light of an Argand lamp. On a cross-beam, over the entrance, was written in black letters:

Hôtel of the Little Blue Hand.

XLIX

FREDERIC GAUTRUCHE was a workman of the jovial, ne'er-do-weel, good-for-nothing kind, a workman who makes his life a holi-day. Filled with the joyousness of wine, his lips perpetually damp with a last drop, his inside befouled with tartar like an old cask, he was one of those whom the Burgundians energetically call "red guts." Always a little drunk, drunk from over night if not drinking during the day, he looked upon life through the liquor which af-fected his head. He smiled at his lot, he gave himself up to it with the heedlessness of the drunkard, smiling vaguely at things as he followed in the track of the wine-seller, at life, at the road stretch-ing away into the night. Weariness, anxiety, neediness, had taken no hold upon him; and when a gloomy, a serious thought came to him, he would turn away his head, give a sort of "psitt" which was his way of saying "Hell!" and raising his right arm towards Heaven in caricature of the gesture of a Spanish dancer, send his melan-choly over his shoulder to the devil.

He possessed the superb philosophy that comes after drinking, the jolly serenity of the bottle.

He knew neither wish nor desire. His dreams were served to him across the counter. For three sous he was sure of having a small glass of happiness, and for twelve a quart of the ideal. Satis-fied with everything, he liked everything, and found laughter and amusement in everything. Nothing in the world seemed sad to him except a glass of water.

To this tipster-like expansiveness, to the gaiety of his health, and of his temperament, Gautruche united the gaiety of his condition, the good humor and high spirits of that free and non-fatiguing oc-cupation out of doors and in mid-air, which amuses itself by singing, and perches a workman's humbug on a ladder over the heads of the passers-by. He was a house-painter and painted letters. He was the only, the single man in Paris who could attack a sign-board without measuring with string, without a blank outline, the only one who could at first trial put every letter inside the border of a placard into its place, and without losing a minute in arranging them, could trace out the capital off-hand. He was rioted, further, for "monster" let-ters, whimsical letters, shaded letters, picked out in bronze or gold to

llows in stone. Thus he would make from fifteen to twenty
e day. But as he drank it all he was none the richer, and he
arrears against him on the slates in the wine-shops.

.ıc was a man brought up by the street. The street had been his
mother, his nurse, and his school. The street had given him his assurance, his language and his wit. All that an intellect belonging to
the people can pick up on the pavement of Paris, he had picked up.
All that sinks from the upper portions of a great town to the lower
— filtrations, fragments, crumbs of ideas and of knowledge, all
that is borne by the subtle atmosphere and laden kennel of a capital
— the rubbing up against printed matter, the scraps of feuilletons
swallowed between two half-pints, the dramatic morsels heard on
the boulevards, had imparted to him that lucky intelligence which,
without education, grasps everything. He possessed an inexhaust-
ible, imperturbable confidence. His speech abounded and gushed
in happy expressions, in funny images, in such metaphors as issue
from the comic genius of crowds. He had the picturesque natural-
ness of open-air farce. He was brimful of funny stories and jokes,
rich with the richest stock of the "Joe Millers" of the house-painting
business. A member of those low caves of harmony called "lists,"
he knew all the airs and songs, and he sang them unweariedly. In
short he was a droll fellow from top to toe. And only to look at him,
people would laugh as at a comic actor.

A man with this gaiety, with these high spirits, "suited" Germinie.

Germinie was not the working animal which has nothing but
its duties in its head. She was not a servant to stand open-mouthed
with frightened features and doltish demeanor of unintelligence
while the words of her employers passed unheeded. She, too, had
been formed, had been trained, had been drawn out by the education of Paris. Mademoiselle de Varandeuil, being without occupation, and having an old maid's curiosity about the stories of the
neighborhood, had long made her relate her gleaning of news, all
that she knew about the lodgers, the whole chronicle of house and
street; and this habit of narration, of chattering as a sort of companion with her mistress, of depicting people, of sketching silhouettes,
had in time developed in her a facility for lively expressions, for
happy, unconscious touches, a piquancy and sometimes a keenness
of observation remarkable in the mouth of a servant.

She had often surprised Mademoiselle de Varandeuil t͟ liveliness of comprehension, her promptness to grasp half-ut͟ tered thoughts, her happiness and readiness in finding such words as would be employed by a good speaker. She knew how to jest. She understood a play on words. She expressed herself without mispronunciation, and when there was any orthographical discussion at the dairy, she decided the question with an authority equal to that of the registrar of deaths at the Town Hall, who used to come there for his breakfast. She had also that foundation of miscellaneous reading which women of her class possess when they read. In the service of the two or three kept women with whom she had been, she had spent her nights in devouring novels; since then she had continued to read the feuilletons cut from the bottom of the papers by all her acquaintances; and from these she had retained a sort of vague idea of many things, and of a few kings of France. She had preserved enough to inspire a wish to talk of it to others.

Through a woman belonging to the house who looked after the establishment of an author in the same street, and who used to have tickets, she had often been to the play; as she returned home she used to recall the whole piece, and the names of the actors that she had seen on the programmes. She liked to buy penny songs, and novels, and read them.

The atmosphere, the living breath of the Breda quarter with all its vitality of artist and studio, art and vice, had quickened these intellectual tastes in Germinie, and created needs, requirements within her. Long before the time of her loose habits, she had separated herself from virtuous society, from the "respectable" people of her condition and caste, from those who were silly, stupid, and worthy. She had withdrawn from surroundings of steady, narrow-minded probity, of sleepy gossipings over the teas given by the old servants of the old folk who knew mademoiselle. She had shunned the tediousness of maids dulled by the consciousness of service and the fascination of the savings bank. She had come to require from those who were to associate with her a certain intelligence corresponding to her own and able to understand it.

And now, when she was emerging from her brutishness, when she was recovering and reviving amid diversion and pleasure, she felt that she must amuse herself with her equals in capacity. She would have about her men who made her laugh, violent merriment, spirituous wit that intoxicated her like the wine that was poured out for her. And it was thus that she turned towards the low Bohemia of the people, noisy, bewildering, intoxicating as all Bohemias are: it was thus that she fell to a Gautruche.

L

AS Germinie was coming in one morning at daybreak, she heard a voice call to her through the shadow of the gate as it closed behind her:

"Who's that?"

She darted to the back staircase; but she perceived that she was being pursued, and soon felt herself seized by the concierge's hand at the turning of a landing. As soon as he recognized her, he said:

"Oh! beg pardon, it's you; don't put yourself about! My word, you're going it! It astonishes you, does it, to see me afoot so early? It's on account of the robbery lately in the room of the cook belonging to the second floor. Well, good-night! I can tell you it's lucky for you that I'm no gossip."

A few days afterwards, Germinie learnt through Adèle that the husband of the cook who had been robbed was saying that there was no need to search, for the robber was in the house; people knew what they knew. Adèle added that this was making a great stir in the street, and that there were people to repeat it, and believe it.

Germinie, in indignation, went and told the whole story to her mistress. Mademoiselle, in still greater indignation, and feeling personally affected by the insult, instantly wrote to the servant's mistress to put an immediate stop to calumnies directed against a girl whom she had had in her service for twenty years, and for whom she would answer as for herself. The servant was reprimanded. In his anger, he spoke still more strongly. He scolded, and, for several days, spread through the house his intention of going to the Commissary of Police, and through him of finding out from Germinie with what money she had stocked the dairy-woman's son, with what money she had hired a substitute for him, with what money she had met the expenses of the men that she had had.

For a whole week the terrible threat hung over Germinie's head.

At last the thief was discovered, and the threat fell to th
But it had had its effect upon the poor girl. It had wro¹
evil in this disturbed brain in which, under the afflux anᵤ
mounting of blood, reason tottered, and was clouded at the slightes.
shock of life. It had deranged the head that was so ready to go astray
under the influence of fear or annoyance, so quick to lose judgment, discernment, clearness of vision and appreciation of things,
exaggerating everything to itself, falling into foolish alarms, evil
forebodings, and despairing prospects, feeling its terrors as though
they were realities, and momently lost in the pessimism of such delirium that finally it could find no other phrase or safety than this:
"Bah! I'll kill myself!"

During the whole week, the fever of her brain led her through
all the modifications of that which she imagined must come to pass.
Day and night, she could see her shame exposed, published; she
could see her secret, her ignominy, her faults, all that she bore hidden
about her and locked in her heart, she could see it shown, displayed,
and discovered to mademoiselle. Her debts for Jupillon increased
by her debts for Gautruche's eating and drinking, and by all that she
was now buying on credit, her debts to the doorkeeper and to the
tradespeople, were all about to come out and ruin her! The thought
made her shiver: she could feel mademoiselle driving her away.

Throughout the week she imagined at every moment of her
thought that she was before the Commissary of Police. For seven
whole days she revolved the idea and utterance of "the court!" the
court as it appears to the imagination of the lower orders, something terrible, undefined, inevitable, which is everywhere, and in
the shadow of everything, an omnipotence of misfortune appearing
dimly in the black of a judge's robe between the constable and the
executioner, with the hands of the police and the arms of the guillotine! She who had all the instincts of these terrors of the people,
she who used often to repeat that she would rather die than appear
in court, she could see herself seated on a bench with gendarmes on
each side of her! in a court, in the midst of all that great unknown
of the law which her ignorance made a terror to her. Throughout
the week her ears could hear footsteps on the staircase coming to
arrest her!

The shock was too great for nerves so diseased as hers. The
moral strain of that week of anguish cast her, and surrendered her

to a thought which hitherto had been continually fluttering about her — the thought of suicide. With her head between her hands, she began to listen to what spoke to her of deliverance. She lent her ear to the sweet sound of death, which is heard behind life like the distant fall of mighty waters descending and disappearing into vacancy. The temptations which speak to discouragement of all that kills with such quickness and facility, of all that takes away suffering with its hand, solicited her, and pursued her. Her gaze rested and lingered upon all those things around her which might be a cure for life. She made them familiar to her fingers, her lips. She touched them, handled them, brought them close to her. She sought in them a trial of her courage, and a foretaste of her death.

She would remain for hours at her kitchen window, her eyes fixed upon the pavement of the courtyard five stories below, pavement which she knew, which she would have recognized! As the light faded she would lean farther out, bending her whole person over the badly fastened windowbar, ever hoping that this bar might give way with her, praying for death without the necessity of that desperate spring into space for which she did not feel that she had the strength —

"Why, you will fall!" said mademoiselle to her one day, holding her back by the petticoat, with a first, frightened impulse. "What are you looking at in the courtyard?"

"I? Nothing — the pavement."

"Come now, are you mad? You gave me a fright!"

"Oh! people don't fall in that way," said Germinie, in a strange tone. "It takes a real wish to make you fall!"

LI

GERMINIE had not been able to induce Gautruche, who was pursued by a former mistress, to give her the key of his room. When he had not returned, she was obliged to wait below, outside, in the street and the night and the winter.

She would at first walk up and down in front of the house. She used to pass backwards and forwards, taking twenty steps and returning. Then, as though she were lengthening out her expectation, she would take a longer turn, and continually increasing the distance, would at last reach the two extremities of the boulevard. She often walked for hours in this way, ashamed and muddy, beneath the gloomy sky, in the suspicious horrors of an avenue near the city gate and of the shadow of everything. She went along by the red houses of the wine-sellers, the bare arbors, the public-house trellises supported by dead trees such as are to be seen in bears' pits, the low, flat hovels pierced at random with blindless windows, the cap manufactories where shirts are sold, the sinister houses in which there are lodgings by the night. She passed in front of shops, shut up, sealed, dismal with failures, of accursed wall-sections, of dark iron-barred passages seeming to lead to those abodes of murder the plan of which is handed to the gentlemen of the jury in the assize court.

As she proceeded there came funereal little gardens, crooked buildings, mean structures, large mouldy entrances, palings enclosing in a plot of waste ground the disquieting whiteness of stones as seen at night, corners of buildings with salpetrous stinks, walls fouled with shameful placards and fragments of torn notices in which the rotting advertisements were like a leprosy. From time to time, at an abrupt turning, a lane would appear which seemed to sink after a few steps into a hole, and from which there issued the breath of a cellar; blind alleys cast the dark rigidity of a great wall upon the blue of the sky; streets ascended dimly, where at distant intervals the light of the street-lamps oozed out upon the bleak plaster of the houses.

Germinie still walked on. She trod the whole of that space wherein the debauched grow drunk on their Mondays, and find their loves, between a hospital, a slaughter-house, and a cemetery: — Lariboisière, the Abattoir, and Montmartre.

Those who passed that way, the workman coming whistling from Paris, the workwoman returning after her day's toil with her hands under her armpits to keep herself warm, the prostitute wandering about in a black bonnet — crossed her path and looked at her. Strangers seemed to be recognizing her; the light made her ashamed. She would escape to the other side of the boulevard, and follow the dark and deserted road beside the boundary wall; but she was soon driven away again by horrible shadows of men and brutally amorous hands.

She would fain have gone away; she abused herself inwardly; she called herself coward and wretch; she swore to herself that this should be the last turn, that she would go again as far as that tree, and that then there should be no more of it, that if he had not then come in there should be an end of it and she would go away. And she did not go away; she still walked and still waited, devoured by a longing and passion to see him that increased in proportion as he delayed.

At last as the hours went by, and the boulevard emptied of passengers, Germinie, exhausted, worn out with fatigue, would approach the houses. She dragged herself from shop to shop, went mechanically where there was still gas burning, and stood stupidly before the flaming windows. She dazed her eyes, and strove to kill her impatience by deadening it. She was arrested for a long time by what is to be seen through the succeeding window-panes of the wine-sellers. The kitchen utensils, the punch-bowls standing in tiers between empty bottles from which issue sprigs of laurel, the glass-cases in which the colors of the liquors are brilliantly displayed, a half-pint measure full of little plated spoons. She would spell over the old advertisements of lottery-drawings placarded at the back of a wine-shop, the announcements of brandied coffee, the inscriptions in yellow letters of: *"New Wine, genuine, 70 centimes."* She would gaze for a quarter of an hour at a back room in which there were a man in a blouse seated on a stool before a table, a stove pipe, and a slate and two black trays on the wall. Her fixed and vacant gaze wandered through a reddish mist to blurred silhouettes of cobblers leaning over their benches. It fell and became absorbed on a counter that was being washed, on a pair of hands counting the pence that the day had brought in, on a funnel that was being scoured, on a water-can that was being rubbed with sandstone. She had ceased to think. She stood there, riveted and growing weak, feeling her heart giving way with the fatigue of being on her feet, seeing everything in a sort of swoon, hearing as in a humming noise the mud-splashed cabs rolling along the soft boulevard, ready to fall and at times obliged to prop herself with her shoulder against the wall.

In the state of strain and sickness in which she found herself, in that semi-hallucination of giddiness which rendered her so fearful of crossing the Seine and which made her cling to the balustrades of the bridges, it would happen that on certain rainy evenings these weaknesses which she experienced on the outer boulevard assumed the terrors of a nightmare. When the flames of the street-lamps, flickering in a watery vapor, cast lengthening and wavering reflections upon the wet ground as on the mirror-like surface of a river; when the pavement, the footpaths, the earth seemed to be disappearing and softening beneath the rain, and nothing solid appeared to be left in the drenching night, the poor wretch, almost mad from fatigue, thought that she could see a deluge swelling in the gutter. A mirage of terror suddenly showed her water all round her, water advancing and drawing near from every direction. She shut her eyes, no longer daring to stir and dreading to feel her feet slip from under her, and beginning to weep, continued weeping until some one passed by and was willing to lend her an arm as far as the *Hôtel of the Little Blue Hand.*

LII

THEN she ascended the staircase; it was her last refuge. She fled there from rain, snow, cold, fear, despair, fatigue. She ascended and sat down on a step against Gautruche's closed door, drawing her shawl and petticoat closely in order to allow a passage to those going and coming along this steep ladder, gathering up her person and shrinking into a corner to lessen the room occupied by her shame on the narrow landing.

From the opened doors issued and spread upon the staircase the odor of the airless rooms, and of the families massed together in a single apartment, the exhalations from unhealthy occupations, the greasy, animalized fumes from meat-warmers heated on the landing, a stench of rags, the dank unsavoriness of linen drying on strings. The broken-paned window which Germinie had behind her transmitted to her the fetidity of a sink into which the whole house emptied its filth and liquid refuse. Every moment her heart heaved at a gust of infectiousness, and she was obliged to take from her pocket a bottle of carmelite water which she always had about her, and drink a mouthful to keep herself from feeling ill.

But the staircase also had its passers-by: honest wives of workingmen coming up with a bushel of charcoal or with the wine for supper. They pushed her with their feet, and the whole time that they took to ascend Germinie could feel their looks of contempt winding round the well of the staircase and crushing her from a greater height at every story. Children, little girls with kerchiefs on their heads passing along the dark staircase with the light of a flower, little girls causing her to see her little daughter again, alive and grown, as she appeared to her in dreams — she used to watch them stop and look at her with widely opened eyes that shrank from her; then they would run away and pant upstairs, and when at the very top would lean over the banister and fling impure abuse at her, revilings such as came from children of the people.

Insults, spit out from those lips of roses, fell upon Germinie more painfully than anything else. She would half raise herself for a moment; then, dejected and self-abandoned, would sink back, and, drawing her plaid over her head so as to hide and bury herself in it, would remain like one dead, crouched, inert, insensible, coiled up on her shadow like a bundle thrown down for everybody to walk on, her senses gone and no life left throughout her body save for a sound of footsteps for whose coming she listened — but which never came.

At last, after hours had elapsed, hours which she could not number, she seemed to hear the stumbling of footsteps in the street; then a thick voice stuttering up the stairs:

"Rascal! — rascal of wineseller! shold me wine — makes fler drunk!"

It was he.

And the same scene was repeated nearly every day.

"Ah! you're there, Germinie," he would say on recognizing her. "Tell you what it is — I'm going to tell you — we were a bit drowned —" and putting the key into the lock — "I'm going to tell you, 'tis not my fault."

He went in, kicked away a turtledove with clipped wings that was hopping lamely about, and shut the door.

"D'ye see? 'Twasn't me. It was Paillon — you know Paillon? The little stout chap who's as fat as a madman's dog. Well! 'twas his doing, it was, on my honor. He *would* stand me a six-teen-sou bottle. He offered me civility, and I offered him politeness in return. Then, naturally, we put a little comfort into our coffee — over and over again? By and by we fell out — there was the devil's own row — And so that rascal of a publican chucked us out of doors like lobster shells!"

During the explanation, Germinie had lighted the candle standing in a brass candlestick. The unsteady light showed the dirty papering of the room, covered with caricatures from the "Charivari," which had been torn out of the journal and pasted on the wall.

"You're a love," Gautruche would say to her as he saw her place a cold chicken and three bottles of wine on the table. "For you must know some wretched soup is all that I've got in my stomach. Ah, it would have taken a proper fencing-master to put out that fellow's eyes."

And he began to eat. Germinie, with both elbows on the table, drank and looked at him, and her look grew dark.

"Good! there's an end of those chaps!" said Gautruche at length, draining the bottles one by one. "Bye! bye! children!"

And between these two beings there were love-passages, terrible, desperate, funereal, wild frenzies and gratifications, furious indulgences, caresses possessing the brutality and wrath of wine, kisses that seemed to seek for the blood beneath the skin like a wild beast's tongue, prostrations that engulfed them and left them but the corpses of their bodies.

To this debauchery Germinie brought an element of madness, of delirium, of desperation, a sort of supreme frenzy. Her inflamed senses turned upon themselves, and passing beyond the appetites of their nature, were driven to the point of suffering. Satiety wore them out without destroying them; and, exceeding excess, they were forced into anguish. In the unhappy creature's paroxysm of excitement, her head, her nerves, the imaginings of her raging body, no longer sought even for pleasure in pleasure, but for something beyond it, more harsh, more poignant, more severe — for pain in voluptuousness. And momentarily the word "death" escaped from her compressed lips, as though she were invoking it in a whisper, and seeking to embrace it in the agonies of love!

Sometimes at night, rising up suddenly on the edge of the bed, she set her naked feet upon the coldness of the floor and remained there, wild, listening to the breathing of a sleeping room. And gradually all that was about her, the darkness of the hour, seemed to enwrap her. She appeared to herself to be falling and rolling into the unconsciousness and blindness of the night. The willpower of her thoughts disappeared; all sorts of dark things, having as it were beings and voices, beat against her temples. The sombre temptations, which dimly display crime and madness, caused a red light — the lightning-flash of a murder — to pass close before her eyes; and at her back there were hands pushing her from behind towards the table on which the knives lay. She would close her eyes, move a foot; then in fear, hold herself back by the sheets; and finally, turning round, would fall back into the bed, and link her sleep once more to the sleep of the man whom she had been wishing to assassinate; why? — she did not know; for nothing — for the sake of killing!

And thus until day the rage and struggle of these mortal loves strove still in the meanly-furnished room — while the poor lame and limping dove, the infirm bird of Venus, nestled in an old shoe belonging to Gautruche, and waking from time to time at the noise, uttered a startled coo.

LIII

GAUTRUCHE had at this time something of a distaste for drinking. He had just felt the first attack of the liver complaint, which had long been lurking in his fired and alcoholized blood under the brick-red color of his cheek-bones. The frightful pains which had gnawed his side and griped the pit of his stomach for a week had brought him to reflect. With resolutions of wisdom there had come to him almost sentimental notions about the future. He had told himself that he must put a little more water into his life if he wished to die in an old skin.

While he turned and twisted himself in his bed, with his knees drawn up in order to diminish the pain, he had surveyed his hovel — the four walls within which he spent his nights, into which without a candle sometimes he brought back his drunkenness at evening, and from which he escaped in the morning at daybreak; and he had thought of making himself a home. He had thought of a room in which he should have a woman — a woman who would make him a good stew, would nurse him if he were ill, would mend his things, would prevent him from beginning a new score

at the wine-shop, a woman, in short, who would have all the quali-
ties of a good housekeeper, and who would, furthermore, be no
fool, who would understand him and laugh with him. This woman
was already found — she was Germinie. She must surely have a
little hoard, a few sous laid by during the time that she had been a
servant to her old mademoiselle, and with his own earnings they
would live comfortably and "be snug." He had no doubt about her
assent; he was sure beforehand that she would accept the proposal.
Moreover, her scruples, if she had any, would not withstand the
proposal of a marriage to terminate their *liaison,* with which he
intended to dazzle her.

One Monday she had just come to see him.

"Look here, Germinie," Gautruche began, "what do you say to
this, eh? A good room — not like this box of a place, but a proper one
with a little one off it — at Montmartre in the Rue de l'Empereur,
with two windows and a view that an Englishman would give you
five thousand francs to take away with him! — something smart and
cheerful, in fact, that a fellow might spend a whole day in without
being worried, because, d'ye know, I'm beginning to have enough
of moving about only to change the fleas. And then, that's not all.
I'm sick of hanging out in furnished lodgings all alone. Friends are
no company — they fall into your glass like flies when you pay,
and there's an end of them. First of all, I don't intend to drink any
more, I really don't, as you'll see. I don't want to kill myself, you
know, with that sort of life. Nothing of that sort. Mind you, a man
has no right to muddle his brains. I've been feeling these times as
if I'd swallowed corkscrews, and I don't want to step straight into
the grave just yet. So this was the idea that ran through me like the
threading of a needle:

"I'll make a proposal to Germinie. I'll treat myself to a little furniture, and you've got what's in your room. You know there's not
much laziness about me; my hands are not too soft to work. Then
we might look to be not always working for other people, but to
set up a little shop of our own. If you've anything laid by, it would
help. We'd settle down nicely together, ready to have ourselves put
to rights some day before the mayor. That's not so bad, eh, my lass,
is it? And she'll leave her old woman, straight away, won't she, for
her old darling of a Gautruche?"

Germinie, who had been listening to Gautruche with her head

advanced towards him and her chin leaning on her hand, threw herself back with a burst of strident laughter.

"Ha, ha, ha! you thought that! — You actually tell me that! You thought that I'd leave her! — her! Mademoiselle! You really thought so? You are a fool, do you know that? Why, you might have hundreds and thousands, you might have pocketfuls of gold — pocketfuls, do you hear? — and I wouldn't do it. It's a perfect farce. Mademoiselle! But you don't know — I've never told you. Ah! it would be a nice thing to have her die and these hands not there to close her eyes! That would be a pretty sight! And you really thought that?"

"Confound it! I fancied — being with me the way you were — I thought you cared more about me than that — in fact, that you loved me," said the painter, baffled by the terrible, hissing irony of Germinie's words.

"Ah! so you thought that too — that I loved you?" and as though suddenly plucking remorse, and the wound caused by her love, from the bottom of her heart, she went on: — "Well, yes, I do love you, I love you just as much as you love me, and no more. I love you like something that's at hand, and that's made use of because it's there. I'm accustomed to you, as I might be to an old dress that was always being put on. That's the way I love you. How would you have me care about you? You or another? I'd like to know what difference that makes to me? For, after all, what have you been more than another to me? Well, yes, you took me, but what then? Is that enough to make me love you? Why, what have you done to make me fond of you, you just tell me that? Did you ever sacrifice a glass of wine for me? Have you as much as had pity on me when I was running about in the mud and snow at the risk of my life? Yes, and all that was said to me, all that was flung in my teeth, till my blood was in a boil from one end to another, all the insults that I've swallowed when waiting for you — precious little *you* were affected by them. There! I've been wanting this long time to tell you all this — my heart has been full with it. Why," she went on, with a cruel smile, "do you think you've made me crazy with your appearance, with the hair that you've lost, and that head of yours? Not likely! I took you — I'd have taken any I one — I was at one of those times when I must have somebody, when I know nothing and see nothing, and it's not myself that wills. I took you because it was hot — there!"

She paused for a moment.

"Go on," said Gautruche, "pitch into me all round. Make yourself comfortable while you're about it."

"Eh?" Germinie resumed, "you fancied I was going to be delighted to settle down with you? You said to yourself: 'That good fool! How pleased she'll be. And then I'll only have to promise to marry her and she'll leave her place there and then. She'll give up her mistress.' Just imagine! Mademoiselle! Mademoiselle, who had no one but me. Ah! you know nothing about it, and you wouldn't understand it either. Mademoiselle, who is everything to me! Why, since my mother, I've had no one but her to be kind to me. Except her, who ever said to me when I was sad, 'Are you sad?' or when I was ill, 'Are you ill?' No one. There was nothing and nobody but her to take care of me, or trouble about me.

"You talk about loving on account of what there's between us. Why, there's somebody — mademoiselle — who did love me, ay, loved me! And it's killing me, I can tell you, that I've become a wretch such as I am, a — "She uttered the word. "And to deceive her, to rob her of her affection, to go on allowing her to love me like her own daughter, — me! me! Ah, if ever she heard anything — but never mind, it wouldn't be for long. There's someone who'd take a fine jump from the fifth floor, as sure as God's my master! But you may make sure of *this* — you are not my heart, you are not my life, you are only my pleasure. But I had a man once. Ah, didn't I just love him! I might have been cut to pieces for his sake and I'd have said nothing. Ay, he was the man of my misfortune. Well, when I was most taken with him, when I never breathed but when he wished, when I was mad, and if he'd trodden on my body I'd have let him do it, if at that time mademoiselle had been ill and had signed to me with her little finger, I'd have come back — yes, for her sake, I'd have left him! I tell you, I'd have left him!"

"Well, then, if that's so, my dear, and you're so fond of your old woman, I have only one piece of advice to give you: you oughtn't to leave your good lady any more, d'ye see?"

"This is my dismissal?" said Germinie, rising.

"Faith! something like it."

"Well, good-bye. I've no objection."

And going straight to the door, she went out without another word.

LIV

AFTER this rupture, Germinie fell, as she was bound to fall, below shame, below nature itself. Step by step, the miserable, burning creature sank to the street. She picked up the loves that are worn out in a night, such as pass, such as are met with, such as are revealed to a wandering woman by the chance of the pavement. She no longer needed to take time for her desire: her caprice was frenzied and sudden, kindled at the instant. Hungry for the first comer, she scarcely looked at him, and would have been unable to recognize him afterwards. Beauty, youth, that appearance in a lover wherein love of the most degraded women seek a kind of base ideal, all this had ceased to tempt or to move her. Among all men, her eyes could see only man; the individual was indifferent to her. The last remaining modesty and the last human sentiment in debauchery, preference, choice, and even — what is left to prostitutes to serve as conscience and personality — disgust itself was lost in her!

And she passed along the streets, roaming through the night, with the suspicious, furtive fashion of animals searching the shade with seeking appetite. As though an outcast from her sex, she herself attacked, she solicited brutality, she took advantage of intoxication, and the yielding was to her. She walked along, smelling around her, going to the ambushed impurity of stretches of waste ground, to the opportunities of evening and solitude, to the hands that were waiting to pounce upon a shawl. The midnight passers could see her by the light of the street lamp, sinister and quivering, gliding and as it were creeping along, stooped, unobtrusive, her shoulders bent, hugging the darkness, with such a look of insanity and sickness, such an infinite wildness as will cause the heart of the thinker and the thought of the physician to be occupied with abysses of sadness.

LV

ONE evening when she was roaming along the Rue du Rocher, passing in front of a wine-shop at the corner of the Rue de Laborde, she saw the back of a man who was drinking at the counter: it was Jupillon.

She stopped short, turned towards the street, and leaning her back against the grating of the wine-shop, set herself to wait. With her shoulders against the bars, she had the light of the shop behind her, and she stood motionless, one hand holding up her skirt in front and the other hanging at the end of her idle arm. She was like a statue of shadow seated on a boundary stone. In her attitude there was terrible resolution and what seemed like eternal patience for waiting there for ever. Passers-by, vehicles, street, she saw them all dimly and distantly. A white horse, the trace-horse of the omnibus used in the ascent of the street, was in front of her, motionless, wearied, sleeping where it stood with its head and two forelegs in the full light from the doorway; but she did not see it. It was drizzling. The weather was such as it sometimes is in Paris, dirty and rotten, the falling water seeming muddy even before it has fallen. The gutter was rising over her feet. She remained thus for half an hour, a mournful sight, moveless, menacing and desperate, dark and featureless like a statue of Fate placed by Night at a dramseller's door.

At last Jupillon came out. She stood up in front of him with folded arms.

"My money?" she said to him. She had the face of a woman with whom there is no longer conscience, God, police, assize court, scaffold — anything!

Jupillon felt his nonsense sticking in his throat.

"Your money?" he said. "Your money isn't lost. But you must give me time; just now, work is not doing well. My shop came to an end long ago, as you know. But I promise to repay you in three months. And how are you getting on?"

"You rascal! Ah! I've got you! So you wanted to be off. It's you that's been my curse, that's made me what I am, robber! thief! pickpocket! It was you —"

Germinie hurled this into his face, pushing against him, facing him, pressing her bosom against his. She seemed to be giving herself to the blows that she called for and challenged; and, stretching quite over to him, she cried:

"Beat me. Tell me what I must say to you to make you beat me?"

She could no longer think. She did not know what she wanted; she had only a kind of desire to be struck. There had come to her an instinctive, irrational longing to be brutally ill-used, to be bruised, to suffer in her flesh, to feel a shock, a concussion, a pain that might silence what was throbbing in her head. Blows — she could think of nothing else to put an end to it all. Then, with the clearness of a hallucination, she could see all kinds of things happening after the blows — the arrival of the police, the police-station, the commissary; the commissary before whom she could tell everything, her story, her miseries, what this man had made her suffer, what he had cost her! Her heart swelled in anticipation at the thought of emptying itself with cries and tears of all that made it ready to burst.

"Beat me!" she repeated, still walking close after Jupillon, who was trying to get away, and was throwing caressing words to her, as he drew back, just as we do to an animal which does not recognize us and which wants to bite us. A crowd began to gather round them.

"Come, now, old tippler, let's have no annoyance of the gentleman," said a policeman, grasping Germinie by the arm and roughly turning her round. At the brutal insult of the policeman's hand, Germinie's knees gave way: she thought that she was fainting. Then she grew frightened, and began to run down the middle of the street.

LVI

PASSION has insane recurrences, inexplicable returns. That accursed love which Germinie thought had been killed by all Jupillon's wounds and blows was reviving. She was terrified to find it again within her as she re-entered the house. The mere sight of the man, a few minutes near him, the sound of his voice, the breathing of the air that he breathed, had been sufficient to turn back her heart, and to surrender her wholly to the past.

In spite of everything, she had never been able wholly to tear out Jupillon from her heart; he had remained rooted in it. He was her first love. She belonged to him, in opposition to herself, by all the weaknesses of memory, all the cowardliness of habit. Between them there were all the bonds of torture which chain a woman for ever — sacrifice, suffering, humiliation. He owned her for having outraged her conscience, trampled upon her illusions, martyred her life. She was his, eternally his, who was the master of all her sorrows.

And this shock, this scene which ought to have given her a horror of ever meeting him, rekindled within her a frenzy to see him again. All her passion seized upon her once more. The thought of Jupillon filled her so as even to purify her. She checked the vagrancy of her senses: she wished to belong to nobody, since in this way only could she still belong to him.

She began to watch him, to study the hours of his going out, the streets through which he passed, the places to which he went. She followed him to Batignolles, to his new lodgings, walking behind him, happy to set her foot where his had trod, to be guided by his route, to see him a little, to catch a gesture that he made, to snatch one of his glances. That was all: she dared not speak to him; she kept at a distance behind, like a lost dog that is pleased at not being repulsed with kicks from the heel.

For weeks, she made herself thus the shadow of this man, a humble and fearful shadow, shrinking back and returning a few paces when she thought that she was seen; then drawing near with timid steps, and, at a sign of impatience from the man, stopping again, and seeming to ask his forgiveness.

Sometimes she waited for him at the door of a house that he entered, rejoined him when he came out, and accompanied him home again, always at a distance and without speaking, with the look of a beggar-woman who begs for leavings and gives thanks for what she is allowed to pick up. Then she used to listen at the shutter of the ground-floor apartment in which he lived, to find out whether he was alone, whether anybody was there. When he had a woman on his arm, she was obstinate in the pursuit of him, in spite of what she might suffer. She went where the couple went, to the very end. She followed them into public gardens and into balls. She walked in their laughter and their speech, lacerated at seeing and hearing them, yet remaining at their backs with all her jealousies sore within her.

LVII

IT was the month of November. For three or four days Germinie had not met Jupillon. She came to spy him out, to look for him near his lodgings. On reaching his street she saw a broad streak of light streaming through his closed shutter; she approached and heard bursts of laughter, the clinking of glasses, women, then a song, a voice, a woman, one whom she hated with all her heart, one whom she would fain have seen dead, one whose death she had so often looked for in the lines of fate, in a word, his cousin!

She pressed against the shutter, breathing in what they said, sunk in the torture of hearing them, starving and feeding herself upon pain. A cold, wintry rain was falling. She did not feel it. All her senses were devoted to listening. The voice that she detested seemed at times to grow weak, and be smothered by kisses, and what it was singing took to flight as though stifled by lips laid upon a song. The hours went by. Germinie was still there. She never thought of going away. She waited without knowing what she was waiting for. It seemed to her that she must continue to remain there until the end. The rain was falling more heavily. Water from a broken spout above her was beating upon her shoulders. Big drops were gliding down the back of her neck. An icy coldness was spreading through her back. Her dress was sweating water upon the pavement. She did not perceive it. Nothing was left to her in all her limbs but the suffering of her soul.

Far in the night there was a noise, a stirring, footsteps coming towards the door. Germinie hastened to hide herself a few steps off in the angle of a wall, and she saw a woman led away by a young man. As she looked at them moving off, she felt something soft and warm in her hand that at first frightened her: it was a dog licking her, a big dog which when quite small she had held in her lap many an evening in the back-shop at the dairy.

"Here, Molossus!" shouted Jupillon's impatient voice two or three times into the shadow of the street.

The dog barked, ran off, turned back frisking, and went in again. The door closed. The voices and songs brought Germinie back to the same spot against the shutter, and the rain soaked her and she allowed it to soak her as she continued to listen until the morning, until daybreak, until the hour when some bricklayers going to their work with their bread under their arms, burst out laughing at the sight of her.

LVIII

TWO or three days after this night spent in the rain, Germinie had a face rendered frightful by pain, a ghastly colour and burning eyes. She said nothing, made no complaint, and did her work as usual.

"Here! just look at me," said mademoiselle; and drawing her abruptly to the light: "What is this?" she went on. "You look as if you had risen from the grave? Come, you are ill? Good gracious! how hot your hands are."

She took her wrist, and threw back the arm a moment after:

"Why, you wretched fool, you are in a high state of fever. And you are keeping it all to yourself."

"Why, no, mademoiselle," stammered Germinie, "I think it's simply a bad cold. I fell asleep the other night with my kitchen window open."

"Oh, as for you," returned mademoiselle, "you would die without so much as saying: 'Ah! wait —' "

And putting on her spectacles and wheeling her easy-chair up to a little table beside the fire-place she began to write a few lines in her big handwriting.

"Here," she said, folding up the letter, "you will be kind enough to give this to your friend Adèle to have it taken by the concierge. And now, to *bed* with you!"

But Germinie would never consent to go to bed. It was not worth while. She would not tire herself. She would remain seated the whole day. Besides, the worst of her sickness was over; she was better already. And then with her, bed meant death.

The doctor, summoned by mademoiselle's note, came in the evening. He examined Germinie, and ordered the application of croton oil. The disorders in the breast were such that he could as yet say nothing. It was necessary to await the effect of the remedies.

He returned after a few days, made Germinie go to bed, and examined her for a long time with the stethoscope.

"It's extraordinary," he said to mademoiselle, after he had come downstairs again, "she has had pleurisy, and has not kept her bed for a moment. Is the girl made of iron? What energy women have! How old is she?"

"Forty-one."

"Forty-one? Oh, it's impossible. Are you sure? She looks fifty."

"Oh, for that matter, she looks any age. What can you expect? Never in health — always ailing — sorrow — worry, and a disposition that is always torturing itself."

"Forty-one! it's astonishing!" repeated the doctor.

After a moment's reflection he resumed:

"Have there been any chest affections in her family to your knowledge? Had she any relations who died?"

"She lost a sister from pleurisy, but she was older. She was forty-eight, I think."

The doctor had become grave.

"After all, the chest is becoming clear," he said in a reassuring tone. "But it is absolutely necessary that she should have rest. And then, send her to me once a week. Let her come to see me, and let her choose a fine, sunny day."

LIX

IT was in vain that mademoiselle spoke, entreated, desired, scolded: she could not induce Germinie to leave off her work for a few days. Germinie would not even hear of a helper to do the chief part of her work. She declared to mademoiselle that it was impossible and useless, that she could never reconcile herself to the idea of another woman approaching her, and serving her and taking care of her; that the mere thought of it in her bed put her into a fever, that she was not dead yet, and that so long as she could put one foot before another she begged to be allowed to go on as she was doing. Her tone was so tender as she said this, her eyes were so beseeching, and her invalid's voice was so humble and impassioned in its request, that mademoiselle had not courage enough to compel her to have an assistant. She only treated her "as a wooden-headed fool," who believed in common with all country folk that a person is dead if she spends a few days in bed. Bearing up with an appearance of improvement due to the doctor's energetic medication, Germinie continued to make mademoiselle's bed, her mistress assisting her to raise the mattress. She continued to prepare her food, and this was more horrible to her than anything else.

When she was getting ready mademoiselle's breakfast and dinner, she felt herself dying in her little kitchen, one of those wretched little kitchens found in large towns, which make so many women consumptive. The embers which she kindled and from which rose slowly a thread of acrid smoke, would begin to make her heart grow faint; then the charcoal — which the dealer next door sold her — strong Paris charcoal full of smoking pieces, wrapped her in its giddy odor. The dirty, badly drawing stovepipe and the low chimney-cover sent back into her lungs the unhealthy respiration of the fire, and the corroding heat of the breast-high stove. She choked, she could feel the redness and heat of all her blood rising to her face and making patches on her forehead. Her head swam. In a state of semi-asphyxiation like that of laundresses ironing amidst the steam from their heaters, she would dash to the window, and inhale a little of the icy air.

As an inducement to being astir when suffering, and her activity continuing in spite of her weakness, she had more than the repugnance of those belonging to the people to keeping her bed, more than the wild, jealous disinclination to suffer the attentions of another to be about mademoiselle; she was in terror of the accusation that might find an entrance with a new servant. It was necessary that she should be there to watch mademoiselle, and prevent anyone from coming near her. Then again it was necessary that she should show herself, that the neighborhood should see her, that she should not be like a dead woman in the eyes of her creditors. It was necessary that she should make a pretense of being strong, even that she should act the appearance and cheerfulness of life, that she should confide in the whole street with an adaptation of the doctor's language, with a look of hopefulness, with a promise not to die. It was necessary that she should put a good face on the matter to reassure her creditors, to prevent the alarms of the money from ascending the staircase and having recourse to mademoiselle.

This horrible and necessary comedy she sustained. She was

heroic in bringing her whole body to lie, drawing up her sinking figure in front of the shops that were watching her, hastening her dragging footsteps, rubbing her cheeks with a rough towel before going downstairs in order to bring the color of blood into them again, in order to disguise on her face the paleness of her disease and the mask of her death!

In spite of the fearful cough that racked her sleeplessness throughout the night, in spite of the loathing with which her stomach rejected food, she passed the whole winter in thus conquering and subduing herself, in struggling with the ups and downs of her illness.

Whenever the doctor came he told mademoiselle that he saw none of the organs essential to life seriously attacked. The lungs indeed were somewhat ulcerated, but that was curable. "Only, her body is much impaired, much impaired," he would repeat in a certain tone of sadness, and with an almost embarrassed air which struck mademoiselle. And at the end of his visits he always spoke of change of air and of the country.

LX

IN the month of August this was all that the doctor had to advise and order — the country. Notwithstanding the reluctance which old people have to move, to change their surroundings, their habits, the laws of their lives; in spite of her domestic temperament and of the species of wrench which she felt in tearing herself away from her home, mademoiselle resolved to take Germinie into the country. She wrote to a daughter of the "chick's," who was living with a nestful of children on a pretty little property in a village in Brie, and who had for years been soliciting a long visit from her. She requested her hospitality during a month or six weeks for herself and her sick maid. They took their departure. Germinie was happy. On her arrival she felt better. For a few days her illness appeared to be diverted by the change. But the summer of that year was uncertain, rainy, mixed with sudden variations and sudden blasts. Germinie caught a chill; and mademoiselle soon heard the frightful cough which had been so intolerable and painful to her in Paris, beginning again overhead, just above where she slept. There were urgent, and, as it were, strangled fits, pausing for a moment and then beginning again, fits the intervals in which left ear and heart nervously waiting and anxious for what would return, for what always did return, burst forth, break down, and die away once more, vibrating however, even when abated, without ever becoming silent or stopping.

Nevertheless Germinie rose after these horrible nights with an energy and activity which astonished, and at times reassured, mademoiselle. She was afoot with everybody. One morning at five o'clock she went three leagues off in a car with the man-servant, to get some fish at a mill; another time she dragged herself to the holiday ball with the maids belonging to the house, returning with them only at daylight. She waked and assisted the servants. Sitting on the edge of a chair in a corner of the kitchen, she was always engaged in doing something with her fingers. Mademoiselle was obliged to make her go out, to send her to sit in the garden. Germinie used then to go and place herself on the green bench, with her parasol open over her head, and the sunshine on her skirt and feet. Perfectly still, she forgot herself in breathing in the day, the light, the warmth, in a sort of passionate inhaling and feverish happiness. Her lips relaxed, and partially opened to the breath of the open air. Her eyes burned without moving; and in the bright shadow glancing from the silk of the parasol, her worn, emaciated, funereal countenance looked forth like a death's head in love.

Weary as she was in the evening, nothing could induce her to go to bed before her mistress. She wished to be there to undress her. Seated beside her, she used to get up from time to time to wait on her as well as she could, assist her to take off a petticoat, then sit down again, collect her strength for a moment, and once more rise and try to help her in something. Mademoiselle had to make her sit down again by force and order her to remain quiet. And the whole time that this evening toilet lasted there was always the same repetition in her mouth about the servants of the house.

"Do you know, mademoiselle, you have no idea what eyes the cook and man servant make at each other when they think they are not seen. They still restrain themselves when I am there; but the other day I surprised them in the bake-house. They were kissing, only fancy! Fortunately madame here does not suspect it."

"Ah! there you go again with your stories! But good gracious," mademoiselle would say, "whether they make fools of each other, or not, what affair is that of yours? They are kind to you, are they not? That is all that's wanted."

"Oh! very kind, mademoiselle; in that respect I have nothing to complain of. Marie got up last night to give me a drink, and as for him, whenever there is any dessert left it is always for me. Oh! he is very good to me; Marie even doesn't quite like his being so attentive to me — you understand, mademoiselle."

"Come, be off to bed with all your nonsense," mademoiselle would say abruptly to her, being sorrowfully impatient to see a sick person so eagerly occupied with the loves of others.

LXI

ON their return from the country the doctor, after examining Germinie, said to mademoiselle:

"It has been rapid, very rapid. The left lung is quite gone. The right one is attacked in the upper part, and I am greatly afraid that the mischief has spread through her entire system. She is a lost woman. She may live another six weeks, or at the very most two months."

"Ah! Heavens," said Mademoiselle de Varandeuil, "all that I have loved will go before me! Must I go after everybody else?"

"Have you thought of placing her anywhere, mademoiselle?" said the doctor after a moment's silence. "You cannot keep her. It would be too much trouble for you — it would be a grief to you to have her there," the doctor added in reply to a gesture from mademoiselle.

"No, no, I have not thought of it. Ah! yes, to send her away! But you have seen that she is not a maid or a servant to me; she is like the family that I never had. How can you expect me to say to her: 'Now be off!' Ah! it is the first time I have so keenly regretted that I am not rich, and that I have such wretched rooms. But it is impossible for me to speak to her about it! And then where could she go? To Dubois? To Dubois indeed! She went there to see the servant that I had before her and that died there. You might as well kill her at once! The hospital, then? No, not there: I will not have her die there!"

"Upon my word, mademoiselle, she would be a hundred times better off there than here. I would enter her at Lariboisière under the care of a doctor who is a friend of mine. I would recommend her to a house-surgeon who is a good deal indebted to me. She would have a very kind sister in the ward where I would have her placed, and if necessary she would have a private room. But I am sure that she would prefer to be in a general ward. You see, mademoiselle, it's a step that must be taken; she cannot remain in the room upstairs. You know what these horrible servants' rooms are. I go so far as to think that the sanitary inspectors ought to force the owners into humanity on the point; it is shameful! The cold weather will soon be here; there is no fireplace, and with the skylight and the roof, it will be an icehouse. You see that she is still keeping up — Oh, yes, she has astonishing courage, prodigious nervous vitality. But in spite of it all she will have to take to her bed in a few days, and she will never get up again. Come, be reasonable, mademoiselle. Let me speak to her; will you?"

"No, not yet. The thought of it — I must grow accustomed to it. And then seeing her about me I think that she will not die so soon as that. We shall have plenty of time. Later on, we can see about it, yes — later on."

"Forgive me, mademoiselle, but permit me to tell you that you may make yourself ill by nursing her."

"I? — Oh! I! — " and mademoiselle made a gesture like that of one whose life is quite done for.

LXII

AMID the despairing anxieties caused to Mademoiselle de Varandeuil by her maid's illness, there crept in a singular feeling, a certain fear in the presence of the new, strange, mysterious creature which the disease had evoked out of Germinie's inner nature. Mademoiselle felt a sort of uneasiness beside a face that was absorbed, buried, almost hidden in implacable hardness, and that seemed to recover and return to itself only transitorily, in gleams, in the effort of a wan smile. The old woman had seen many people die; her long and sorrowful memory brought back to her many expressions of dear, doomed faces, many sad, downcast, distressed expressions of death, but none of the countenances that she remembered had in its decline assumed the sombre appearance of one retiring into seclusion within itself.

Locked in her suffering, Germinie continued solitary, stiff, concentrated, impenetrable. She had the immobility of bronze. As she looked at her, mademoiselle would ask herself what she was thus brooding quietly over, whether it was disgust of her life, horror of death, or perhaps some secret, some ground for remorse. Nothing external seemed to affect the sick woman. Her perception of things was going from her. Her body was becoming indifferent to everything; it no longer sought for comfort or seemed desirous of being cured. She made no complaint, and found no pleasure or diversion in anything. Even her yearnings after affection had left her. She never bestowed a mark of endearment, and every day something of humanity quitted this woman's soul which appeared to be growing petrified. Often she sank into a silence that prompted waiting for the anguish of a cry, of an utterance; but after casting her eyes around her she would say nothing and again set herself to gaze at the same spot, in vacancy, before her, fixedly, everlastingly.

When mademoiselle returned from a friend's house where she had been dining, she used to find Germinie sunk in an easy-chair, in the dark, without any light, her legs stretched out upon a chair, her head bowed upon her breast, and herself so deeply absorbed that sometimes she did not hear the opening of the door. As Mademoiselle de Varandeuil advanced into the room it seemed to her as though she were disturbing a terrible interview between Sickness and Shade, wherein Germinie was already seeking the terror of the invisible, the blindness of the grave and the darkness of death.

LXIII

THROUGHOUT the month of October Germinie persisted in her unwillingness to stay in bed. Every day, however, she was feebler, weaker, more deserted by her bodily powers. She could with difficulty ascend the flight that led to her sixth story, drawing herself up by the banister. At last she used to fall down on the stairs, and the other servants lifted her up and carried her to her room. But this did not stop her: the next day she came down again with that gleam of strength which the morning gives to the sick. She prepared mademoiselle's breakfast, made a pretense of working, and still went about the room holding on to the furniture and dragging herself along. Mademoiselle used to take pity on her, and make her lie down on her own bed. Then, Germinie rested in it for half an hour, without sleeping or speaking and with open, motionless and unsettled eyes, like a person in pain.

One morning she did not come down. Mademoiselle ascended to the sixth floor, turned down a narrow, evil-smelling corridor through the servants' quarters, and reached Germinie's door, which was No. 21. Germinie asked her forgiveness for having made her come up. She had found it impossible to set her foot to the ground. She had great pains in the stomach, which was quite swelled. She begged mademoiselle to sit down for a moment, and, to make room for her, took away the candlestick which was on the chair at the head of the bed.

Mademoiselle sat down, and remained for a few moments looking at this wretched servant's room, one of those rooms in which the doctor is obliged to lay his hat upon the bed, and in which there is scarcely room to die! It was a garret a few feet square without a fireplace, in which the skylight (kept open by a rack) gave passage to the breath of the seasons, the heat of summer and the cold of winter. The lumber of old trunks and carpetbags, a towel-basket, and the little iron bedstead on which Germinie had laid her niece, were heaped together under the sloping roof. The bed, a chair, and a small, rickety dressing-table with a broken hand-basin, formed the whole of the furniture. Above the bed hung the daguerreotype of a man, in a frame painted to resemble rosewood.

The doctor came during the day.

"Ah! peritonitis," he said when mademoiselle had informed him of Germinie's condition. He went up to see the patient.

"I am afraid," he said on coming down again, "that there is an abscess in the intestine communicating with an abscess in the bladder. It is very serious, very serious. She must be told not to make any great movement in the bed, and to turn herself with caution. She might die of a sudden in the most frightful pain. I proposed to her that she should go to Lariboisière, and she acquiesced at once.

She has no aversion to doing so. The only thing is that I do not know how she will stand the moving. But after all, she has such energy; I never knew anyone like her. Tomorrow morning you shall have the order for admission."

When mademoiselle went up again to see Germinie, she found her smiling in bed, cheerful at the thought of going away.

"Come, mademoiselle," she cried to her, "it's only a matter of six weeks."

LXIV

AT two o'clock on the following day the doctor brought the admission order. The invalid was ready to set out. Mademoiselle proposed to her that she should go on a stretcher, which would be brought from the hospital.

"Oh! no," said Germinie eagerly, "I should believe myself dead." She was thinking of her debts; she must show herself to her creditors in the street, alive and afoot until the end!

She got out of bed. Mademoiselle de Varandeuil assisted her to put on her petticoat and her dress. As soon as she had left her bed, the life disappeared from her face, and the fire from her complexion; it seemed as though earth were suddenly rising under her skin. Clinging to the banister, she descended the steep flight of the back-staircase, and reached the rooms below. They made her sit down on an easy-chair in the dining-room near the window. She wished to put on her stockings quite by herself, and as she drew them up with a poor, trembling hand whose fingers knocked together, she showed a little of her legs which were so thin as to be frightful. The charwoman, meanwhile, was putting up into a bundle a little linen, a glass, a cup and a tin case containing knife, fork, and spoon, which Germinie had wished to take with her. When this was done Germinie looked for a moment all around her; she took the room into a last embrace which seemed as though it would carry the things away. Then her eyes rested on the door through which the charwoman had just gone out: "At least," she said to mademoiselle, "I leave you someone who is honest."

She got up. The door closed behind her with a sound of good-bye, and supported by Mademoiselle de Varandeuil, who almost carried her, she went down the five stories by the principal staircase. At every landing she stopped and took breath. In the entrance-hall she found the concierge who had brought her a chair. The stout fellow laughed and promised her health in six weeks. She moved her head with a stifled: "Yes! yes!"

She was in the cab beside her mistress. The cab was hard, and jolted over the stones. She kept her body advanced to avoid the shocks of the jolting, and clung to the hand of the concierge's wife. She watched the houses gliding past, and kept silence. On reaching the door of the hospital she would not be carried.

"Can you go as far as that?" asked the porter, showing her the reception room twenty paces off.

She made a sign of assent and went in; it was a dead woman walking because she desired to walk!

At last she reached the large lofty room, cold, rigid, spotless, and terrible, the wooden benches in which formed a circle round the stretcher in waiting. Mademoiselle de Varandeuil made her sit down on a straw easy-chair near an office window. A clerk opened the window, asked Mademoiselle de Varandeuil Germinie's name and age, and spent a quarter of an hour in filling ten sheets of paper, marked at the top with a religious figure, with writing. This done, Mademoiselle de Varandeuil turned and kissed her; she saw an attendant take her under the arm, then she saw her no more, hastened away, and falling upon the cushions of the cab burst into sobs, giving free course to all the tears that had been stifling her heart for an hour past. On his seat at the back the coachman was astonished to hear such loud weeping.

LXV

WHEN Thursday, which was the day for visitors, had come, Mademoiselle de Varandeuil set out at half-past twelve to see Germinie. She wanted to be at her bedside at the very moment of admission, at one o'clock precisely. Passing again through the streets which she had traversed four days before, she recalled the frightful journey of Monday. It seemed to her that in the vehicle in which she sat alone, she was inconveniencing the body of a sick person, and she kept in the corner of the cab as though to leave room for the recollection of Germinie. How was she going to find her? Would she so much as find her? What if her bed were to prove empty?

The cab threaded a little street full of carts of oranges, and women who, sitting on the footpaths, sold biscuits in baskets. There was something wretched and lugubrious in this open-air display of fruits and cakes, delicacies for the dying, viaticums for the sick, looked for by fever, hoped for by the last agony, and taken in the black hands of toil to be brought to the hospital as a tit-bit for death. Children were bringing them as though they understood, gravely, almost piously, and without touching them.

The cab stopped in front of the railing of the court-yard. It was five minutes to one. At the gate thronged a file of women in their work-day dresses, crowded, sombre, sorrowful and silent. Mademoiselle de Varandeuil took her place in the file, advanced with the rest and entered. She was searched. She asked for the Sainte-Joséphine ward, and was directed to the second pavilion on the second floor. She found the ward, then the bed, bed No. 14, which, as she had been told, was one of the last on the right. Moreover she was, so to speak, summoned to it from the end of the ward by Germinie's smile, the smile of a hospital patient at an unexpected visit, which says so gently, as soon as the visitor enters:

"Here, here I am."

She bent over the bed. Germinie tried to repel her with a gesture of humility and the modesty of a servant

Mademoiselle de Varandeuil kissed her.

"Ah!" said Germinie to her, "the time appeared very long to me yesterday. I had fancied it was Thursday — and I was wearying for you."

"Poor girl! And how are you?"

"Oh! it's all right now — the swelling in my stomach has gone down. I've three weeks to be here, mademoiselle. They say I've a month or six weeks but I know about myself. And then I'm very comfortable; I'm not dull. I sleep at night now. I *was* thirsty when you brought me on Monday! They won't give me wine and water."

"What have you there to drink?"

"Oh! the same as at home — the white of an egg. See, mademoiselle, will you pour me out some? Their tin things are so heavy."

And raising herself by one arm by means of the little stick hanging over the middle of her bed, and holding out the other, bared by the drawing back of the night-dress, thin, shivering, for the glass which Mademoiselle de Varandeuil handed to her, she drank.

"There," she said when she had finished, laying her two arms at full length on the sheet outside the bed-clothes. "Poor mademoiselle," she resumed, "must I give you all this trouble? It must be downright dirty at home."

"Don't mind about that."

There was a moment's silence. A colorless smile came upon Germinie's lips:

"I've been smuggling," she said to Mademoiselle de Varandeuil, lowering her voice, "I've confessed in order to feel comfortable."

Then, putting her head forward on the pillow so as to be closer to Mademoiselle de Varandeuil's ear, she went on:

"There are tales to be told here. I have a funny neighbor, there, see," with a glance and a movement of her shoulder she indicated the sick woman, towards whom her back was turned. "She has a man who comes to see her here. He spoke to her yesterday for an hour. I could hear that they had a child. She has left her husband. He was like a madman, that man was, while he was talking to her."

And as she said this Germinie grew animated as though she were still quite full of this scene and quite tormented by it, quite feverish and jealous, though so near death, at having heard love beside her!

Then suddenly her countenance changed. A woman was coming toward her bed. The newcomer acted embarrassed on seeing Mademoiselle de Varandeuil. After a few minutes she kissed Germinie, and, as another woman was coming, took leave in haste. The new-comer acted in the same manner, kissed Germinie and left her immediately. After the woman a man came; then there was another woman. They all, after a moment, bent down to kiss the patient, and in every kiss Mademoiselle de Varandeuil vaguely gathered a muttering of words, an exchanging of utterances, a low question from those who were kissing, and a rapid reply from her who was kissed.

"Well!" she said to Germinie. "They're looking well after you, I hope!"

"Ah! yes," repeated Germinie in a strange voice, "they are looking after me!"

She had no longer the same lively appearance as at the beginning of the visit. A little blood which had mounted into her cheeks had remained there only in the form of a spot. Her countenance seemed to be shut; it was cold and dead like a wall. Her lips were drawn in and as though sealed. Her features were hidden beneath the veil of mute and infinite suffering. There was no longer anything caressing and speaking in her motionless eyes which were occupied and filled with a thought. It seemed as though a boundless internal concentration, a wish born of the last hour brought back within her person all the external tokens of her ideas, and that her whole being remained despairingly fastened upon a grief that drew everything to itself.

For the visits that she had just received were those of the fruiterer, the grocer, the butter-woman, and the laundress — of all her living debts! These kisses were the kisses of all her creditors coming to scent out their dues and blackmail her death-agony in an embrace!

LXVI

MADEMOISELLE had just risen on Saturday morning. She was about to make up a little basket of four pots of Bar-le-Duc preserve which she intended to take to Germinie the next day, when she heard low voices, a colloquy in the ante-chamber between the charwoman and the concierge. Then almost immediately the door opened, and the concierge came in.

"Sad news, mademoiselle," he said.

And he held out a letter which he had in his hand; it bore the stamp of the hospital of Lariboisière: Germinie had died that morning at seven o'clock.

Mademoiselle took the paper; she saw nothing in it but the words saying to her: "Dead! dead!" And it was for nothing that the letter repeated to her: "Dead! dead!" for she could not believe it. Like those of whose end we are informed with suddenness, Germinie appeared to her full of life, and her person which was no more came before her with the supreme presence of someone's shadow. Dead! She would see her no more! There was no longer a Germinie in the world! Dead! she was dead! And the person who would now move about in the kitchen, would be no longer she; the person who would open the door for her would be no longer she; the person who would roam about in her room in the morning would be another!

"Germinie!" she cried at last, with the cry with which she used to call her; then she recovered herself: "Machine! Thing! What do you call yourself?" she said harshly to the disconcerted charwoman. "My dress — I must go there!"

So rapid an issue of the illness was such an abrupt surprise that her thoughts could not accustom themselves to it. It was with difficulty that she could conceive this sudden, secret and vague death, which, to her, was wholly comprised within this scrap of paper. Was Germinie really dead? Mademoiselle asked herself the question with the doubtfulness of those who have lost at a distance some one that is dear to them and, not having seen the death, are unwilling to believe in it. Had she not seen her full of life, on the last occasion? How had this happened? How had she suddenly become that which is good for nothing but to be put underground? Mademoiselle dared not think about it, and yet did think about it. The unknown nature of this death, concerning which she was in complete ignorance, frightened and attracted her. The anxious inquisitiveness of her affection went out to her maid's last hours, and she tried in groping fashion to raise the veil and horror that shrouded it. Then she was seized with an irrepressible longing to know everything, to be a spectator, through what was told her, of what she had not seen. She must learn whether Germinie had spoken before dying, whether she had expressed a desire, or testified a wish, or given utterance to one of those words which are life's last cry.

On reaching Lariboisière, she passed the concierge, a stout man reeking of life as one reeks of wine, traversed the corridors in which pale convalescents were gliding about, and at the very end of the hospital rang at a door draped with white curtains. It was opened, and she found herself in a parlor lighted by two windows, in which a plaster image of the Holy Virgin stood on an altar between two views of Vesuvius which seemed to be quivering there against the naked wall. From an open door behind her issued a prattling of sisters and little girls, a sound of young voices and fresh laughter, the merriment of a clean room wherein the sunshine sports with children at play.

Mademoiselle asked to speak to the Mother of the Sainte-José-phine ward. A little, half-deformed sister came to her, with a face that was ugly and good, a face like the mercy of God. Germinie had died in her arms.

"Her pain was almost gone," the sister told mademoiselle; "she was better; she was feeling relief; she had hope. About seven o'clock in the morning, just after her bed had been made, and without realizing that she was dying, she was suddenly seized with a vomiting of blood during which she passed away."

The sister added that she had said nothing, asked for nothing, wished for nothing.

Mademoiselle rose, freed from the horrible thoughts that she had had. Germinie had been saved from all the dying agonies which she had imagined. Mademoiselle blessed such a death from the hand of God which gathers the soul at a single stroke.

As she was going out, an attendant coming up to her said: "Will you identify the body?"

The body! The expression was a frightful one to mademoiselle. Without waiting for her to reply the attendant began to walk before her until he reached a large, yellowish door, above which was written: *"Amphitheatre."* He rapped; a man in his shirt-sleeves and with a cutty-pipe in his mouth half opened the door, and told them to wait for a moment.

Mademoiselle waited. Her thoughts frightened her. Her imagination was on the other side of this door of terror. She tried to see what she was going to see. Filled with confused images and conjured terrors, she shuddered at the idea of entering in there, and of recognizing amid others that disfigured countenance, if indeed she could still recognize it! And yet she could not tear herself from the spot: she told herself that she would never see her again!

The man with the pipe opened the door. Mademoiselle saw nothing but a bier, the covering of which, reaching only as far as the neck, allowed Germinie to be seen with open eyes, and with hair lying straight back from her head.

LXVII

BROKEN down by these emotions, and by this last sight, Mademoiselle de Varandeuil took to her bed on going home, after giving money to the concierge for the sad proceedings, the burial, the concession of a private grave. And when she was in bed, what she had seen came back before her. Horrible death was always near her, and the frightful countenance framed in its bier. Her gaze had brought away this unforgettable head within her; beneath her closed eyelids she could see it, and was afraid of it. Germinie was there, with the discolored features of a murdered face, with her hollow sockets, and her eyes which seemed to have shrunken into holes! There she was, with the lips still distorted by the pain of vomiting forth her last breath! There she was with her hair, her terrible hair, brushed back straight from her head!

Her hair! It was this that especially pursued mademoiselle. The old maid thought, without wishing to think, of things dropped into her ear when a child, of popular superstitions lost in the depths of her memory, and she asked herself whether she had not been told that the dead whose hair is thus carry away a crime with them when they die. And at times this was the hair that she saw on this head, hair of crime, upright with terror and stiffened with horror before the justice of Heaven, like the hair of a man condemned to death when in presence of the scaffold on the Place de Grève!

On Sunday mademoiselle was too ill to leave her bed. On Monday she sought to rise, in order to go to the funeral, but she was seized with weakness, and was obliged to lie down again.

LXVIII

"WELL, is it over?" said Mademoiselle from her bed, on seeing the concierge coming into her apartment from the cemetery at eleven o'clock, in a black frock-coat, and with a look of compunction suited to a return from a funeral.

"Yes, indeed, mademoiselle. God be thanked, the poor girl is out of pain."

"Here! I have not my wits about me to-day. Put the receipts and the remainder of the money on my night-table. We'll count it another time."

The concierge remained standing in front of her without stirring or going away, changing a blue velvet skull-cap, cut out of the dress of a girl belonging to the house, from one hand to the other. After a moment he made up his mind to speak.

"It's dear, mademoiselle, getting buried. First there's — "

"Who told you to calculate it?" interrupted Mademoiselle de Varandeuil, with a pride of haughty charity.

The concierge continued:

"And then, moreover, a grant in perpetuity, as you told me to get, is not to be had for nothing. For all you've a good heart, mademoiselle, you are not over-rich; people know that, and they say to themselves: 'Mademoiselle will have plenty to pay, and we know mademoiselle — she will pay.' Well, what if this were saved her? It will be so much to the good, and *she* will be all right underground. Besides, what would give her most satisfaction up above? Why, to know, worthy girl, that she's not wronging anybody."

"To pay what?" said Mademoiselle de Varandeuil, rendered impatient by the concierge's circumlocutions.

"Why, it's not of any consequence," replied the concierge, "she was very fond of you all the same. And then when she was so ill, it was not the time, — dear me, it's not right to trouble you about it — there's no hurry — it's the money she had been owing for sometime. Here it is."

And he drew a stamped paper from the inside pocket of his coat.

"I did not want her to give a note — it was her own doing."

Mademoiselle de Varandeuil seized the stamped paper, and at the bottom of it saw the words:

I certify that the above statement is correct.
GERMINIE LACERTEUX

It was an acknowledgement for three hundred francs, payable in monthly instalments, the latter to be entered on the back of the paper.

"There's nothing, you see," said the concierge, turning the paper round.

Mademoiselle de Varandeuil took off her spectacles.

"I shall pay it," she said.

The concierge bowed. She looked at him: he remained where he was.

"That is all, I hope?" she said in an abrupt tone.

The concierge had again begun to gaze steadily at a square in the floor.

"That's all — if — "

Mademoiselle de Varandeuil felt afraid, just as she had felt afraid when passing through the door behind which she was to see her maid's body.

"But how is it that she owes all that?" she exclaimed. "I gave her good wages. I almost dressed her. Where did her money go?"

"Ah! there it is, mademoiselle. I'd rather not have told you, but it's as well told to-day as tomorrow. Besides, it's better you should learn beforehand; when people know about things, they can make arrangements. There's an account with the poultry-woman. The poor girl owes a little everywhere; she wasn't very regular towards the end. The laundress left her book the last time — it mounts up rather high, but that's all I know about it. It seems that there's a bill at the grocer's — oh! an old bill, going years back. He'll bring you his book —"

"How much to the grocer?"

"Somewhere about two hundred and fifty."

All these revelations falling upon Mademoiselle de Varandeuil one after the other drew from her deep exclamations. Raising herself on her pillow, she was left speechless in presence of this life whose veil was being torn away, piece by piece, and whose shames were being revealed one by one.

"Yes, somewhere about two hundred and fifty. There's been a deal of wine, by what he says."

" I always had some in the cellar —"

"The dairy-woman," resumed the concierge, without replying — "Oh! nothing very much — the dairy-woman — seventy-five francs. There was absinthe, and brandy —"

"She drank!" exclaimed Mademoiselle de Varandeuil, who at this word guessed everything.

The concierge did not seem to hear.

"Ah! you see, mademoiselle, it was her misfortune to know the

Jupillons — the young man. It was not on her own account that she did it; and then, what with sorrow and so on, she took to drinking. You must know she hoped to marry him, she fitted up a room for him, and when people go in for furniture, money soon disappears. She was destroying herself, and it was all no use my telling her not to drown herself in drink as she was doing. As far as I was concerned, I was not going to tell you, as you may believe, when she came in at six o'clock in the morning. It's like her child — oh!" the concierge went on, in reply to the gesture from mademoiselle, "it was precious lucky the baby died. There's no harm in telling you she led a fearful life, a gay old time ... And so about the ground that's — why, if I were you, I'd — why, she cost you enough, mademoiselle, as long as she was eating your bread, and so you may as well leave her where she is — along with everyone else."

"Ah! so that's the way of it! That's how it was. She stole for her lovers, and ran into debt, did she? Ah! she did well to die! And I have to pay! A child! Just to think of that, the trollop! Yes, indeed, she may rot where she lies! You did well, Monsieur Henri! Steal! She stole from me! It's a good thing for her that she's in her coffin! And to think that I used to leave her all my keys. I never expected that she'd — good gracious! that's what comes of putting trust in one. Well, yes, I'll pay, not on her account but on my own. And I gave her my finest pair of sheets to be buried in. Ah! if I had known, I'd have given you a dish-cloth — nicely swindled as I am!"

And mademoiselle went on for some minutes until the words choked her and were strangled in her throat.

LXIX

AFTER this scene, Mademoiselle de Varandeuil remained for a week in bed, sick and furious, filled with an indignation that shook her entire heart, that overflowed her lips, that wrung from her at times some coarse insult which she would ejaculate with an outcry at the foul memory of her servant. Night and day she revolved the same imprecatory thoughts, and her very dreams stirred the anger of her slender limbs in her bed.

Was it possible! Germinie! her Germinie! She could not get over it. Debts! A child! All sorts of disgracefulness! The profligate! She abhorred and detested her. Had she lived she would have gone and denounced her to the commissary of police. She would have liked to believe in hell, that she might commend her to the tortures which chastise the dead. Her maid was such a character as that! A girl who had been in her service for twenty years, and whom she had loaded with kindness! Drunkenness! She had sunk so low as that! The horror that follows upon an evil dream came to mademoiselle, and all the disgust rising from her soul cried shame upon this dead woman whose grave had vomited her life and rejected her filthiness.

How she had deceived her! How the wretch had pretended to love her! And that her ingratitude and knavery might be displayed still more clearly, Mademoiselle de Varandeuil recalled her endearments, her attentions, her jealousies which seemed as though they worshipped her. She could see her bending over her when she was sick. She thought again of her caresses. And it was all a lie! Her devotion was a lie! The happiness of her kisses, the love of her lips were lies! Mademoiselle told herself this, repeating it to herself, and persuading herself of it; and yet from these awakened memories, from these evocations whose bitterness she sought, from the distant sweetness of bygone days, there rose up gradually and slowly within her a first softening of pity.

She drove away the thoughts which allowed her anger to flag; but her musing brought them back again. There occurred to her those things to which she had paid no attention during Germinie's lifetime, such trifles as the tomb suggests and death illumines. She had a dim recollection of certain singularities on the part of this girl, feverish outpourings, agitated embraces, kneelings that seemed preparatory to confessions, movements of lips upon which a secret seemed to hang. With the eyes which we have for those who are no more, she reviewed Germinie's sad looks, the gestures and attitudes that she displayed, her countenances of despair. And she could now divine beneath them wounds, sores, rendings, the tortures of her agonies and repentances, the blood-tears of her remorse, all kinds of stifled sufferings throughout her life and her person, a passion of shame which dared not ask for forgiveness save by its silence!

Then she scolded herself for thinking this, and blamed herself as an old fool. Her rigid, straightforward instincts, the severity of conscience and harshness of judgment: due to a faultless life, all that prompts a virtuous woman to condemn a female, all that must inevitably prompt a saint like Mademoiselle de Varandeuil to be pitiless towards her servant, rebelled against forgiveness. Within her, justice, stifling her kindness, cried out: "Never! never!" And with an implacable gesture she drove Germinie's infamous spectre away.

At times, even, to render the damnation and execration of this recollection still more irrevocable, she accused her and crushed her, and calumniated her. She added to the frightful inheritance of death. She reproached Germinie with even more than she had to reproach her with. She lent crimes to the darkness of her thoughts, and murderous desires to the impatience of her dreams. She wanted to think, and did think, that she had wished and looked for her death.

But at this very moment, amid the blackest gloom of thought and supposition, a vision rose and shone before her. An image approached that seemed to advance towards her gaze, an image from which she could not protect herself, which passed through the hands wherewith she sought to repel it, and Mademoiselle de Varandeuil saw her dead servant once more. She saw the face of which she had had a glimpse at the amphitheatre, that crucified face, that tortured countenance to which had mounted both the blood and the agony of a heart. She saw her with that soul which the second-sight of memory evolves from things. She appeared as though stripping herself of terror and horror. Suffering alone remained to her, but it was a suffering of expiation, almost of prayer, the suffering on the face of a dead woman who would fain weep. And as the expression of this countenance grew constantly softer, mademoiselle could at last see in it a beseeching supplication, a supplication which in time ensnared her pity. Insensibly there crept into her reflections, allowances, palliating thoughts at which she was herself astonished. She asked herself whether the poor girl were as guilty as others, whether she had chosen the evil, whether life, and circumstance, and misfortune of body and destiny, had not made her the creature she had been, a being of love and sorrow. And then she suddenly checked herself, for she was ready to forgive!

One morning she sprang out of bed.

"Here you! whatever you're called!" she cried to her charwoman, "the mischief take your name, I always forget it! My things, quick, I have to go out."

"Lord! mademoiselle, just look at the roofs. They're quite white."

"Well, it's snowing; that's all."

Ten minutes afterwards Mademoiselle de Varandeuil was saying to the driver of the cab that she had sent for:

"The Montmartre cemetery!"

LXX

A WALL stretched in the distance, a boundary wall perfectly straight and continuous. The thread of snow which striped the coping gave it the color of dirty rust. In the corner to the left, three bare trees reared their dry, black branches to the sky. They rustled mournfully with a sound of dead wood clashing in the north wind. Above these trees, behind the wall and right opposite, rose the two arms on which hung one of the last oil lamps in Paris. A few roofs stood at intervals here and there; then began the slope of the hill of Montmartre, its shroud of snow rent by streaks of earth and sandy patches. Little grey walls followed the line of escarpment, topped by thin, meagre trees whose clusters were violaceous in the mist, and reached away as far as two black mills.

The sky was leaden, washed with the cold, bluish tints of ink spread with a brush, while for light there was a clear and perfectly yellow rift over Montmartre of the color of the water of the Seine after heavy rain. Across this wintry ray passed and repassed the arms of a hidden mill, arms that were slow and undeviating in their movement, and that seemed to be revolving eternity.

In front of the wall, which was overlaid with a bush of dead, frost-reddened cypress, extended a large tract, upon which, like two great mourning processions, there descended two thick rows of serried, crowded, huddled, overturned crosses. These crosses touched and hustled and crowded one another. They bent, and fell, and were crushed by the way. In the centre there was a sort of strangulation which had forced them out and to one side: they could be seen covered, only raising by the thickness of their wood the snow that lay on the paths, which, somewhat trodden in the middle, ran down the length of the two files. The broken ranks undulated with the

167

fluctuation of a crowd, with the disorder and serpentine movement of a long march. The black crosses, with their outstretched arms, assumed an appearance of shadows and persons in distress. These two straggling columns suggested a human overthrow, a desperate and terrified army. They were like a terrible rout.

All the crosses were laden with wreaths of immortelles, wreaths of white paper with silver thread, black wreaths with gold thread; but the snow beneath made them show out worn and all tarnished, horrible as mementoes rejected by the other dead and picked up to trick out the crosses with the gleanings of graves.

All the crosses bore names written in white letters; but there were also names which were not even written on a bit of wood; and a tomb might be seen there formed of the bough of a tree broken off and planted in the ground, with the envelope of a letter tied round it!

On the left, where a trench was being dug for a third row of crosses, a workman's pick was throwing up black earth, which fell back upon the whiteness of the embankment. A great silence, the dull silence of the snow, enfolded everything, and two sounds only were audible, the deadened sound of the shovelled earth, and the heavy sound of a regular footstep: an old priest who was in attendance, with his head in a black cowl and wearing a black camail, a black stole, and a dirty yellow surplice, was trying to warm himself by stamping his big goloshes on the pavement of the main avenue in front of the crosses.

It was the common grave that day. The ground, the crosses, the priest expressed these words:

"Here sleeps the Death of the people, and the Nothingness of the poor."

O Paris! you are the heart of the world, you are the great human city, the great charitable and fraternal city!

You have gentleness of spirit, ancient clemency of manners, and sights which give alms! The poor man is your citizen as well as the rich. Your churches speak of Jesus Christ; your laws speak of equality; your newspapers speak of progress; all your governments speak of the people; and it is there that you fling those who die in your service, who kill themselves in creating your luxury, who perish from the mischief of your industries, who have sweated out their lives in working for you, in giving you your comfort, your pleasures, your splendors, who have made your animation, your noise, who have placed the chain of their existences in your duration as a capital, who have been the crowd in your streets and the people of your greatness!

Each one of your cemeteries has a like shameful corner, hidden at the end of a wall, where you hasten to bury them, and where you cast the earth upon them in such niggardly shovelfuls that the foot of their coffins may be seen coming through. It is as though your charity were checked at your last sigh, as though your only free gift were the bed of suffering, and as though, the hospital apart, you who are so enormous and superb had no further room for these folk! You keep them, and crowd them, and mingle them in death as a hundred years ago you mingled their dying agonies beneath the sheets in your public Hospitals! Even yesterday you had not so much as the priest on duty to throw a little, common holy water upon all comers, nor the smallest prayer!

But what this priest blesses is still the same: a hole wherein the deal knocks together, and the dead are not at home! Corruption is common there; no one has his own, but each one has that of all; 'tis the promiscuousness of the worm! In the devouring soil a Montfaucon hastens for the Catacombs. For the dead have neither time nor space to rot; the earth is taken from them before the earth has finished! — before their bones have the color and as it were the ancientness of stone, before the years have effaced a remnant of humanity upon them and the memory of a body! The clearing is made while the earth is still themselves, and they are the damp mould into which the spade sinks. The earth that is lent them — why, it does not enclose so much as the odor of death! The summer, the wind which passes across this scarcely buried human sewer, wafts the impious miasma from it over the city of the living. In the burning days of August, the keepers prevent us from going so far, for there are flies that have the poison of the charnel-house, flies that are carbuncled and that kill!

Mademoiselle arrived here after passing the wall and vault which separate the perpetual from the temporary concessions. Following the direction of a keeper, she went up between the last file of crosses and the newly opened trench. And there, walking upon buried wreaths, and upon the oblivion of the snow, she came to a hole, to the opening of the grave. It was stopped up with old rotten planks and a sheet of oxidized zinc upon which a digger had thrown his blue blouse. The earth sank behind to the bottom, where it left visible three coffins outlined in their sinister elegance: there was a large one and two smaller ones a little way back. The crosses of the week, of two days before, of the previous day, descended along the channel of earth; they were slipping, and sinking, and seemed to be making great strides, as though they were being hurried down the slope of a precipice.

Mademoiselle began to go up past these crosses, bending over each, spelling out the date, seeking for the names with her bad eyesight. She reached some crosses of the 8th of November; it was the day before that of Germinie's death, and Germinie must be close by. There were five crosses of the 9th of November, five crosses huddled together; Germinie was not among the crowd. Mademoiselle de Varandeuil went a little further on, to the crosses of the 10th, then to those of the 11th, then to those of the 12th. She came back to the 8th, and again looked everywhere: there was absolutely nothing — Germinie had been buried without a cross! Not even a piece of wood had been set up by which she might be known!

At last the old lady let herself fall on her knees in the snow between two crosses, one dated the 9th of November, and the other the 10th. What remained of Germinie must be close by. Her uncared-for tomb was this uncared-for soil. To pray over her it was needful to pray at haphazard between two dates — as though the poor girl's destiny had willed that there should be as little room on earth for her body as there had been for her heart!

THE END

Books
Published by Mondial

The Rougon-Macquart

Les Rougon-Macquart is the collective title given to French novelist Emile Zola's greatest literary achievement, a monumental twenty-novel cycle about the exploits of various members of an extended family during the French Second Empire, from the coup d'état of December 1851 which established Napoleon III as Emperor through to the aftermath of the Franco-Prussian War of 1871 which brought the Empire down.

The ten volumes published by Mondial:

1. La Fortune des Rougon (1871)
   The Fortune of the Rougons
   (Mondial; ISBN 9781595690104)

2. Le Ventre de Paris (1873)
   The Fat and the Thin (The Belly of Paris)
   (Mondial; ISBN 9781595690524)

3. La Conquête de Plassans (1874)
   The Conquest of Plassans
   (Mondial; ISBN 9781595690487)

4. La Faute de l'Abbé Mouret (1875)
   Abbé Mouret's Transgression
   (The Sin of the Abbé Mouret)
   (Mondial; ISBN 9781595690500)

5. Son Excellence Eugène Rougon (1876)
   His Excellency
   (Mondial; ISBN 9781595690555)

6. Une Page d'amour (1878)
   A Love Episode (A Page of Love)
   (Mondial; ISBN 9781595690272)

7. La Joie de vivre (1884)
   The Joy of Life (Zest for Life)
   (Mondial; ISBN 9781595690470)

8. Le Rêve (1888)
    The Dream
    (Mondial; ISBN 9781595690494)

9. L'Argent (1891)
    Money
    (Mondial; ISBN 9781595690630)

10. Le Docteur Pascal (1893)
    Doctor Pascal
    (Mondial; ISBN 9781595690517)

Other Books

For more information please visit our website at
www.mondialbooks.com

Emile Zola: Fruitfulness (ISBN 1595690182 / 9781595690180)

Malama Katulwende: Bitterness
(An African Novel from Zambia. ISBN 159569031X /
9781595690319. *Julius Chongo Award 2006 for Best Creative Writing.* Tribal and social affiliations and the student riots at the University of Zambia, in a captivating and intelligent story about love, political involvement and individual responsibilities.)

Martin Andersen Nexø: Pelle the Conqueror (Complete Edition,
Parts I to IV. ISBN 159569028X / 9781595690289)

Martin Andersen Nexø: Ditte Everywoman
(Trilogy: Girl Alive. Daughter of Man. Towards the Stars.
ISBN 9781595690333)

Victor Hugo: The Man Who Laughs (By Order of the King. ISBN
1595690131 / 9781595690135)

Victor Hugo: History of a Crime
(ISBN 1595690204 / 9781595690203)

Honoré de Balzac: Ursula (Ursule Mirouët)
(ISBN 1595690530 / 9781595690531)

Honoré de Balzac: Maitre Cornelius
(ISBN 1595690174 / 9781595690173)

Anatole France: Penguin Island
(ISBN 1595690298 / 9781595690296)

Anatole France: The Crime of Sylvestre Bonnard
(ISBN 9781595690593)

Anatole France: The Gods are Athirst
(Les Dieux ont soif. ISBN 9781595690128)

Gustave Flaubert: Salammbo (Salambo)
(ISBN 1595690352 / 9781595690357)

Jules Verne: An Antarctic Mystery
(The Sphinx of the Ice Fields. (ISBN 1595690549 / 9781595690548)

Romain Rolland: Pierre and Luce (ISBN 9781595690609)
Andre Gide: Strait is the Gate
(La Portre étroite ISBN 9781595690623)

André Gide: Prometheus Illbound
(Le Prométhée mal enchaîné. ISBN 9781595690807)

André Gide et al.: Recollections of Oscar Wilde
(ISBN 9781595690814)

Johann Wolfgang von Goethe: The Sorrows of Young Werther
(ISBN 159569045X / 9781595690456)

Theodor Storm, Adelbert von Chamisso, Adalbert Stifter: Famous German Novellas of the 19th Century
(Immensee. Peter Schlemihl. Brigitta. ISBN 159569014X / 9781595690142)

Sigmund Freud: Dream Psychology
(Psychoanalysis for Beginners. ISBN 1595690166 / 9781595690166)

Frederick (Friedrich) Engels: Socialism: Utopian and Scientific
(Appendix: The Mark; Preface: Karl Marx. ISBN 1595690468 / 9781595690463)

Karl Marx: The Eighteenth Brumaire of Louis Bonaparte
(ISBN 1595690239 / 9781595690234)

Gabriele D'Annunzio: The Child of Pleasure
(ISBN 9781595690581)

Getrude Stein: Three Lives (With an Introduction by Carl Van Vechten. ISBN 9781595690425)

Jack London: War of the Classes. Revolution. The Shrinkage of the Planet. (ISBN 9781595690401)

Jack London: Before Adam. Children of the Frost.
(ISBN 1595690395 / 9781595690395)

Jack London: The Iron Heel (ISBN 1595690379 / 9781595690371)

Susan Coolidge: Clover (ISBN 1595690263 / 9781595690265)

Oscar Wilde, Anonymous:

Teleny or The Reverse of the Medal (Gay erotic classic)
(ISBN 9781595690364)

**Agatha Christie: Two Novels
(The Mysterious Affair at Styles. The Secret Adversary.)** (ISBN 9781595690418)

Jerome K. Jerome: Idle Thoughts of an Idle Fellow
(ISBN 9781595690241)

Oscar Wilde: The Critic as Artist.
Upon the Importance of Doing Nothing and Discussing Everything. (ISBN 9781595690821)

Carl Van Vechten: Firecrackers. A Realistic Novel.
(ISBN 9781595690685)

Coming soon

Bruce Kellner: Winter Ridge (ISBN 9781595690692)

Carl Van Vechten: Caruso's Moustache and Other Writings About Music (ISBN 9781595690708)

Heinrich Heine: Germany. A Winter Tale. (Deutschland. Ein Wintermärchen. ISBN 9781595690715)

Printed in the United Kingdom
by Lightning Source UK Ltd.
127544UK00001B/247/A